I0598829

Zulu
Six

Strike Force Zulu
Book 1

Laura Acton

ISBN: 978-1-951713-03-4 (ebook)
ISBN: 978-1-951713-12-6 (hardcover)
ISBN: 978-1-951713-02-7 (paperback)

Zulu Six is a work of fiction. Names, characters, places, and events are products of the author's imagination or are used fictitiously. Any resemblance to actual persons, living or dead, events, locales, or organizations is entirely coincidental.

Three Fates Publishing

Novels by Laura Acton

For details on all Laura's novels, sneak peeks of work in progress, and to be notified when her next book is released, visit www.lauraactonauthor.com

Strike Force Zulu
ZULU SIX
BLOOD BONDS
WOUNDED HONOR
BLURRED LINES

Blackweld Saga
Trail to Bitterbend

Guardian Chronicles
The General's Son

Beauty of Life
FORSAKEN: On the Edge of Oblivion
SOLACE: Behind the Shield
BELONGING: Hope, Truth, and Malice
OUTLIER: Blood, Brotherhood, and Beauty
PURGATORY: Bonds Forged in Hellfire
SERENITY: A Path Home
GUARDIANS: Mission to Rescue Innocence
SECRETS: Passion, Deceit, and Revenge
OUTCAST: Trust, Friendship, and Injustice
WHITEOUT: Above and Beyond
BREAKPOINTS: Slow Spiral Down
TREASURES: Vows Vengeance Valor
BLACKOUT: Devotion to Duty

Acknowledgments

Kate, Martha, Lisa, Angel, and Valarie
you ladies are awesome, and I sincerely
appreciate all your support and keen eyes.
THANK YOU!

Contents

Zulu Six

1

Let the Dart Fly

FINN McBride glared at the five photos pinned to the corkboard. Calloused fingers of one hand raked through his ginger locks while his other hand fiddled with a dart as he attempted to make his choice. Zach and Grant had thrown theirs without hesitation, and one picture now possessed two darts while the other four remained pristine.

"Throw the damned dart, Finn." Master Chief Jake Marshall leaned against the table and eyed his newly anointed number three. Like the rest of his teammates, Jake was not ready to choose a new Zulu Six. He would prefer to operate as a five-man team and not replace Levi, but Lockwood over-rode his desire, threatening to make the selection if he didn't pick a replacement today.

"Haud yer wheesht! Still deciding." In truth, Finn didn't want any of them, nor did he aspire to be Jake's new Three. Zulu Four suited him better. Three was too close to One and Two. Leading a team would never be his style, and he didn't fancy Three's responsibilities either.

Finn had no desire to mentor, shepherd, or whatever politically correct term was presently applied to babysitting the team rookie. But short of leaving Zulu, which would never happen while he could do his job, the position was his, earned via capability, seniority, and the trust of his team leader.

He shifted his moss-green eyes to the opposite wall, the one with photos of the men who had gone before, previous members of the Navy's elite strike force who died or were discharged due to injury. Team Zulu was a one-way street, unlike most SEAL teams. Once in, always in.

Yes, men retired, but by an unwritten law, no one ever transferred out of Zulu while able-bodied, which made selecting a new member a challenging task. They needed to be a tight-knit unit to accomplish the missions assigned to them. If they chose wrong, team dynamics would suffer, and that got people killed.

Finn settled his gaze on Levi's photo, which was added last month after he received a medical discharge. Though Finn never truly got on with Levi, he never wished for any brother to be taken out of action the way the previous number three had. His hand dropped to his left side and absently rubbed his most recent scar as his mind returned to the night all hell broke loose.

Flashback – Three Months Ago – Village in Algeria

Pinned down, bullets flying, Finn growled as he applied pressure to his wound while Jake radioed for ETA on the Quick Response Force. Since their usual support team hadn't traveled with them, they were reliant on whatever QRF happened to be in the AO. Taking another peek at Levi's position, Finn noted the RPG destroyed the side of the building with stairs.

Though wanting to make a run for Three's location, it would be suicide, especially with a bullet in his side. Finn groused, "Intel was shit. Supposed to be ten, not a whole army."

"I hear ya, brother, but quit the chatter and focus," Zulu Two said as he took aim at another tango, creating a fine pink mist when his bullet found a home in the militant's head.

Finn shut his mouth, but his mind didn't quiet. Their intel package indicated only ten of Sayed Massi's guards would be here, not the fifty or more who came out of nowhere. The drone overhead had not picked up their heat signatures, which led Finn to believe a tunnel system existed in this village.

This should've been a somewhat routine snatch and grab, nothing as covert as their typical missions. The poor intel made him wonder if Massi set a trap for them, but that would remain a mystery unless a miracle happened and they managed to get the hell out of here alive, which, at this point, seemed highly unlikely.

As they snatched Sayed and put a hood over the high-value target's head, Levi alerted them from his overwatch position right before the shit hit the fan, and armed men swarmed out of the surrounding buildings. Zulu Three cleared an exit path for them until the explosion took out half the roof of Levi's sniper perch. Before Levi's radio quit working, he communicated both legs had been busted, and he couldn't walk, so he would lay down cover for them as long as possible.

With no way to reach their teammate, Massi's men would capture Levi before they could rescue him, and his death wouldn't be quick since Massi's faction was known for slowly hacking their enemies to pieces as they filmed the torturous process. Although knowing Levi, the SEAL would go out in a blaze of glory, schwacking as many of the bastards as he could before he would allow himself to be taken alive.

Currently trapped in a tiny structure in the middle of the village with Massi's force surrounding them, the only reason the rest of them still lived is they had the elder Massi, and none of his men dared to send an RPG into their location for fear of being cut-up by their boss' equally sadistic brother, Anwar.

Finn wished they could've snagged both brothers, but to maintain control of their faction, Sayed and Anwar never resided in the same place. His thoughts halted as Zulu One relayed, "QRF five mikes out. Prepare to exfil south."

"What about Three?" Finn asked as his eyes drifted north to where Levi continued taking potshots at tangos who dared lift their heads enough.

"Our priority is to bring in Massi." Jake's gut twisted. He never wanted to leave a man behind and, under other circumstances, would defy orders, but he must protect the other four men.

"WE DON'T LEAVE NO ONE BEHIND!" Finn yelled. He and Levi butted heads from the day they both joined Zulu as Five and Six, but Finn refused to abandon him.

"QRF is sending someone to try to reach him," Jake explained, not happy with the situation but not seeing a way for them to retrieve Levi without being killed. He ran every scenario he could think of in his mind. With no cover between here and Zulu Three and the stairs obliterated, even if they managed to run the gauntlet without ending up full of holes, they would be easy pickings as they attempted to scale the outside wall to the roof.

"Four, Five, prepare the smoke," Jake directed. "I'll take the high-value target. Two, on point. Six, bring up the rear."

"Roger," they all responded, none of them happy, as each glanced at Levi's building, hoping the QRF reached him in time.

Finn gaped and pointed. "What the … who the hell?"

Gunfire erupted as a lone figure sprinted towards Levi's position, bullets kicking up dust around him. Gaining speed as he went, the man vaulted upward using available handholds and structures to climb the wall parkour-style … no ropes and quicker than they'd ever seen.

Recognizing the runner as friendly, Jake communicated to Levi, though thus far, all attempts to raise him after learning he was injured resulted in no response. "Zulu One to Three, if you can hear me, friendly climbing up the east side. I repeat, friendly coming in from your east."

When the crazy man made it to the rooftop without falling, Finn shook his head and quipped, "Hell, whoever he is, he's faster than a speeding bullet."

Although his headset still functioned, Levi didn't bother to reply to Jake. Unable to stand after the blast shattered his kneecaps and aware no one would be coming to save him, he had not wanted to say awkward goodbyes, so he pretended he couldn't respond. However, now thankful for a working comms yet unwilling to be taken alive in case Jake got it wrong, Levi faced east and leveled his weapon, preparing to shoot.

Rolling for cover after pulling himself over the edge, Maxwell Stirling called out, identifying himself as Foxtrot Five. Upon receiving the necessary response, Max moved toward the downed SEAL. He took a knee and scanned the man he volunteered to rescue. "Gonna get you out of here in a bit. Just gotta clear a way for your buddies first."

"How the hell did you climb without a rope?"

Max only gave Zulu Three a cocky grin in answer. He unslung the rocket-propelled grenade launcher and sniper rifle before tossing a med-pack to Three. "Morphine's in there. You're gonna need it. Our ride will be here in about six mikes."

Noting Foxtrot Five carried no ropes, Levi asked, "Plan on tossing me off the roof?"

"Nah." Shouldering the rocket launcher, he targeted the abode, which his team lead indicated most likely housed the tunnels, and from the angle of destruction, this building is where the RPG came from. Max fired, then switched out for his rifle and began picking off tangos as they fled the burning structure. Shifting his focus, Max helped his teammates clear a path for the rest of Zulu to escape to the south.

Once Zulu and Foxtrot piled in the trucks and made a hasty departure, Max turned his attention to the severely injured man. "It sucks we don't have time to splint your legs, but I need to harness you to me before the helo arrives."

Levi nodded, recognizing how they would be getting off the roof now. The morphine kicking in, he tried to help the young SEAL but ended up passing out before he was fully hitched.

"Foxtrot Five to Chalk One. Ready for pickup."

"Chalk One, incoming."

Max slung the launcher and his rifle over his shoulders and did one last check to ensure Zulu Three was secured to his front. When the line dropped to him, he clipped his carabiner into the metal ring embedded in the rope and wrapped his arms around Three. Max grinned as they were lifted, enjoying the adrenaline rush of swinging in mid-air under the helicopter.

Present – Zulu Team Room

Finn let his dart fly, joining the other two in the face of Stewart Babcox, Sierra Seven, from their support team. Although Babcox possessed skills, otherwise, he wouldn't be part of Sierra, or in the candidate pool today, Finn didn't like the self-aggrandizing guy. He believed him to be too much of a loner, a glory hound, and pretty much a ballbag. When Jake and Dave added theirs to the same photo, Special Warfare Operator Babcox had been summarily eliminated from the selection.

Now they had only two more to disqualify before debating the merits and shortcomings of the final two contenders and voicing their opinion to Marshall on who should become Zulu Six. The next two rounds went swiftly, knocking out Harris and Paulson, both men exceptional operators but not the best fit.

"Okay, boys, were down to Axel Chase and Hector Morales. You've all reviewed their files. Anyone got anything to say about either?" Jake took a seat at the table and flipped open the two personnel jackets, prepared to listen as his men expressed their views. Selecting the right man wasn't easy, particularly in a team of badass individuals who understand the value of teamwork.

Everyone on his team had been selected to fill a niche or a skill they required. Zulu, as a whole, added up to more than the sum of their parts. They had to. They were the Navy's premier strike team, created and resourced for dangerous, covert missions.

Before anyone spoke, Lieutenant Commander Lockwood strode in, followed by Lieutenant Farris and Logistics Specialist Draper. "Sorry to interrupt. Got us a situation."

Kira Draper pursed her lips as she spied five darts in Babcox's photo. She never doubted the guys' good sense. Babcox might be okay for the support team, but he would never be on par with Zulu. She noted the remaining two, and if she had a vote, which she didn't, she would pick Chase. Taking her seat beside Finn, she said under her breath, "Whittled it down to two already?"

"Aye." Finn kicked back and focused on the Naval Intelligence Officer at the front of their room. "We goin' after Anwar Massi?"

Nicole Farris wanted to find Anwar as much as Zulu, but the man went to ground, and none of her sources had pinpointed his location. And his brother Sayed continued to remain tight-lipped despite interrogation. She clicked a button to display a map. "No, still haven't ferreted him out. We have another urgent mission."

She halted and turned to Lockwood. "Where is he?"

"He should be here any minute. Needed to be escorted through gate security," Bryan answered.

"Where's who?" Jake questioned.

Nicole stated with a bit of aloofness, "Your strap for this mission. He possesses certain qualities required for this op."

"What qualities?" Jake asked as the door opened. He turned along with the rest of his team and stared at the newcomer. A man wearing a form-fitting, short-sleeved t-shirt, faded jeans, and cowboy boots. He possessed a mop of light-blond, unruly curls and ocean-blue eyes. His clean-shaven face made him appear young and handsome enough to be a member of a pop music band, but the hard planes of his muscular body and rock-solid biceps bespoke of a well-honed sailor.

"Special Warfare Operator Stirling, you're late. Take a seat so I can begin," Lieutenant Farris ordered.

Maxwell Stirling moved forward as seven pairs of eyes sized him up. Used to being judged, he held his head high and set it at a cocky tilt as he strode to an empty chair.

"Not there!" Finn growled as he yanked Levi's chair away. "In the back where straps belong."

Changing direction, Max sighted an open spot near a dog. The brown-haired sailor petting the Belgian Malinois sported a patch on his left arm, indicating him as Zulu Five. Lowering himself into the seat, Max focused on the lieutenant commander, still unaware of why he received a temporary assignment to Jake Marshall's legendary Zulu team.

2

Cut From the Same Cloth

Zulu Plane En Route to Argentina

ZACHARY Connors, now Zulu Five, happy to shake the rookie mantle after several years, scratched behind Rocketeer's ears as his bored dog nudged his leg. He sat with the rest of Zulu near the front of the plane while the minimal support team and their strap were buckled in at the rear.

He listened to Finn griping about Stirling. Their gruff breacher of Scottish descent got his dander up whenever a strap came along on missions. Zach, however, typically didn't have a problem with them. They were useful on occasion when they needed a skill set the team didn't possess. And in this case, Stirling fit the bill. The young SEAL had the fresh face of a fraternity pledge, so he could pull off the role of a university student on holiday.

Zach tuned in when Lockwood, who usually stayed out of their banter, must've reached his limit with Finn's bellyaching because he said, "You do realize Stirling is the man who saved Levi's life in Algeria? He volunteered to make that run. Took balls."

Jake crossed his arms, unhappy with the turn of events. "Just means he is as reckless as his old man. And you all know what his lack of caution caused."

"No, what?" Zach asked as his eyes sought out the blond at the rear of the plane, who appeared to be reading a book.

"Wiped out an entire Zulu team. Himself included."

"Come on, brother. It isn't fair to paint him with the brush of his father. That kid has only been in the teams for two or three years. Whatever Preston Stirling did or didn't do should have no bearing on his son. Hell, the kid couldn't have been more than six or seven when his father died."

Dave eyed his best friend before continuing, "Hell, you got your shot at Zulu when they had to reform from scratch. Youngest ever drafted. You might not be part of or leading Zulu today if things had gone differently. So, don't be putting boulders in Stirling's rucksack, which aren't his to bear."

"Cut from the same cloth ... all I'm saying." Jake closed his eyes, refusing to discuss it further.

Max buried his nose in a book, one method he used to avoid confrontations and appear to be unfazed by comments about his father. Though he tried hard not to be affected, the hot barbs still burned. He clenched his jaw to bite back words he desired to yell in Dad's defense. If anyone noticed his tension, Max would claim reading in low light gave him a headache, but no one ever did.

Besides always being judged, Max was also all too familiar with being alone. Sure, he had teammates, and on the battlefield, Foxtrot watched out for one another, but once home, he was on his own. They had their wives, girlfriends, whatever, and no one sought to associate with the son of a pariah.

Although he endeavored to accept his lot in life, Max still yearned for what he once had—a caring family. His father was not who everyone claimed. The man Max remembered was kind, intelligent, strong, loving, and one badass SEAL. Max could never prove what he knew to be the truth, and after eighteen years, nobody except him cared to set the record straight.

Max sucked up his pain and ignored the snide remarks about Master Chief Preston Stirling, which cast an oppressive shadow over him all through the SEAL pipeline and into his current position as Foxtrot Five. He would follow in his dad's footsteps—become the best-damned operator he could be, and perhaps one day vindicate his father's name and restore his honor.

Dealing with Zulu for one mission would be tolerable. Nobody, especially Master Chief Marshall, wanted to draft him to Zulu. Not when his legacy included a father accused of getting an entire team blown up. Once this op was completed, he'd go back to Foxtrot, and things would return to what passed as normal.

"What ya reading?" Lester asked after getting up the nerve to talk to one of the SEALs. The man might not be Zulu, but there was no question in Lester's mind; he was just as lethal.

Lowering his book, Max almost gaped at the man two seats down from him. He took in the slight man with black, plastic glasses over brown eyes, who wore khaki trousers, a blue polo shirt, and loafers. "A language book. Brushing up on Argentinian Spanish. It's a bit different from what is spoken in Spain. In some ways, it sounds more like Italian."

"Wow, learn something new every day. Oh, by the way, I'm Info Systems Technician Owen Lester. I work with Farris."

"I'm Max. Nice to meet you."

Not the most socially adept, Lester liked that Max didn't bite his head off for talking to him, so he asked, "Do you speak other languages? I mean, like other than English and Spanish."

"Yeah."

"Like what?"

Max grinned as the image of Mr. Hartrum came to mind. The foreign language teacher had taken a frightened eight-year-old boy under his wing and given him something to focus on during his lonely years at Fairwinds Military Academy. The boarding school became his home after his uncle decided he was too much trouble. Though honestly, Max preferred the impersonal school over living with Uncle Dick Asshole … um, Richard Athole.

"The mainstays, like French, Italian, Spanish, Russian, and German. Plus, I studied many of the Middle Eastern languages, Arabic, Uzbek, Pashto, Urdu, Dari, and several major African languages and some minor dialects."

Lester's eyes widened. "You're joshing me, right?"

Max shrugged. "No. I'm a polyglot. I learn languages fast."

Virginia – Zulu Team Room

Lugging several cases of beer and water to restock the fridge, Stewart Babcox entered the room, which had been assigned solely to Zulu. Other teams shared briefing rooms, but Zulu, being the best of the elite, warranted a dedicated one. He was miffed to be left behind again. The whole shitshow in Algeria might've given him a foot up to take Levi's spot. He could've shown Marshall what he was made of, but Sierra had been left here in Virginia.

He came to a halt when he spied five photos on the corkboard, three of them filled with five darts. Anger surged forth when he recognized his face. He ripped out the darts and tore his picture down. "Goddammit. I shouldn't have been eliminated this round. I deserve the spot."

Senior Chief Robert Powers, Sierra One, leaned on the door. "Maybe next time. You've only been on my team for a while. And so you know, they don't always select from Sierra. Depends on what they require and who is best to fill the niche." He noted Chase's and Morales' photos. "Bet they go with Chase. They need another sniper, and he speaks Arabic. He's seasoned, too. The Mighty Finn won't have to babysit him much, which he'll like."

"I also speak Arabic, and I'm a better sniper than Chase. Hell, I'm much better than Zulu Two. I can outshoot Katz any day. Plus, I'm a helluva lot better swimmer than that overgrown Scottish terrier McBride." Stewart stormed out of the room without putting the beverages in the refrigerator.

Rob shook his head and moved to put things away. Stewart was a great shooter, but his head tended to inflate, making it hard to be in the same room with him. Every so often, Rob wished he had done a little more digging into Stewart's personality before selecting him for Sierra. With Babcox's attitude, Marshall would never choose Sierra Seven for Zulu.

Marshall wanted well-rounded men who valued being a team player. Only someone willing to give his all because he recognized he was part of something greater than himself, not a glory-seeker, would ever become a member of Zulu's family.

Zulu Plane En Route to Argentina

Max woke with a crick in his neck. Sleeping sitting up was a pain in the … well, neck. He stood and stretched his stiff muscles, noting the members of Zulu rolling out of their comfy hammocks. He averted his gaze when the red-haired, burly guy glared at him. Max overheard McBride's snarky comments when they boarded the plane … and long after, too.

Yeah, being a strap was no fun. And although Foxtrot wasn't much better, at least they didn't openly direct hostility towards him. Reaching for his rucksack, Max pulled out a water bottle, uncapped it, and sat on the webbing again. He wondered who offered him up for this crap assignment.

Though unsubstantiated, a part of him believed his maternal uncle might have a hand in this. Captain Richard Athole enjoyed making his life hell. It all began when his father died. His mother's brother never wanted kids, hated them in fact, and when at the tender age of six, Maxwell was orphaned, Uncle Asshole became saddled with a worthless brat … Athole's words, not his.

For two years, Max tried everything in his power to prove he was worthy of being loved. He grabbed at any scrap of affection tossed to him, which only came while in public view, never in private. No, privately, he endured neglect, harsh words, and punitive discipline.

The first of many battles started when he was eight and overheard a conversation not meant for his ears. He learned the truth of what happened when his dad died and who was responsible. But no one listened to a little boy, especially when his uncle was a well-respected Naval Intelligence Officer who took every opportunity to inform his cronies how much of a burden Max was and how he did everything under the sun to help his troubled, undisciplined nephew.

After one terrifying incident, Max found himself shipped off to Fairview. Since that fateful day, until he was fifteen, he only stayed at his uncle's house during school breaks when other arrangements like summer camps couldn't be made.

Everything came to a head when he turned fifteen. After one hit too many, unwilling to put up with Dick Asshole's verbal and physical abuse any longer, Max cold-cocked his uncle. He never returned to Athole's house again. Mr. Hartrum allowed him to stay with his family during two winter breaks, and he attended camps during the summer, which prepared him physically for entering the Navy and his sole desire to become a SEAL.

Yeah, Max could see his asshole uncle arranging this assignment. Athole would get his jollies by knowing Max had to work with men who would hold what they believed his father did against him. If he failed in his task, it would be a black mark on his record, possibly costing him his place on Foxtrot.

"Stirling?"

Max tabled his thoughts and peered up at Lieutenant Commander Lockwood. "Yes, sir?"

"We'll be landing soon. Do you have any questions about your role? Any concerns?"

"No, sir."

"Okay." Bryan studied Stirling's eyes. He disliked this operation. It was not a typical one for Zulu, and it hinged on this young man. A sailor who wore a huge scarlet letter for something which was not his fault. Much like the stigma carried by children born out of wedlock in the old days. Tarred with the moniker of 'bastard' for their parents' indiscretions and forever viewed as trash and unworthy of respect. An unfair label and something Bryan wished would change for Stirling.

"Anything else, sir?" Max maintained the gaze, unsure why Lockwood continued to stare at him.

"No." Bryan pivoted and strode to the front, hoping Jake's mindset towards the kid wouldn't affect how he approached this mission. He halted the thought. Jake Marshall was many things, and not all of them wholesome, but the master chief would never intentionally put an operator under his command at risk, regardless of his personal opinion.

3

Blond Bait

SMIRKING, Finn studied Stirling as the baby-faced strap slung the backpack over one shoulder. Freshly shaven and dressed in a faded maroon t-shirt with Harvard emblazoned across the chest, dark gray cargo shorts, and black canvas skate shoes, Stirling appeared to be a typical college student. "Well, Chad, don't go getting lost on us," he taunted.

After shooting McBride a scowl, Max turned his attention to Marshall as Zulu One approached him wearing a glower of his own. Though twenty-four, without his beard, Max could still pass for an eighteen-year-old, which meant he was about the only SEAL who could pose as a young university student. Max wished he didn't fit the bill so well.

"We'll be tracking your every move." Jake surveyed Maxwell. Although he didn't care for Stirling, he didn't like that this op put him in a risky position with no back up close at hand. Yes, they would be around, but they couldn't be too near, or whoever was abducting male university students would not go after the kid.

"Yeah, I'm aware. Draper put GPS trackers in the wallet, shoes, and the waist of my boxers." Max shifted the knapsack.

"I still say we should implant a subdermal one," Finn chimed in. "Like the microchips for dogs."

Kira Draper grinned. "I could do that."

Incensed by the taunting banter, which made him believe they didn't trust him to do the job, Max allowed a bit of acid to leach into his tone, "No. You're acting like I can't handle myself. I'm a trained SEAL like the rest of you. Might not be as old and decrepit as you all, but I'm not some untried greenie."

"Did you just call me decrepit?" Finn pulled up to his full height, which was still shy about two inches of Stirling's six-foot frame, and squared off, ready to pound the cocky upstart. With his broad chest and powerhouse biceps, the little turd would go down with one solid punch.

Max didn't back down as he met McBride's challenge head-on. "If the shoe fits."

"Why you—" Finn began to ball up a fist, but Jake stepped in and pushed Finn back.

His timbre stern, Jake said, "Not now! Don't give a rat's ass if you don't like each other, but a pissing contest will get someone killed. Stow it and focus on the mission. Is that clear?"

Finn pivoted and strode off without a word as Max hissed, "Crystal, Master Chief."

Nicole strolled up and handed Max two cards. "Your ID and credit card. Just don't go wild. Your cover is Chad Davenport, a student at Harvard. Your mother is Senator Davenport, and your father is a leading neurosurgeon."

After sliding the cards into slots in the tagged wallet, Max shoved it in his hip pocket and nodded. Striding down the plane's rear ramp to the taxi, he mentally reviewed what he must do. *Act like a carefree, rich kid out to have fun with Mom and Dad footing the bill.* Though his appearance fit the role, none of the rest of his cover story even remotely mirrored his own life.

Zulu was assigned this operation when the local law enforcement turned a blind eye to five missing young men in the past month. One of whom happened to be Dexter Clovis, the twenty-year-old son of a highly influential senator. It remained unclear what befell them since no ransom demands were ever presented, and their bodies never turned up.

After a brief investigation, they determined the disappearances to be a recent occurrence. No one from any other country went missing, and Farris believed whoever orchestrated the abductions targeted Americans only. Max would act as bait, and Zulu would track him when he vanished. With any luck, they would locate the missing students and bring them back alive.

Dave placed his hand on Jake's back, noting the tense muscles. Although his best friend groused a lot about Stirling on the flight, Jake remained a consummate professional and took care of the men under his command, which is one of the reasons Dave would follow Marshall anywhere. "He'll be okay."

Pivoting, Jake eyed his second-in-command, whom he relied on more than anyone outside of his team would ever guess. "Stirling better not do something stupid like his reckless father."

"Jake, stop. Give the kid his due. Lockwood's right. Took guts to save Levi. Kid's got skills ... like his father."

Any further discussion halted as Draper called out, "All three trackers transmitting."

Nicole turned to the rest of the team. "Cover has been set for each of you. Grant, Zach, you'll be joining a singles tour group staying at Iguazu Resort." She handed them their tickets.

Eyeing the bikini-clad woman on the ticket given to Grant, Finn grumbled, "Why don't I get to go with the hot lasses?"

"Because you'd be too distracted," Jake replied.

"Besides, they'll be doing a trek into the jungle ... and we know how much you *loooove* the flora, fauna, and creepy crawlies in jungles," Kira teased as she kept her eyes on the monitor.

Smiling, Lieutenant Farris handed documents to Jake, Dave, and Finn as she explained, "You are businessmen taking a break from your meetings in Oberá to do some sightseeing."

"I don't have to wear a suit, do I?" Finn had no desire to put on one in this hot, humid weather.

Nicole chuckled. "No. What you're wearing is appropriate." She liked McBride as much as she did all the guys. He kept things lively and lightened the mood with his unguarded comments.

Iguazu Bar, Argentina – 2100 Hours

Max wandered up to the bar, ordered a beer, then turned and leaned on the counter as he scanned the mass of people in the only venue hopping tonight. Most of the day, he lounged at the pool, but he also wandered off to view the falls. He learned from reading the placards that Iguazu was the most extensive waterfall system in the world, and the swift-moving river delineated the border between the Argentine province of Misiones and the Brazilian state of Paraná.

So far, he chatted with anyone near him. With no idea how the abductees were targeted, he had no clue who might be a friend or a foe. Throughout the day, Max noted each member of Zulu at one point, but they gave him a wide berth and never approached him. Spying an open high-top table, he ambled over and settled on the stool after receiving his beer. Max wished he could've enjoyed his honeymoon here with Lacey, but fate had other plans.

He peered into the amber ale, the color of Lacey's hair, and let sorrow wash over him. For a second brief time in his life, he had someone who cared. She supported his desired life as a SEAL. Gung-ho, running with him, going to the gym, pushing him to be and do better, Lacey had been his shining beacon.

But he was doomed to be alone. Lacey unexpectedly dropped dead from a ruptured brain aneurysm as they jogged one afternoon, a week before he departed for Green Team. He used his grief to push through training, pouring every ounce of himself into doing whatever it took to earn a slot on a top-tier team.

A hand on his shoulder pulled him from his reverie. Max smiled at the dark-haired woman and launched into casual conversation. A half-hour later, Arcilla Ramirez tugged on his hand, wanting him to dance, and although reluctant, he grinned and played along as if she thoroughly enthralled him.

Once on the dance floor, his body got into the groove, but his mind never stopped analyzing if she might be involved. Being approached by a beautiful woman would be an easy way to target men. Max scanned, noting Marshall and Katz not far away.

Alert for any signs of others watching him, Max spotted two bouncer-like men near the front door who seemed to keep staring at him. *Perhaps they work here.*

Several songs later, when Arcilla excused herself to go to the ladies' room, Max returned to the table to find his unfinished drink sitting there. Aware someone might've tampered with his beer, he flagged down a waitress and ordered another one since ending up drugged would hamper his ability to complete his mission.

Upon returning at the same time as his drink arrived, Arcilla smiled and reached for the mug. "Do you mind? I'm thirsty."

"No. You want one?" Max asked.

While taking a long drink, Arcilla turned in a complete circle, her body moving with the beat of the music as she viewed all the people. Returning her gaze and the beer to Max, she smiled. "No, thanks. I'm not a big drinker." With innocence exuding from her brown eyes, Arcilla said, "Can you believe the crush of people in here tonight? So exciting."

"Not sure what it is usually like. This is my first night here." Max noted the heavy coating of red lipstick on the mug's rim. Turning the glass to drink from the other side, he wondered if he should give Arcilla the brush-off since she didn't seem like a threat, but decided it might be out of character to ditch a woman who appeared to be interested in him.

So he remained, and they conversed in Spanish while he drank his pint and covertly scanned the bar for potential threats. Once he finished the last swig, Arcilla dragged him out on the dance floor again. Max grimaced when the ambient lighting dimmed, and bright red, blue, green, and yellow spotlights pulsed sickeningly fast as a mirrored ball lowered and began to spin.

Max blinked, trying to maintain his equilibrium as he tilted to one side. Arcilla's face swam in front of his as the realization he'd been drugged dawned on him. He spun in a circle, searching in the chaotic lighting for a glimpse of one of the guys but not finding any of them. Becoming increasingly dizzy, his ability to control his muscles waned, and Max sank to the floor.

Relief, brief and fleeting, surged when two sets of strong hands gripped his arms and hauled him to his feet. Turning to the right, expecting to find Marshall or Katz, dread replaced the prior feeling as the face of the man he had noted by the entrance earlier sneered at him. He barely translated the man's words, *'It will be fun hunting you,'* before his head lolled forward, his legs gave way, and he blacked out.

Dave restrained Jake from moving forward. "Stop, brother. Draper's tracking him. This is the plan. We must allow this to play out. Otherwise, we won't find the others."

Outside Iguazu Bar – 2300 Hours

Finn watched Stirling being dragged to a vehicle and his limp body shoved into the back. One man went to the driver's side and hopped in while the other guy and the woman Max danced with climbed into the rear. "They put him in a black van. The license is covered in mud. I'm following."

"Hold. Don't move too fast. Give them space, or we won't be able to follow them." Bryan commanded though he didn't like the idea. "But don't lose him."

Grant and Zach disengaged from the women they were talking with outside as a cover for their observation positions. Spotting Dave and Jake exiting the bar, they converged at the rented cars.

Jake hopped into the front passenger seat, and Dave scarcely closed the back door as Finn put his foot on the gas. Zach slid behind the wheel of the other sedan and turned the key while Grant hurried around to the other side.

Each somewhat surprised the strap managed to be kidnapped on the first night. They wanted to keep him in view but held back so as not to spook the target. As they lost sight of the van on the twisting road, Jake kept an eye on the mobile GPS tracker. All three blips were centered together.

"They're maintaining a steady speed. Likely unaware we're following," Jake voiced his hope, only to have it plummet in the next moment. "TOC, you seeing the same thing?"

From the plane, Kira responded, "Yeah, one of the trackers is stationary. It is the one I put in his billfold."

Finn spotted the white wallet on the road as the headlights reflected off the glossy surface. "There. Son of a bitch. They threw it out. We need to decrease the distance."

"Maintain the gap," Lockwood ordered as he observed the blips on the monitor over Draper's shoulder.

Shortly after the second tracker halted, Dave spied Max's shoes in the roadway, along with the kid's shirt and shorts. "What the hell?! Are they stripping him?"

"We should've implanted the kid," Zach said as he followed behind Finn. Both increased their speed, disregarding Lockwood's command to hold back.

When the last beacon stopped moving, Finn romped on the gas pedal a fraction of a second after Jake yelled, "FLOOR IT! I'M NOT LOSING THE KID."

Speeding down the access road to the falls, they approached the intersection of the main Route 101. Coming to a halt, they scanned left and right, searching for signs of taillights, finding none. "Go left, Three. Five, you take a right," Jake directed, wanting to cover both possible paths.

The cars sped off in opposite directions. Each man's guts roiled because despite three trackers, they lost the strap, and that didn't sit well with any of them, regardless of the fact Maxwell happened to be the *infamous* Preston Stirling's son.

4

Let the Hunt Begin

Somewhere in Iguazu National Park

MAX began to rouse from a thick fog. His head throbbed mercilessly, and he believed lifting his lashes would be next to impossible and cause more pain. His senses lethargically emerging, Max became aware of the chirps and thrills of unknown birds in the distance. Leaves rustled in a slight breeze, and a faint crackling—a fire based on the scent of burning wood, bacon, and coffee filling his nose.

Ever so slightly, Max shifted, trying to bring his aching arms forward, but found his wrists trussed up behind him. Likewise, his ankles had been bound. When he moved a bit more, striving to straighten his limbs, he became frustrated when he discovered his hands had been hog-tied to his feet.

He didn't need to open his eyes to discern that he lay on his side, buck-assed naked in a bed of ferns, dead leaves, and moist dirt. Recalling blacking out while on the bar's dance floor, Max struggled to lift his heavy lids and squinted when presented with daylight filtered through a dense canopy of trees.

Blinking to focus, he espied five men in sleeping bags around the fire and the woman from the bar squatting to turn bacon in a pan. Continuing his silent scan, he found several rifles, three regular string bows, and one crossbow leaning against tree trunks, plus four quivers of arrows hanging from branches.

Arcilla must've sensed his waking because she turned and peered at him, her face morphing into a wicked smile. Gone was the amiable woman of last night, and in her place, a disturbing facsimile. Her malevolent laugh sent a shiver down Max's spine. *What the hell is going on?*

"You're conscious." Arcilla rose and kicked one bag-clad lump on her way over to Max. "Wake up. Playtime." She crouched in front of her prey. "I hope you are a challenging hunt. Sadly, most are so ... how do you say ... soft and easy to catch."

"Untie me!" Max demanded, glaring at the brown-eyed witch, refusing to show fear. Though at a disadvantage and vulnerable given his current state, he wrestled himself upward, settling his bare shoulder against the rough trunk of a towering tree. From his new position, he caught sight of something which almost made him hurl. Dangling from a tree were four human heads. On another tree, tied by their feet, dangled the corresponding headless bodies riddled with arrows.

"You've found my trophies. You'll be joining them soon enough." Arcilla stood and strolled back to her spot, accepting a plate of food from the man she roused.

Max breathed slowly to quell the rising sense of panic when he comprehended that Marshall's team wouldn't be able to track his location without his clothes. Centering himself, Max realized this was one more time where he must rely solely on himself to survive. He tuned out the conversation around the firepit and focused inward to assess his options. *I need to break this rope and disappear into the jungle before I become one of Arcilla's trophies.*

When two of the men moved towards him, Max tensed as the deranged woman ordered them to drug him. He fought the only way he could, flinging his head back and forth and clenching his teeth. His efforts resulted in three others coming over to restrain him while one pried open his jaw and the last shoved several pills inside and poured in water. Max tried to spit them out, but one hand pinched his nose shut while another clamped over his mouth, making him choose between swallowing or suffocating.

Max swallowed as they continued to hold him down. He bucked and twisted with all the force he possessed when a syringe appeared. But, like with the pills, resistance was futile, and they injected the contents into his arm. Once released, Max glared at each man, memorizing their faces. He would make them pay for forcing drugs into his body.

Arcilla laughed as her men returned to the fire. "Hope you enjoy the trip my LSD concoction will take you on."

Max searched the surrounding woods. His thoughts ran a mile a minute, wondering if Dexter Clovis ended up as prey. He stole another glance at the heads, but they were too decomposed to make out features.

While his captors ate, Max rifled through his mind to find a way out of this nightmare. He started rubbing the thin rope that bound his wrists against the rough bark, gouging his forearms with each stroke. *Keep your shit together, Stirling. Zulu is probably searching for you, but it's on you to get the hell out of here.*

Minutes later, with no discernible progress on the binding, Max's world began shifting as the drug's effects kicked in. Colors altered and spun, making him nauseous as his pulse and body temperature increased. Intense fear of impending death threatened to overwhelm him as he thought about the lifeless bodies of those hunted before him.

Not giving in or up, two things which weren't part of his DNA, Max renewed his efforts, uncaring if he made a bloody mess of his arms. When the twine snapped apart, he scarcely registered the freeing of his hands. As he brought them to the front, the dangling rope took the form of an anaconda. He scuttled back, attempting to move away, but the snake came with him.

A grain of lucidity allowed him to realize the anaconda was the rope. He slunk into the foliage and unwrapped the line that was restricting his ankles. With one glance back, Max noted his abductors remained unaware of his escape. Gaining his feet, he began to run. To where, from where, Max had no clue. He only knew if he stayed, he would be dead.

Iguazu National Park – Hotel Room – 0700 Hours

Jake paced in the tiny space between the twin beds and the small table against the wall in his and Dave's room. He tried to sleep last night when they returned to the hotel near zero three hundred but gave up hours ago. With no trail and no friggin' clue in which direction the abductors took Stirling, reluctantly, he called off the search and brought his men back for some rest.

The confines of the room pressed in uncomfortably around Jake, so he went to the little balcony and slid open the door. Arizona-born and raised, Jake preferred dry heat and vast spaces, so he grimaced as he stepped out into the muggy air. He gripped the railing, staring at the panoramic view of the falls, but his thoughts were thousands of miles and eighteen years away.

He recalled how Commander Droit approached him one sunny day, the hard set of the man's jaw unreadable as always. Everyone in the SEAL community heard what happened to Team Zulu. Six men were blown to smithereens in the blink of an eye because Master Chief Stirling decided to enter the building despite the intelligence officer's warning. Stirling's *'no guts, no glory'* attitude had been something Jake emulated once upon a time.

Hell, Jake earned the moniker 'Mars' in his early years as a SEAL. Though short for Marshall, it also referenced his God of War approach to every mission. The death of an entire team and the subsequent guidance of Master Chief Derek West squelched his brash behavior and honed him into a leader. Under West's tutelage, Jake learned to temper his impetuous reactions and develop the skills necessary to enable a successful outcome while maintaining his men's safety as a primary concern.

And he had Droit to thank for the opportunity of a lifetime. The brief conversation with the officer on that beautiful, bright day changed the direction of his life. Although eagerly anticipating going home to his wife Valarie and newborn son Jamie after returning from deployment, Droit's unexpected offer to join a reformed Zulu took him away from her for a full six months until they relocated from California to Virginia.

Jake's mind shifted again. His eldest son was almost the same age as the senator's son, two years shy. However, on his pay, James would attend community college instead of some Ivy League university if he chose the higher-education route. Jake wanted to locate Dexter because it was his mission, and as a father, he also understood the dread associated with a missing child.

His teenage daughter's disappearing act last month, sneaking out to meet a boy she talked to online, nearly sent him over the edge. Luckily, Dave kept him calm, and with the rest of the guys, they tracked her down and put the fear of God into the jackanape, who turned out to be a thirty-year-old predator. The bastard now sat in jail awaiting trial, and Eve learned a valuable lesson, fortunately only frightened and not harmed.

Jake blew out a breath and raked fingers through his chestnut brown hair. A man accustomed to taking action, he didn't do well cooling his heels. Lockwood, Draper, Farris, and her techie Lester were working the issue and trying to find them something, anything to go on ... a direction in which they could begin searching for Stirling.

"You sleep at all?" Dave asked as he joined Jake on the balcony and offered him a paper cup with coffee.

"Not really," Jake admitted to his best friend.

"Didn't think so. Stirling's a trained SEAL. He'll be fin—"

"NO! Don't go there. He may be trained, but he was drugged when they took him. We lost him. That's on me. He can't be much older than Jamie ... still a kid. Twists my gut."

Dave nodded. "We didn't count on them stripping him. That was wholly unexpected."

"Should've let Draper implant a tracker," Finn said as he squeezed in beside Dave on the small balcony.

Jake eyed Finn. "How'd you? Never mind."

"Not a door in this world that can keep me out. Though I do prefer blowing them open to picking locks." Finn's green eyes twinkled. "Any word from Lockwood yet?"

As if Finn's words were a premonition, Jake's phone buzzed.

Somewhere in Iguazu National Park

Stumbling, disoriented, lights and colors playing havoc with his vision, making everything distorted and surreal, Max's breaths came in short pants. Drug-induced fear continued to mix with confusion and drove him forward. The sticks, rocks, and foliage underfoot tore into his unprotected feet, but he kept going. The thick, oppressive, humid air made breathing more difficult, yet an internal desire to survive propelled him onward.

A quickly silenced cry of agony wrenched from him as his left ankle twisted in a hole. His arm slammed into a tree trunk as he fell, and the bark hungrily ate up his exposed skin as he slid down. Max reached out in an attempt to keep his face from smacking the dirt. Only partially successful, the impact not as forceful as it could've been, Max rolled to his back and grabbed for his throbbing ankle.

Sunlight filtered through the dense canopy of leaves above him, creating a kaleidoscope of colors which, if he hadn't been so shit out of luck and running for his life, would've been beautiful. He rocked on his unclothed back as he clung to his lower leg, riding the downward crest of pain.

Wild blue eyes with pupils blown darted around, searching for something to wrap and support his ankle so he could keep going. Fighting a losing battle against the anxiety-producing drugs, Max released his foot, twisted his body, and raised himself to his scraped and bloody knees. Hissing as one landed on a pointy rock, he crawled into the underbrush to hide.

Safely ensconced and concealed by bromeliads, orchids, and ferns clustered around trees, Max lay his head on a bed of damp moss. The drugs working their way through his system produced frightening hallucinations of predatory animals about to pounce, so he squeezed his eyes shut to block them out.

But in doing so, other visions, real ones, assaulted him. The blood-soaked face of his mother, seen through the lens of his five-year-old self, came first. Some images had been tattooed in his brain ... his mom after the car accident being one of them.

Buckled safe and sound in his three-point harness car seat in the rear of their sedan, Max stared at the rearview mirror reflection of Mom. Her blue eyes remained open, but even at five, he grasped they held no life. Vacant and unseeing as blood trailed down her cheeks. *Mommy, don't go. Please don't leave me.*

The mental picture shifted, and he stood in the middle of the living room of his childhood home, the one before everyone he loved disappeared. Now only a few months older than when Mom died, he clung to the phone he used to dial 911, wishing he could contact his dad and be hugged by his strong arms.

He trembled as Nanna lay on the carpet on her back, her eyes shut and her blouse open with wires stuck to her. Adults rushed around him, saying things he didn't understand. Max had no idea what a heart attack meant, but comprehended death visited again and took his beloved grandmother.

A flag-draped coffin came next. Max couldn't stop the tears from running down his cheeks as his six-year-old body stood erect and held a salute for his father. He finally lowered his hand as a stern man came forward and offered him the folded flag. Max clutched it to his chest as, one by one, men in uniform proceeded to pound golden eagle pins on the top of the casket.

His world dissolved at that moment. Max went from having everything to nothing too damned fast. In less than a year, he lost his mom, grandma, and dad—everyone who loved and cherished him was gone. All his happy, carefree days vanished, never to be revisited after being sent to live with Uncle Athole.

"Go away!" Max ordered as an apparition of Uncle Asshole formed. Max shivered as the man who made his life a living hell gripped his scrawny arms and shook him violently before locking him in his bedroom without dinner again. No matter what he did, he seemed to anger Athole. He could do nothing to protect himself or please his uncle.

"Maxers. Hey, come on, kiddo. Open your eyes."

The warm and caring voice, distantly familiar, Max obeyed and was greeted with an unexpected specter. "Dad?"

"Up now, kiddo. You're not safe here. You need to keep moving."

"You can't be here. You're dead."

Preston tapped Max's forehead. *"I'm here."* He moved his index finger to his son's heart. *"And here. Always. Time to dig deeper and move, or the bitch will find you."*

"She drugged me. You're only a figment of my imagination."

"Perhaps, but it doesn't change the fact your mission is to stay alive. Use the broad leaves to wrap your ankle."

Max pushed himself up and reached for a bunch of leaves. He glanced at the mirage of his father, who remained in a crouching position beside him. Real or imagined, it didn't matter. He wasn't alone, and he drew strength from the confidence radiating from Preston Stirling's face.

Tapping a potent reservoir deep within, Max determined to do whatever was necessary to survive. He padded his ankle with a clump of moss, then covered it in several layers of the pliant and rubbery fan-like leaf. He tugged on a nearby vine, gathering a length, which he wound around his foot and up his shin. His makeshift brace wouldn't impress a medic but would stabilize his injured appendage enough to hobble.

Using the tree to assist him, Max clawed his way to his feet. Supporting his weight on his right leg, he sucked in a breath and exhaled gradually, trying to maintain his grasp on reality. Alone, naked, injured, drugged, and scared out of his mind, Max continued his flight, limping off, hoping he selected a direction that would save his life.

5

Drugs or Batshit Crazy

Somewhere in Iguazu National Park

A CHING and thirsty, Max forced himself to keep going. Whenever clarity and logic filtered into his brain, he stopped to listen to determine if anyone followed him. Relieved each time he determined Arcilla and her men had not located him, Max pushed aside the fronds of a plant and spied a godsend.

Reaching the narrow and shallow creek, Max dropped to his knees and cupped his hands to drink greedily. Once sated, he sat on his butt to scan his environment as he swatted another bug. If Arcilla didn't kill him, he would be eaten alive by the mosquitos and other flying nuisances. Shifting again, he rested his throbbing ankle in the cool water, hoping it might reduce the swelling or at least numb his pain a bit.

For the most part, Max managed to repress the unexpected fear and hallucinations, but physically, his heart still raced, and he felt hotter than usual. Swaying as his head hammered painfully, Max shut his eyes and used a hand to prop himself upright.

"Only a short break, kiddo. They'll catch you if you linger in one place too long."

"Yeah. I know." Max squinted at his dad, thankful for the company even if he was not real.

"You're too visible. You don't blend into your surroundings as a sniper should."

Max chuckled. "I'm naked. How the hell am I supposed to blend in, Dad?" He fell over in the next moment. Lying on his back, he stared up at his father. "Why'd you knock me down?"

"Use your head. Think. Solve the problem."

His father disappeared as a memory from when he was seven surfaced. He and a neighbor boy found a mud puddle after a storm and crawled through it as they pretended to be doing SEAL training. Uncle Asshole blistered his hide with the paddle when he traipsed through the house covered in muck.

He had difficulty sitting for almost a week and never got to play with Jerry again. His uncle lectured him about not fraternizing with kids of enlisted sailors. It never made sense to Max because Dad was enlisted … not a cake eater.

The recollection sparked an idea. Max wallowed in the mud at the edge of the stream, covering himself before rolling in the dead foliage. Sitting up, he scooped up more muck and wiped it across his face and neck, ensuring he covered all parts of his lightly tanned skin. The coating not only provided him camouflage, but it also acted as a mosquito repellant and sunscreen.

Max rinsed his hands, took one more drink of water, and then crawled to a tree to pull himself up on his feet once more. He took about fifteen limping paces before he froze. A snapping twig alerted him to someone or something in his vicinity. Arcilla was not the only danger he faced in the jungle. Dense rainforests were home to anaconda, caiman, and jaguars.

Scarcely breathing, Max waited and listened for another sign of who or what approached. A rustle ahead caused him to meld into the tree, hoping to become invisible. A naked and dirty blond with an arrow shaft protruding from his bicep stumbled into view, and Max couldn't believe his eyes. *Dexter Clovis.*

The missing university student fell to the ground at the creek and drank hastily as his head swiveled back and forth, his expression filled with abject terror. Max's mission changed. Now, he not only had to keep himself alive, but he must also help Dexter. He limped forward. "Dexter, I'm Max."

Campsite in Iguazu National Park – 1200 Hours

"Holy hell!" Jake said, and a loud "Fuck!" came from Finn as the men of Team Zulu gaped at the mutilated bodies.

Dave turned his gaze away. He'd seen terrible things in his time in the military, but this he would classify as one of the worst. "Is the one on the left Dexter?"

Grant shook his head as he studied the one Dave indicated. "Too decomposed to be him, although whoever this is had the same color hair. Poor kid."

Rocketeer sniffed at a tree and alerted Zach. Moving forward, Zach took a knee and examined the blood-stained bark and the disturbed foliage. "Appears a struggle took place here, and someone worked hard to break free." He held up a length of rough, frayed twine covered in dried blood.

Jake's gut churned as he strode over to Zach. This mission went off the rails. Not only did they lose Stirling and fail to locate Dexter, but they also discovered rotting corpses, which most likely belonged to the other missing students.

"TOC, Zulu One. We located the campsite, plus four dead bodies. No joy on Clovis or Stirling. There are signs someone was tied up here recently." He went on to describe what they found as his men searched the camp for any details that might help them determine who and how many they were dealing with.

Jake ended the transmission after being informed that local authorities would deal with recovering the bodies. Anger roiled in him at not being allowed to cut the men down, but accepted the police would probably send investigators to gather evidence and they must leave things as undisturbed as possible.

For now, Jake needed to focus his efforts on locating Clovis and Stirling. Preferably alive. "Zach, did Rocky find his scent?"

Coming out of the brush, Zach said, "Yeah, this way."

Grim expressions covered their faces as they moved deeper into the forest, following their furry rocket. All business, they took note that Finn had not made a single comment about all the ways the jungle might kill him, and no one teased him either.

Zulu Plane – TOC

Kira swallowed the bile rising in her throat as photos of the deceased were sent to her from Grant. She bit the bottom of her lip when she thought about Stirling ending up like them. *I should've implanted him with a tracker.*

Aware of Draper's distress, Bryan laid a hand on her shoulder as he said, "Subcutaneous GPS implants aren't allowed for SEALs. You did all you could to ensure Stirling's safety."

"Not enough. He's lost because I didn't anticipate—"

"Draper, this isn't your fault. It isn't anyone's, though Jake most likely will believe differently. If Stirling is anything like his father, he will adapt."

Kira stared at the lieutenant commander. "Did you work with Preston Stirling?"

"No. Before my time, but Captain Kendrick and Admiral Droit did. Don't believe everything people say about the elder Stirling. I'm not sure what went down years ago, but you don't become Master Chief of Zulu if you don't possess the right stuff."

Nodding, Kira gave Lockwood's words some thought, and they held merit.

Bryan blew out a breath. "As far as Maxwell Stirling, your efforts, which identified a potential location, may lead to his rescue and perhaps Clovis too."

"I didn't do much." Kira deflected.

"Don't sell yourself short. The guys rely on us here as much as we do them out there. They couldn't do their job without the logistical support you provide. And you're the one who found a thin trail of smoke in the middle of a jungle." Lockwood grinned as Kira blushed.

They lucked out when Draper joined their support staff. Kira did the work of three, was quick-witted, and possessed the ability to acquire what they required out of thin air … often before they realized they needed it. She earned the respect of the entire team, himself included.

Somewhere in Iguazu National Park

Max knelt beside the unconscious man and touched him to determine if he was another illusion like his father and the dozen or so jaguars, anacondas, and dinosaur-sized caimans his mind continued to conjure. Finding flesh and blood, he peered at his father, who crouched on the other side. "Shit. I didn't expect him to pass out."

Preston laughed as he sat back on his heels. *"Kiddo, you look like a freaking mud monster. Be thankful he didn't run. You'd have a hard time catching him if he did."*

"Yeah, there's that." Max studied the wound in Dexter's arm, noting it appeared infected and at least a couple of days old. The heat radiating off Dexter also supported an infection. Debating whether to wait until he roused or try to bring him around with a splash of water or gentle tapping on his cheek, lashes fluttering up saved him from making a decision.

Spying the nightmare beast hovering over him, Dexter scurried backward on his butt and elbows, scared shitless and wondering why the hallucinations returned. His voice shook, trying to make the apparition disappear with words. "You're not real."

"I'm real ... I think." Max wavered in place, but he maintained eye contact as a new round of nausea assaulted him, and the thumping in his head escalated.

Halting his backward movement, Dexter tentatively reached out to touch the figment of his imagination. When his fingers landed on a solid mass, his eyes widened. "Shit. You are real. Fucking hate drugs. They messed me up good. Still not sure what exists and what's in my mind."

Max glanced at his dad, who smiled at him. "Yeah. I hear ya."

"Why are you covered in mud?"

Staring down at his playmate, Max stated earnestly, "A good SEAL uses mud for camouflage. Come on, Jerry, roll around and cover yourself before Uncle Asshole finds us." Max's eyes darted to where he came from. "Unsure how far off he is, and unfortunately, I left a trail for him to follow."

Confused, Dexter gaped at the similarly naked man. "What? Are you related to that crazy bitch and her goons?"

"Huh?" Max lost his battle with nausea and bent over to hurl as his stomach clenched.

Realization hit Dexter as Mud Monster Max spat and rinsed his mouth with water from the stream. "Arcilla drugged you too."

Max returned his gaze to Jerry, but his seven-year-old playmate morphed into Dexter Clovis. He squeezed his eyes shut and clenched his fists. Whatever drugs ran through his system thoroughly screwed with his mind. He admitted, "Yeah."

"How long ago?" Dexter asked as he scooped up a handful of mud to rub on his face, recognizing the man might be tripping as badly as he had, but the muck would make him less visible than his lily-white skin.

"No idea. Sometime in the morning … maybe."

"Well, if it is anything like what she gave me, you're in for one hell of a ride."

Ten minutes later, Dexter, now covered in mud, stood and asked, "I'm totally lost. Any idea how we get out of here?"

Having crawled to a tree, Max used it to pull himself up once again. He held on until the waves of dizziness subsided a bit. Max peered at his dad, reassured by his presence. It reminded him of SERE training when his father appeared to him and helped him deal with the mock captivity. "Which way do I go?"

"Without a compass, maps, or a point of origin, pick a direction and keep the sun on the same side so you don't go in circles," Preston suggested.

"Sound advice. Thanks." Max hobbled forward on his swollen ankle. "This way, Dexter."

Dexter's mouth gaped again. "Who are you talking to?"

"My dad. Best damned SEAL who ever lived. I'm following in his footsteps." Max stumbled onward, not realizing Dexter stared at him like he was bat-shit crazy.

With no clue where to go and glad to have company, Dexter followed, hoping like hell they got out alive.

After what seemed like a few hours later, sunlight peeking in from lower on the horizon, Dexter worked hard to stay with Max. He wondered how in the hell Max continued to walk on an injured foot, though the man did grab tree after tree for support as he moved through the lush vegetation.

More than once, Dexter thought about suggesting they stop so Max could redo the leaves wrapped around his ankle. Mostly, they had come off, revealing significant swelling and ugly bruising, which appeared to be getting darker. But he didn't because Max scarcely registered his presence as he carried on a one-sided conversation with his father, the Navy SEAL.

Dexter worried about Max's sanity and believed the drugs Arcilla gave the guy must be more potent or a higher dose than the ones he received. He shuddered at the thought of the evil bitch catching them and becoming one of her trophies. About to halt, needing a break, weak from days without food, Dexter could only watch as Max fell to the ground in front of him.

Max struggled to keep his mind present as his world became a chaotic mess of hallucinations. Anacondas slithered across his path. Jaguars sat in every tree, ready to pounce. Fire ants covered his lower left leg and kept biting him, causing ungodly pain. A terrifying mud creature followed his every step, and no matter how fast he went, he couldn't lose the tail.

Worst of all, arrows kept flying past his head, and he figured it was only a matter of time before one hit him, and he would be strung up by his feet and his head chopped off by the insane woman. Moving to the next tree, Max misjudged the distance, and instead of clasping the trunk, he grabbed air and crashed to the jungle floor.

His eyes squeezed shut as pain washed through him. An unexpected piece of him wanted to admit defeat and let fate decide his end. "I'm done. She wins."

"Hey, none of that. Get your ass up. Now!"

Max opened his eyes at his father's harsh tone. "Dad?"

"Yeah. Now you heard me. Up."

"I can't."

"I'm not gonna let you give up, Son."

"You told me before to let go ... I'm letting go."

"The hell you are! That was different. You needed to forget your past and the grip your uncle had on you. Now, you need to hang on. Zulu is coming for you. We never leave a brother behind."

"Done fighting ... it's too hard. And I'm not one of them. They hate me because they think you screwed up. No one cares. Everyone I loved is dead. Might as well join them." Max groaned as every part of his body ached, and his head did a magnificent job of trying to detach itself with every beat of his heart.

"Maxers, kiddo, you got the shaft early on. No denying the facts. Hold on. Better things are coming your way. But you gotta save yourself and Dexter until Zulu arrives. You're never out of the fight, so haul yourself to your feet, sailor."

"Dexter?" Max's face scrunched in confusion.

"The mud creature. Your mission is to rescue him. Remember? He's counting on you. Don't let him down."

Moving forward, when Max said his name, Dexter asked, "Are you okay?"

Max peered up into a concerned face as a moment of clarity came. *Dexter Clovis is my mission.* "Yeah." He rolled to his knees and used another tree to pull himself up. "Which way, Dad?" When Preston didn't answer, Max turned his head, and sadly, his father disappeared again. "Quit fucking leaving me."

"Oh, I didn't leave you ... you left me. Not nice. I see you found Dexter for me. Thought he got away."

Max's blood froze in his veins upon hearing Arcilla's voice. For one moment, he wondered if he hallucinated, but her mention of Dexter set him into action. He lunged for the younger man, using his body as a shield. Max experienced a searing pain as an arrow lodged in his ass. The force of the impact sent both men to the ground with Max on top.

As gunfire erupted around him, Max shut his eyes, accepting the grim reaper finally came for him.

6
Mission Accomplished

J AKE aimed and dispatched the woman who shot Stirling with a crossbow before she could reload. As she fell, he moved to eliminate the other five but discovered his men neutralized four, and Rocky leapt on the fifth, sinking his teeth into the man's forearm, taking his quarry down to his knees before the last tango fired his rifle at Stirling.

Zach moved forward with Finn, and they restrained the tango's hands behind his back. Though they both wanted to put a bullet between his eyes, they needed someone alive to provide intel on the hunters … to find out if there were more.

Angry for arriving too late to stop the strap from being impaled by the crossbow bolt, Jake rushed forward and knelt beside Stirling as the team secured the area. "Found you."

His backside on fire from the recent paddling, Max cringed, pulling away from his furious uncle, as he stammered, "Sorry, I'm sorry. I didn't mean to ruin things. Jerry and me were only playing SEAL in the backyard. Don't hit me anymore." Max moved his hand to cover his stinging rear.

"Hey. Don't touch!" Jake barked and grasped Stirling's hand, holding tight to prevent him from yanking out the arrow. The words coming from the injured strap confused Jake, but when Stirling tried to move again, Jake ordered, "Stop moving!"

Max stilled, afraid to anger Uncle Athole more, knowing the punishment would be severe if he didn't obey.

"He's drugged out of his gourd," Dexter offered.

Jake glanced at the muddy man under Stirling, and recognition lit his face. "You're Dexter Clovis."

"Yeah."

"Okay. Be still for a moment while we take care of Stirling."

"Sure thing."

Returning his gaze to the kid, Jake noted fear reflecting from the frozen, deer-in-headlights eyes as Grant Beckett, Zulu Four, and the team medic shrugged off his medkit and knelt.

"Jake, his pupils are blown. He's been drugged." Grant started to pull out supplies.

"That's what I said," Dexter chimed in. "He's tripping bad. He was talking to his dad and asking for help on which way to go. Thinks he's a SEAL."

"He is," Jake answered before he softened his expression, donning one he used with his kids when they were frightened. "Hey, Maxwell. Hold still."

Max's eyes locked on the steel-blue eyes directly in his line of sight. "I'll behave. Don't hit me again, Athole."

"Did he just call you Asshole?" Zach asked with disbelief.

"Nah, I think he said Athole. A Scottish name which, if said with the right inflection, sounds like asshole," Finn stated as he guarded the prisoner while Dave tried in vain to communicate with the bastard since none of them had command of Spanish.

"Not going to hit you. I'm Jake. Do you remember me?"

Max blinked, and his world shifted into clarity for a brief moment. "Marshall?"

"Yes. Good. We've got you. Grant needs you to hold still so he can examine the arrow in your ass."

Max twisted his head to peer at his backside. "Oh?" He groaned as pain radiated through his body.

"How the hell did you get covered in all this muck?" Grant opened a saline bag to rinse the injured area.

Dexter supplied the answer when Max only clenched his jaw. "At the stream. Max said it would camouflage us, and well, it did, and it stopped the mosquitos from eating me alive too."

Using gauze, Grant stabilized the metal bolt sticking out of Max's glut, unwilling to extract it here, unsure if the bleeding would worsen. The object worked as a plug for the wound at the moment. "Any idea what drugs you were given?"

Shifting his gaze to Beckett, Max racked his disorganized mind for the information required. "LSD … and don't know."

"Well, shit. I'm sorry, but I can't give you anything for the pain. Not sure how painkillers will interact." Grant pulled a roll of gauze out and put it in Stirling's mouth. "Bite on this so you don't crack a tooth when we move you off Dexter."

Once Max bit down, Grant, Jake, and Zach shifted the strap, positioning him on his side. Upon finding the shaft of an arrow in the university student's arm, Grant directed Finn to put together the folding stretcher for Stirling as he turned his attention to Dexter's wound.

Jake stood, leaving Zach in charge of Stirling, and moved over to Dave, who guarded the detainee. "Hiking out of here will be painful for the kid."

"Which one?" Dave eyed both young men.

"Both, but mostly Stirling."

"Yeah." Dave didn't say anything more as he noted the softening of Jake's attitude towards Stirling. Jake might be a hardass, stubborn, and slow to change his mind at times, but he possessed a fatherly soft spot. And with the kid's youthful appearance, he could be Jake's son Jamie, which would hit a little close to home for his best friend.

"Zulu One to TOC." Jake then provided status and requested evac to a local medical facility since both men required treatment now instead of waiting until they were stateside. He grimaced as he lifted one corner of the stretcher, and Maxwell moaned. The trek out would be harrowing, and he wouldn't wish the coming pain on anyone, not even Preston Stirling's offspring.

Hospital de Puerto Iguazu – Waiting Room – 1900 Hours

In a small Argentinian hospital, four exhausted men waited for word on Dexter and Max while Zach took Rocketeer outside. Frustrated by their lack of ability to communicate in the local language, the guys assumed Rocky disturbed the sensibilities of the medical staff based solely on the aggressive shooing motions from one of the nurses.

Restless, unsure if the strap and the student were receiving proper care, Grant groused, "Wish we had a terp with us."

Dave nodded. "Axel speaks both Arabic and Spanish. He would be an asset to the team."

"We're talking about who replaces Levi now?" Finn grumbled.

"Well, it will keep our minds occupied, and Lockwood will pick if we don't." Dave stretched his stiff back.

Jake stood and paced the tiny room, tuning out the chatter from his men. He couldn't keep his thoughts from returning to the godawful hike. Stirling let out only a few soft moans when they jarred him, but other than those times, he remained stoic with a clenched jaw. The drugs that had been forced on him prevented them from relieving his pain and also induced severe anxiety. Jake found it hard to watch him struggle with fear.

As Jake leaned against the wall, Dave's words during the flight to Argentina began to roll through his mind. Usually, he was more open-minded and slower to judge people. It concerned him why he, as Dave put it, *painted Maxwell with the same brush as Preston.*

In truth, he never met Preston nor been briefed on the AAR of the mission, which resulted in the team's death. Thinking back, neither Admiral Droit nor Captain Kendrick ever badmouthed Preston, and they had been captain and lieutenant commander, respectively, at the time and oversaw Zulu's ops.

The rumors and hearsay started in the ranks and spread as they placed the blame on Preston's shoulders, claiming he either made a bad call or ignored intel. *I've made my fair share of bad calls. Sending Levi to the roof is one. I should've realized it was a trap. Losing the strap and getting him injured is another.*

Jake's musings halted as a man wearing a white lab coat and carrying a clipboard exited the treatment area. Dave, Finn, and Grant all quieted and turned to the doctor.

"Hello. My name is Doctor Albarez. I understand you do not speak Spanish," the physician said in heavily accented English.

"Correct." Jake pushed off the wall, moving toward the man. "How are the two men we brought in doing?"

Albarez reviewed his notes. "The one named Clovis. Besides being dehydrated and malnourished, he is doing well. We cleaned his wound and, well, his entire body because he was so dirty. I also started him on antibiotics and provided him a pain reliever. I would like to keep him overnight as a precaution."

Jake nodded. "Okay. Two of my men will stay with him."

"There is no need. This is a safe hospital." Albarez scanned the fierce-looking men.

"He is under our protection, so yes, it is necessary."

"Alright."

"And the other, Stirling?" Dave asked, more concerned about a fellow brother.

"His ankle is sprained. Sorry to say we do not have the facilities to determine what drugs are in his system, but based on what Señor Clovis shared, I estimate the hallucinogenic effects will be gone by tomorrow morning. Regrettably, we could only use a local while removing the arrow and debriding his wounds. Quite a painful process, but he is resting now. We started antibiotics, but I believe it is best if he also remains here overnight."

"Agreed. Likewise, we will be staying with him. Can you place them in the same room?" Jake slowly unfurled his fingers, not sure when he made a fist.

"No. The rooms are all singles, but across the hall is doable. Two of you can come back now."

"Dave, Grant, you go. I need to contact Lockwood and provide a sitrep." Jake reached into his pocket for his cell. He dialed Bryan as his men followed Dr. Albarez into the treatment area, and Finn motioned he would go outside to update Zach.

Next Day
Hospital de Puerto Iguazu – Stirling's Room – 1100 Hours

Dave nudged Jake, who sat in the corner on the floor of Maxwell's room. "Think he's waking."

Moving his head from shoulder to shoulder, Jake stretched out the cricks in his neck caused by the angle it lolled while catching a few winks. Turning his eyes to the bed, he spied the unmoving strap. "What gives you that impression?"

"His hand gripped the sheet, and his face grimaced for a moment. Think he might be in pain."

"No doubt. The doctor hasn't given him any meds other than antibiotics." Rising, Jake spotted Grant in the other corner of the bare-bones, red-bricked hospital room. Sometime during the early morning, Grant must've switched places with Zach, who would now be with Finn in Clovis' room.

Jake wanted coffee but needed to be in the room when Stirling woke. After giving a lot of thought to why he judged Maxwell, he didn't much care for the answers. He allowed others' opinions and rumors to cloud his reasoning—something Jake rarely did.

He firmly believed every person deserved to be measured on their merits. So, Jake vowed to reassess his opinion of Maxwell, based on concrete evidence of his capabilities and qualities, as he would any other SEAL.

Leaning against the wall and stretching his back, Dave said, "Draper called a few hours ago. She's amazing. Found and rented a vehicle more suitable for us to transport him to the plane. Kira said he'd be more comfortable lying down. Arranged for a gurney too so he won't need to sprawl across several webbed seats or rack out on the aircraft's floor."

Jake grinned. "Kira's always looking out for everyone. We'd be lost without her. I thought about letting him use my hammock, but the gurney will be better."

"Whoa! What's with the one-eighty, brother? Last I heard from you, Maxwell was cut from the same cloth as Preston." Dave gaped with genuine surprise at Jake.

"I'm big enough to admit when you're right, and I'm wrong."

"Hold right there. I need a picture of this momentous occasion." Dave snickered as he pulled out his phone.

Jake flipped double birds as he laughed.

Pushing up from the floor, Grant grinned at their antics. Part of the reason he enjoyed being on this team is they acted more like family. True brothers were not afraid to disagree, admit errors, or razz the hell out of each other while still being the best-damned group of operators within the SEAL ranks. Their success record spoke for itself. If there was a situation anywhere in the world that required an elite strike force, Zulu would get'er done.

Laughter pulled Max from the last vestiges of sleep. His lashes lifted slightly before lowering and raising a bit more on his second attempt. He caught sight of Marshall flipping off Katz while both chuckled with Beckett.

Max wondered if he was the source of their amusement, which wouldn't be a first. However, finding team guys in his room upon waking was unique. Never once had any of his teammates visited him whenever he had been hurt on a mission.

Somewhat disoriented, unsure where he was, a general achiness and lethargy shrouding him, Max shifted on the bed. Pain shot through his hip as he moved his leg, and as much as he tried, Max couldn't stop the low moan from escaping as he squeezed his eyes shut and gritted his teeth.

Grant moved forward. "Hey. Don't try moving. Haven't been able to give you anything for the pain yet."

Max blinked his eyes open at the concerned tone. His gaze met Beckett's. Inhaling and holding his breath for a four-count, Max gradually released it to gain control over his pain. "Where am I?"

"What passes for a hospital in Puerto Iguazu." Jake wiped the humor from his face upon viewing Stirling's scrunched brow. "Grant, he needs something. Is it safe yet?"

"Maybe. Maxwell, look at me," Grant requested as he flicked on his penlight.

"Just, Max."

"Okay, Max." Grant studied the ocean-blue orbs, noting the pupils had returned to normal. He turned to Jake. "Probably safe for over-the-counter painkillers. Until Doc can run the tox screen, I'm not comfortable giving him anything stronger."

Unnerved at being the center of attention, Max said, "Don't need anything. Can handle it."

"Grant, give him whatever you think best." Jake turned his focus on Stirling. "You're going to need something. Not putting you through the hell you endured yesterday again."

"Yesterday?"

Dave stepped closer as Grant rummaged in his medkit for an analgesic. "Welcome back. Do you recall anything after being taken in the bar?"

His mind hazy, Max lifted an arm to rub his face and spied the white gauze which covered it from wrist to elbow. He glanced at his other arm, finding it adorned in the same manner. Eyes moving back to Katz, he said, "Arcilla is a psychopath. She hunted and killed four men, though I think Dexter is alive." Images of the dead men invaded his thoughts, causing his stomach to lurch. Visions Max wouldn't soon forget.

"We located the camp with their bodies. Local authorities don't have any information on her specifically, but suspect she may have been the perpetrator of a series of heinous crimes across Argentina over the past five years," Dave shared.

Max wondered how much he imagined versus what was real. "Did she shoot my ..." Spotting their smirks, he blushed.

"Yeah. You had an arrow in your ass," Jake supplied.

Groaning, Max realized he would be quite literally the butt of many jokes for a long time.

Misinterpreting the reason for the groan, Grant offered two pills. "Here. Take these. They'll help take the edge off. Their roads aren't the best, so it will be a bumpy ride to the plane." After Stirling popped the tablets into his mouth, Grant held a bottle of water to his lips so he could take a sip to wash them down.

"How'd you find me?"

"Rocketeer. After he got your scent off your boxers. If we had been a little faster …" Jake trailed off as he raked a hand through his hair, still upset he failed the strap, and the kid almost ended up dead. "Dave, Grant, prepare him to leave. I'm going to check if Clovis is ready." He strode from the room before he allowed his internal anger to show.

Embarrassment increased as Max remembered he had been buck-assed naked. "You bring me clothes?"

Grant lifted a bag off the floor. "We got ya covered. Sweats and a t-shirt."

Max started to pull himself up, planning on standing since sitting to dress would be out of the question.

"Whoa, no standing. You've got a sprained ankle too." Dave gently pushed the kid down on the pillow. "Let us do the work." He stopped as Maxwell eyed him suspiciously.

"I'll do it myself." Under his breath, Max said, "Always have," as he grabbed the gray sweats Beckett held out to him.

"Fine." Dave stepped back, unwilling to force help on Stirling. He caught the murmured words and added them to things Max uttered while they hiked out of the jungle. Granted, at the time, the kid had been high as a kite, but Dave surmised Stirling must be used to being on his own, which made him wonder how his Foxtrot team treated him.

Dave's thoughts halted as Stirling groaned, unable to bend enough to put on his pants without pulling on the stitches in his backside. Grant intervened and, in his gruff, no-nonsense medic mode, took charge, yanking the sweats from Stirling and dressing the kid.

Once Stirling was clothed, Dave put a pillow on a wheelchair before Grant transferred Maxwell. The expression on the kid's face ran the gambit of disbelief, brooding, and pain. The last struck Dave hard, and he wished they could give him more relief. He tabled his emotions as he gripped the handles and pushed the chair out the door. "Time to blow this joint. Draper arranged a ride, which will allow you to lie down."

7

Sins of the Father

MAX struggled to keep his eyes open, but his lids only managed to lift to half-mast. Though the drug-induced hallucinations had worn off, unwanted images assaulted him each time he allowed them to close. The headless bodies haunted him most, but bits and pieces of his trek through the jungle also filtered in and left him uneasy.

Sleep would allow him to escape McBride's annoying jokes … several of them at his expense. Max possessed a thick hide, needed one being the son of Preston Stirling, and perhaps if his mindset was not still a bit screwed up, he might find McBride's humor funny. But the barbs got under his skin to the point Max desired to shut the man's mouth … with a fist if necessary.

Weary of laying on his stomach, Max shifted, positioning himself on his side. He spied the logistics specialist as Draper sat with Zulu, laughing with a beer in her hand. He owed her a token of appreciation for arranging an old-style camper truck to transport him from the hospital to the plane.

The over-the-cab bed allowed him to stay off his injured backside, and the front window provided him a view, giving him something to focus on during the drive. She also procured several pillows and a gurney topped with egg-crate foam for him, which would make this sixteen-hour flight bearable.

Loud guffawing from the group near the forepart of the aircraft, presumably at another of McBride's witticisms, which Max didn't catch, caused him to inhale sharply and clench his jaw.

"Hey, are you in pain?" Dexter shifted on the seat, moving closer to the man who risked his life to find him.

"I'm fine." Max peered at the young college student, surprised to be asked how he was.

"Sure?"

"Yeah."

Dexter exhaled as his hand rubbed lightly on his still-aching arm. "Never figured I'd end up running for my life while a crazy bitch tried to skewer me with arrows. And those guys with her … well, I didn't realize people like them existed. Thanks for saving me. I'm sorry you ended up shot with a crossbow bolt."

No one ever thanked him before, leaving Max unsure how to respond. "I'm glad you're safe, but I didn't save you. The guys up front did."

"Yes, you did." Dexter leaned forward when Max shook his head. "You probably don't remember 'cause of the drugs, but you kept me going. I gave up hope of ever finding my way out of the jungle, certain I would become one of her trophies. Geez, those poor guys. I ralphed when I saw them.

"Anyway, when you showed up at the stream, you scared the crap out of me at first. But then you said you were there to rescue me, and well, I was no longer alone. Gave me hope. Those drugs sure messed with your head, but you said Zulu would find me, so I believed. And they did … just in the nick of time. Well, a few seconds earlier would've been better. You wouldn't have gotten skewered protecting me."

Dexter sat back but maintained eye contact. "Thanks for that too. I'm pre-med, and I want to be a surgeon like my dad. I've taken a lot of anatomy classes. I wouldn't be alive now if not for you. The bolt would've likely hit my femoral artery, and I would've bled out before we made it to where the trucks picked us up. So, yeah, I'm alive because of you."

Ignorant of those tidbits until now, Max only stared at the college student as they lapsed into an uncomfortable silence, both unaware two people watched them intently. Zulu's medic, with concern, and the team's intel officer, with ambivalence, as Nicole measured what she'd been told about Stirling against what she witnessed on this op.

Grant Beckett tuned out Finn's latest humorous anecdote, something about how he ended up locked out of his apartment wearing only a pair of speedos and his seventy-year-old landlady propositioning him. His eyes sought Stirling, intending to check how he fared. The injuries Max suffered would knock him out of operating for at least a month or two.

He briefly pondered how angry Stirling's team would be that Zulu lost him and almost got him killed. If roles had been reversed, they'd be out for a bit of payback. However, Foxtrot's reaction remained at the low end of his worry. Occupying the top spot, did Stirling receive the right medical treatment?

The local doctor might be a quack, and Grant wished they could do a toxicology panel of the kid's blood so he could adequately medicate him. He had to be in significant pain, given his overall physical state. A couple tabs of ibuprofen wouldn't do much to ease the misery of his cut-up soles, sprained ankle, and the damage done by the arrow.

Rising, desiring to alleviate as much discomfort as possible, Grant snagged his medkit and moved to the rear of the plane. As he approached, he caught sight of Farris staring at Stirling. Their intel officer's expression was always hard to read, but he discerned puzzlement now. Dismissing her, he focused on Max.

Almost to him, Grant held back, waiting to hear Stirling's answer, when he overheard Dexter ask, "So, you must be close with your dad like I am. Bet he taught you all that stuff ... um, like the mud camouflage."

"I was. When I was six, he died proudly serving our country." Max didn't elaborate further.

"Six? Wow, sorry, dude. Must've been hard on your mom."

"No. She died about ten months before him."

"Shit. Geez, sorry. I'm not sure how I would function without my parents. They hover too much sometimes, but I ... God, I couldn't imagine losing them at six."

Max shifted, not wanting to talk anymore. Unfortunately, his movement caused his pain to amplify, and a hiss escaped.

Grant moved forward, dropping his kit on the floor and taking a knee. "You're in pain," he stated the obvious.

Gaining control, Max met Beckett's eyes, surprised to find compassion. No one ever gave a shit about him. "I'm good."

"Like hell, you are!" Grant fished out two pills. "Want to give you something stronger, but I can't until ... well, I just can't yet. But a couple more ibuprofen and some cold packs should help a little." He dug for the instant ice packs after Max took the meds and washed them down with the bottled water Draper had placed on his gurney earlier.

Dexter observed the interaction with a grin. If he didn't have his sights set on becoming a surgeon, he might consider being a military medic. Then again, he didn't like the idea of being shot at, and his parents certainly wouldn't want him to go into such a risky career. Though, the camaraderie and the way these men behaved appealed to him. They might be the brothers he wished he had. Being an only child lacked certain benefits of having siblings.

On his stomach once more, in a somewhat awkward position with his lower leg propped on pillows and cold gel packs tucked around his ankle and on his ass, Max closed his eyes. The visions bombarded him at first, but sleep finally came as he conjured up an image of his dad standing guard to protect him.

Grant turned his attention to Dexter. "How's your pain? Do you need more meds?"

"No. It aches, but the doctor gave me a kick-ass painkiller before we left the hospital." Dexter grimaced as he said, "I'm sorry I asked about his father. I didn't realize he was dead. The way Max talked to his imaginary dad made me think that his father was alive. Can't imagine how much it hurt to lose both parents so young."

Settling in beside Dexter, Grant gazed at Max. He considered Dave's words about putting rocks in Stirling's rucksack, which weren't his to carry. The kid was only six when Preston died. Grant thought back to when he was six. Back then, his father was his superhero and could do no wrong.

Grant was full-grown and out of the house before he understood every human possessed faults. No, it wasn't right to judge Maxwell by Preston's failings. He wouldn't want to be measured by his own father's mistakes, which landed Frank Beckett in jail for driving drunk and almost killing a family when he crashed into a van on New Year's Eve two years ago.

Shaking the memory loose, Grant turned to Dexter. "If you need anything, come see me." He rose, grabbed his bag, and wandered back to where the team sat.

"Why are you bothering with Stirling?" Finn asked as Grant resumed his seat.

"Quit being a jackass. He hurts. You'd be whining and carrying on if you were in his condition," Grant retorted, sick of McBride's comments about Max.

"I'm no pansy. It's only a swollen ankle and a wee hole in his arse," Finn bit back.

Grant glared at Finn.

Aware of that particular expression, Dave stepped in before things became heated. "Might be little, but remember a crossbow bolt made the hole, and the arrow's tip hit his bone. He can't have morphine until the blood tests are done. Show some compassion, Finn. None of our brothers should have to go through something like that without painkillers. Not even one with the last name of Stirling."

"Not one of my brothers," Finn groused, pulled his hat down to cover his eyes, and ignored the rest of the team.

Dave eyed Jake with reproach. He laid Finn's attitude at Jake's feet. His best friend met his gaze head-on, and he didn't see any movement in the hard, steel-blue orbs. *Yeah, he's stubborn. It will take more than one encounter to change Jake's mind about Stirling.*

Lester wandered back from the head and snagged a bottle of iced mocha and an energy drink from the cooler. He settled into a seat beside his superior and handed Farris the mocha before popping the top on his beverage. He noted her concentration on the strap at the back and said, "I'm glad they found him. He'd be a real asset for Zulu."

Nicole uncapped the bottle and shifted her gaze to Owen Lester. He had an aptitude for technology, which came in handy often, but his social skills were a bit lacking. "In what way?"

"He's a polyglot."

"A what?"

"Polyglot."

"I heard what you said. I'm unfamiliar with the term." Nicole sipped her coffee, though often she wished to drink a beer instead. She believed she must maintain a professional distance between herself and the operators she sent into dangerous situations, so she opted not to engage in post-mission beers.

"Oh, um, polyglot refers to a person who speaks, writes, or reads numerous languages. Max told me he's fluent in over a dozen, many from the Middle East and Africa. He said he picks them up fast. It would be quite useful with all the places Zulu goes. Perhaps you might suggest he be added to their support team?"

Nicole didn't want Stirling on this team. He was only selected for this mission for his looks, nothing more. She shrugged, disguising her disdain. "Not up to me. The selection of operators isn't in our chain of command. That belongs to Lockwood."

Lester nodded. "Yeah, of course, but it might be beneficial for interrogations in the field. Or, well, save the guys' lives if they had someone who spoke the local language." He guzzled half his drink, reached for his laptop, and abandoned the topic. Lester had a couple hours of downtime and wanted to work on his latest software project.

Returning her gaze to Stirling, the seed of Lester's suggestion took root. *Perhaps his skill could be used to keep the guys safe. So long as Stirling is never allowed to make command decisions.*

8

Thrown Under the Bus

Three Days Later - Virginia – Zulu Team Equipment Cages

ROCKETEER jumped, catching the ball tossed to him by his packmate. Trotting over to Jake, he dropped the slobbery toy in his lap, waiting for him to throw it again. Rocky could do this all day and never tire of the game, happy that when one of his humans stopped, another would gladly join in unless they were talking serious stuff with pictures on the wall.

He dashed for the airborne projectile again as his master said, "So when is Chase joining us?"

Wiping his wet hand on his pants, Jake peered at Zach. "Should be here tomorrow if all goes well."

Finn grinned, pleased with the selection of Axel Chase. They concluded their discussion on the flight back. The next day, Jake offered the position to Chase, and when he accepted, Lockwood initiated the transfer process. "Won't need to be babysitting him. He's as solid as they come."

Dave only shook his head at Finn's reasoning. One of the things he liked most when he was Zulu Three was mentoring new guys, even the seasoned ones. Making it to this team came with an increased level of expectations. As far as the world knew, becoming a top-tier operator in DEVGRU was the highest position a SEAL could achieve, but in truth and unpublicized, Strike Force Zulu was the tip of the trident.

Being the cream of the crop allowed them to choose any SEAL from any team when they needed a replacement. In the history of Zulu, no one ever turned down the opportunity to join when they received the call. However, by accepting, they became the low man on the totem pole, regardless of their previous position.

Some found the transition difficult, which is why Zulu Three's role as a mentor was so important. Their new member must integrate fast because they might be spun up for a situation at a moment's notice. The process of moving from another team, where the operator may have been number one or two to become number six, sometimes caused a few bumps in the road.

Like when Finn and Levi joined. Transitioning from being Charlie Team's second-in-command and leading men to number five of a six-man team, stuck in Levi's craw for several months and caused friction. Dave sighed, recalling how much effort it took to shift Levi's thinking, but he succeeded, and their team gelled, except when Levi and Finn butted heads.

Years ago, when he mentored Finn, Dave figured out fast the Scotsman was an outspoken guy who didn't take kindly to Levi's overt ambitions to lead Zulu. From the tips of his red hair to his toes, Finn lived and breathed the essence of what it meant to be a fiercely loyal brother.

All the turmoil was moot now. With Levi gone and Axel's temperament more easy-going, the team would mesh better. Zach's next question pulled Dave from his musings.

"We having a team barbeque?" Zach chuckled, recollecting his welcome to Zulu. Almost going broke buying cases of beer for all his firsts with them. He couldn't wait for someone else to be footing the bill.

Jake nodded. "Val's arranging things with Cathy. Probably be next Saturday."

With a grin, thinking about his wife Cathy, Dave asked, "How long is Lockwood giving us to train?"

"Six weeks if we aren't spun up." Jake chucked Rocky's ball across the room again.

The door to their team equipment room opening caused all five men to turn. Finn chuckled as Kira pulled a cart with her. "What ya got for us now?"

"Not yours. Axel sent his list of supplies, so I went ahead and gathered them." Kira pushed the loaded cart into the empty cage, then pivoted and shut the door. She leaned on the wire, kicking one foot behind her as she surveyed the guys. "When's the barbeque?"

"Most likely next weekend." Finn scratched Rocketeer behind the ears after the pup dropped the tennis ball into his lap when Jake tired of playing fetch.

Kira nodded and turned to Grant. "I finally got the word for you regarding Stirling. Doc said no lasting effects from the drugs, and they shipped him back home this morning."

"Why ya checking up on the strap?" Finn asked.

Grant had enough of McBride's bashing of the young man who put his life on the line. "I don't get it. You're the first one to support any brother. Why are you ragging on Stirling? What did he ever do to you?"

"He doesn't belong."

"Why, because of something his father did? Hell, Max was only six. How could it be his fault? Shit. He was orphaned when his dad died. Cut the guy some slack. He passed through the same pipeline as you, me, all of us. And he performed his job better than we did on that last mission. We lost him and nearly got him killed." Grant stormed out of the room, leaving his teammates gaping at him.

Jake sighed as his usually calm and collected medic left. "Give it a rest, Finn. Grant is only doing due diligence following up. He takes all injuries seriously."

Shrugging, letting the issue slide since they wouldn't have to put up with Stirling again, Finn turned his attention to Kira. "Wanna join Zach and me at the bar tonight?"

Kira pushed off the cage and grinned. "Not tonight. Some of us have lives outside of the team."

"Suit yourself." Finn winked at her as she rolled her eyes.

Coronado, CA – Max's Apartment

Balancing on crutches, Max fished for his keys to unlock his place. Tugging them out of his pocket, he wobbled. To remain upright, he made a quick decision to grab the knob, unfortunately dropping the keys. Max groaned. Bending would suck, but with no one to help, he must do this on his own.

Clenching his jaw, he lowered his sprained foot to the floor to stabilize himself and bent over. Yep, it sucked ... *big time*. The arrow wound in his gluteus maximus pulled taut, causing pain. After retrieving the keychain, Max straightened and blew out a breath. He inserted the key and let himself in.

Hobbling forward a few steps, he again balanced and reached to shut his door. He halted in the middle of his four-hundred-square-foot studio apartment. Not much, compared to most, but bigger than his room at Fairwinds Military Academy and better than living in the barracks.

Moving to the small kitchenette, he set the bag of medication on the tiny counter before making his way to his queen-sized bed. Ungracefully, he flopped on his stomach and lay there, staring at the blank wall to the left. Exhausted and starving, he closed his eyes and decided to go without eating. He went to bed without meals many times when he lived with Athole.

His mind drifted, reviewing the past three days. As usual, not a single soul came to visit him, but then again, Foxtrot was on the west coast, and he had been hospitalized on the east. Only nurses and a doctor came into his room while in Virginia. Luckily, the drugs forced on him by Arcilla, a cocktail of things he couldn't recall, wouldn't pose him problems in the future.

The flight home had been hell. Military transport was not known for comfort, and no one took care of his needs like Zulu's logistics officer. He rode the entire way, sitting on a hard metal bench with his foot dangling. In absolute agony, his ankle and rear throbbed mercilessly. Thankfully, his posterior went numb after an hour, although the pins and needles sensation of it coming back to life as he stood to exit almost brought tears to his eyes.

He managed to make the half-mile walk from the tarmac to the base entrance under his own power. He waited twenty minutes for the cab to arrive and chose to stand the whole time since it would be less painful than sitting.

Nobody from Foxtrot showed up to offer him a ride home, though the doctor told him he had spoken with his team leader before he left the hospital and provided Master Chief Baystock with the travel itinerary. The fact that Baystock didn't pick him up didn't surprise Max. If he or one of the other guys had, now that would've shocked him.

Max's phone buzzed as sleep began to draw him down. Not wanting to move a muscle, desiring to ignore it, but realizing he couldn't, he rolled a bit to dig out his cell. His tone held a note of gruffness as he answered, "Stirling."

"Special Warfare Operator Stirling, you are to report to Captain Ridgeway's office in thirty minutes."

"I'm going to be late. It will take me at least an hour to arrive."

"Unacceptable … he's in a foul mood."

Recognizing the haggard voice of the harried yeoman run ragged by their CO, Max said, "Hayden, normally it wouldn't be a problem, but I'm at home and on crutches. I need to call a taxi. I'm not allowed to drive due to medications."

Hayden paused and stared at his superior's closed door. He liked Stirling, though his boss didn't. "Oh, I didn't know. Okay. I'll inform Ridgeway and do what I can to smooth his feathers for you. Just get here as fast as possible."

"Roger." Max sighed as he hung up and thought, *so much for sleeping or eating*. Neither would be happening for several hours. He pulled up the app on his phone and ordered a ride, then got to his feet after grabbing his crutches.

Max glanced at his pain meds, contemplating if he should pop one now, but decided he needed his wits about him when he met with Ridgeway. The captain must be aware of his injuries, and he wondered why Ridgeway ordered him to come in while on medical leave. His gut twisted. This didn't bode well.

Captain Ridgeway's Office

Ridgeway's scowl told Max his prediction would be proven true. Nothing pleasant came when his captain wore that specific expression. He steeled himself for the worst scenario as he entered the room. "Captain, you wanted to see me."

"You're late." Ridgeway motioned to the chair. "Sit."

"Sir, if you don't mind, standing is preferable at the moment." Max held his stoic shield in place, a skill perfected over time.

Ridgeway nodded before launching into his diatribe. He tapped the folder on his desk, emphasizing every which way Stirling screwed up during the mission.

Max listened as he was blamed for being drugged, told he shouldn't have consumed a beer, should've assessed Arcilla as a threat, been aware of his surroundings, and not discarded his GPS trackers. He got harangued for wasting valuable resources when Zulu Team had to locate him *and* take him to a local hospital after he got shot in the ass.

His eyes only wavered from Ridgeway once, flicking to the after-action report on the desk. He couldn't believe Zulu had twisted everything around so much. The comments from Marshall in the Argentinean hospital led him to believe they thought they were at fault for losing track of him, not the other way around.

But this would be par for the course. His father's name had been besmirched for a mistake not of his making. Ridgeway's final statement brought his attention back to the chewing out.

"As a result, you are no longer on Foxtrot. When you are off medical, you'll move to Red Support. If you screw up again, you'll be kicked out of the SEAL teams altogether and be cleaning latrines for the remainder of your enlistment. Dismissed."

Dumbfounded, Max stared a moment, unsure if he heard correctly.

"I'm not in the habit of repeating myself, Stirling."

"Yes, Sir." Max awkwardly pivoted and hobbled out of the office. His dreams were shattered by one damned assignment with Zulu.

9

Red Two

SOUNDS of surf and his blood thrumming in his ears, Max ran along the beach in full tactical gear at the head of the pack of eight men. A cocky smile plastered to his face, happy to be healed with no residual aches or twinges. Although he now possessed a scar on his ass and had been demoted to a support role, he was alive and still a SEAL.

Finding the bright side to a crappy situation was a game he played for so many years it became second nature. He recalled that, as a little boy, his mom told him to make lemonade when life handed him lemons … to make something sweet out of the sour. He learned to make damned-fine lemonade since life gave him bushels of the sour fruit.

Max's stride was easy and smooth. His grin broadened as he continued to run on the sand his father once trod, imagining his father's footprints ahead of him. *I'm following your path, Dad. Might be a bit deviated, but someday, I'm going to restore your honor. You will be vindicated, and the responsible parties will be brought to justice for getting you and your team killed.*

Coming to a halt at the finish line, Max put his thoughts aside and turned to encourage his teammates to bring it home on a high note. He fist-bumped or high-fived each man as they completed the ten-mile training run.

During his six weeks off, while rehabbing, he worried how his new team would receive him, but the first day set him at ease. Senior Chief Gabriel Miller's leadership was a breath of fresh air. The man ran a tight ship, didn't give a damn about his parentage, and judged every SEAL on their merits. The other six men followed his lead, and for the first time, Max believed he might gain true brothers.

"Damn, … Stirling. You set a … hard pace." Lucas Tanner gasped for breath, hating to be the last man.

Max only chuckled. He didn't want to rub it in their faces by gloating that he only ran at about ninety percent of his usual speed. No, he would rather go slower and, through training, help everybody improve. Doing so was in the best interest of the team because they were only as strong as their weakest link.

After pouring water over his head to cool off and taking a sip, Gabriel shook his hair, spraying his guys before raking his hand over his face. As his team gathered around, everyone except Stirling aware of what would come next, Gabriel grinned and directed his gaze to his newest member.

Uncomfortable when all eyes landed on him, Max fought the urge to take a fighting stance. He wondered if their friendliness had all been an act, and he was about to find out what they actually thought of him.

It happened before, though the first time, it was a group of twelve-year-old boys at Fairwinds Academy. They befriended him only to give him a beat-down after class one week later. He bloodied a few of their noses, and the headmaster expelled the instigator, but ever since, Max found it difficult to trust an outstretched hand of friendship without proof.

Gabriel cleared his throat and reached into his pocket. "Max, you've been with us for a week now." Perceiving the wariness in Stirling's expression, he came to the point. "We all agree you got the shaft from Ridgeway, but we agree unanimously on something else, too." Gabe's eyes moved to Caleb and Brett, his most querulous members. "Never happens with these guys."

Max shifted his eyes to Miller's hand as he withdrew it from the pocket, noting the fist. *Shit, here it comes.* Max prepared himself to throw a punch or two and run because seven against one were odds that would get him killed, no matter how much he buffed up in the past weeks with nothing to do but hit the gym every day.

Opening his hand, Gabriel's grin grew. "Max, I want ... we all want you to be Red Two. Anderson was my second, but he got your spot in Foxtrot, which isn't right by any measure. And well, frankly, you have more experience than any of the others. You're a natural leader who understands the value of teamwork."

Max's jaw dropped. Suspicion still clouded his eyes, but he peered at the team patch in Gabriel's hand and at the guys around him, who all nodded with grins. There wasn't a clenched fist or sneering face among them. He reached for the 2RST patch with a small upturn of his lips and quipped, "Perhaps being demoted was not such a bad thing after all."

The men of Support Team Red laughed and offered fist bumps in addition to claps on the back. Max pressed the patch on his sleeve before gripping Gabriel's outstretched hand and giving it a firm shake, believing this to be the beginning of a friendship.

Virginia – Naval Intelligence Office

Nicole sat back and rubbed her aching neck, giving her eyes a short break from the computer screen. Frustration built over the past five months as she was no closer to locating Anwar Massi now than she had been after the trap laid for Zulu.

All the usual haunts of the Massi brothers came up empty. She sent team after team to recon every known and several suspected locales. She never had a target so hard to find. For every step forward, she ended up two steps back—downright maddening.

Zulu counted on her to locate Anwar because capturing him would be a little vengeance for what happened to Levi ... not to mention would put a considerable dent in the arms trade supplying various terrorist activities.

Reaching for her coffee, a slightly raised voice from her CO's office drew her attention, and a habit of her trade naturally took over as she eavesdropped. She frowned as Captain Athole spoke to someone on the phone and mentioned Maxwell Stirling. Athole sounded enraged by whatever the other person said.

She was keenly aware the captain didn't care for his nephew. Athole made no secret that he believed the troubled young man didn't belong in the Navy, let alone the SEALs. When she joined the intelligence branch after graduating from Officer Candidate School roughly nine years ago, on her first day, she got a glimpse into Athole's private life and his struggles with Stirling.

Athole came in sporting an impressive black eye, one delivered by his fifteen-year-old nephew. She heard the gossip courtesy of Yeoman Larro, who had been a clerk in the office for almost a decade. Larro detailed how much Athole did for the problematic son of his sister.

According to Larro, Max had authority issues and turned out to be a reckless know-it-all like his dad. Athole enrolled the unruly child in the best military academy, hoping it would straighten him out. The punch to the face was Athole's last straw, and no one blamed him for limiting his exposure to the hellion afterward.

Nicole pursed her lips in thought. After Lester's suggestion, she pulled Stirling's jacket to familiarize herself with his records. He possessed an astonishing aptitude for languages, but that was not his only skill. When he was in Green Team, before Foxtrot drafted him, he broke several long-standing course records.

Maxwell's reviews ran hot or cold with no in-between. This led her to believe people either liked or hated Stirling. As a data-driven person, Nicole wanted to dig deeper into the incongruity before taking action. Until the Argentina mission, she never had cause to doubt the scuttlebutt regarding Stirling, but what she witnessed no longer fit nicely into a box.

The slamming of Athole's phone as he ended his call brought Nicole out of her reflections, and she refocused on her task of locating Anwar Massi. The Stirling mystery would wait for now.

Zulu Team Room

Camaraderie filled the room as Zulu filtered in and took seats in the chairs, the sofa, or barstools near the small kitchenette's counter. Still sweaty from the practice drills they ran through the shoot house, Axel wiped his forehead, then rubbed his palm on his pants to dry his hand. He settled into a chair at the back of the room, contemplating how to explain to his wife that he owed another case of beer. After seven weeks, he believed they would've let up, but the list of firsts appeared to be endless.

Axel's breath hitched, and he coughed repeatedly. He chalked up the reoccurring hacking to all the dust from running an ungodly number of drills with his new team. Marshall more than lived up to his reputation as a hard taskmaster, but Axel wouldn't want it any other way. Their laser-focus made this team the best.

His eyes moved to the wall and studied the team's emblem emblazoned on a flag as the guys continued to drink and banter during their break. At first, he wondered why Zulu chose an orca as a mascot, one illustrated with unrealistic, massive, sharp teeth, but once Zach explained, he understood.

Axel would rather do anything else than put his face in a book, so the trivia the mostly quiet dog handler supplied surprised him. *Orcas, also known as killer whales, are the largest, most powerful species of dolphin. The black-and-white apex predators are sometimes called wolves of the sea because they hunt in packs.*

Zach shared more than the encyclopedia description, telling him about several dead great white sharks that washed ashore in Africa. Bite mark analysis revealed orcas eviscerated them and only ate their livers. In Axel's book, the orca was an appropriate mascot for a team specializing in precision strikes.

When Axel started coughing again, Jake eyed him. "You sick?"

Taking a swig of his water to wet his throat, Axel shook his head. "Breathed in a lot of dust." His comment left him open for renewed razzing about being the last man up the hills. He laughed along with them, and forty-five minutes later, they were all rising and heading out to hone their razor-teeth with more drills.

Coronado, CA - Pirate's Cove Pub

Enjoying a beer and kicking back with his teammates, Max's attention was drawn to the entrance when he spotted Gabriel entering with the most exquisite woman. Entranced by her feminine curves, silky chestnut hair, pillowy lips that begged to be kissed, smooth, ivory skin, and most striking of all, her bright blue eyes, Max continued to stare as they approached.

She walks in beauty, like the night of cloudless climes and starry skies. And all that's best of dark and bright meet in her aspect and her eyes. His thought seemed clichéd, but Max's well-educated brain failed him at this moment, and he couldn't come up with anything more original than Lord Bryon's poem idolizing a woman's beauty.

Gabriel halted, a smirk on his face as he saw the besotted expressions on his men. Calliope had this effect on all men. He had his hands full as a teen, beating off boys who clamored after her. Slinging his arm over Calliope's shoulder, he said, "I'd like to introduce Calliope, one of my sisters. She's in town for a few days and wanted to hang out tonight. Calliope, this is Lucas, Brett, Caleb, and Max. The rest are over at the pool table."

Calliope smiled and centered her gaze on the handsome, blond-haired man. "Max, you must be the new teammate. Gabe hasn't mentioned your name before."

Max's grin lit his blue eyes. "Yes, I am. A pleasure to meet you, Calliope." He stood and offered her his seat since all the others were occupied.

"How chivalrous," Gabriel chuckled. His other teammates still appeared too tongue-tied to do more than gawk.

"Thanks, and just Cali, please. My full name is a bit formal."

"Beautiful," Lucas mumbled. He shook himself and peered at his team leader. The siblings possessed no resemblance. Her fair complexion contrasted Gabriel's umber-brown skin. "Are you certain she is your sister?"

Cali's hand moved to Gabe's bicep, warning him not to take offense. "Yes. Though me and all my siblings are adopted."

Hoping to learn more about her, Max asked, "How many siblings do you and Gabriel have?" Max almost melted when she graced him with a smile that rivaled brilliant sunshine.

"There are seven of us. Gabe's the oldest. Then comes Liam, me, James, Benny, Xavier, and Ariel."

Max always wished to have at least one brother ... five would've been heaven. He listened as she described life with six siblings and the antics of her protective brothers, laughing when she shared funny stories about Gabriel. He stood, sipping his beer while Cali held court over the team.

He learned Cali lived in Chesapeake, Virginia, and worked for Katsaros Gallery of Fine Art, which meant starting anything with her wouldn't be feasible. Long-distance relationships never worked out. Plus, there was the fact she was his leader's sister. That in itself was a non-starter ... you don't become involved with your CO's family ... ever.

Though drawn to Cali, Max refocused on getting to know his new mates better before they deployed in two days. As the night wound down, Max found himself in a discussion on Greek mythology with Lucas Tanner, who, like himself, enjoyed studying ancient civilizations and their folklore.

Pausing their discussion to bid Gabe and Cali goodnight, both stared as Cali sauntered out. Max finished his third beer as Lucas pondered out loud, "Wonder if she spells her name with a C or K? Although K would be as unique as the bearer, either fits. Surely, she is the goddess of epic poetry and eloquence."

Max laughed and set his mug down. "Careful, buddy. Remember, she has five brothers, and they'd rain holy hell down on you if you mess with her."

Lucas swallowed a lump of fear before flashing a grin. "Might be worth the risk to kiss those lips." He slammed back the last of his whiskey. "Ready to head out?"

"Yeah. Thanks for the ride tonight." Max rose and waved to the others before he and Lucas headed for the bar's exit.

10

Tip of the Spear

L**ISTENING** to Brett and Caleb grousing about the dismal conditions again, Max chuckled softly. Frick and Frack, two practically inseparable buddies who came through the pipeline together, disagreed on almost everything under the sun except this lousy recon assignment. Max now grasped Gabe's comment and glance at these two on the beach when he offered him the 2IC position.

During the past twelve days, they camped in the northeastern part of Algeria, close to the Tunisian border. As for the weather, Max agreed with them. It rained often enough that they didn't possess a single dry or non-muddy item except their weapons.

They swam a mile and made a coastal infil before hiking through the night to the observation target. After arriving, Gabe split the team into two, taking three men into the forest to the south. Max led the second team, consisting of Lucas, Caleb, and Brett, towards the wood's northern section.

For almost two weeks, they logged the comings and goings of the occupants within the five buildings of the walled compound, and Gabe relayed details to TOC every evening. As of yet, they had not positively identified the HVT, so here they would sit until they did, or the cake-eaters decided this recon was a bust and gave them the go-ahead to exfil.

Max sat up and moved toward the scope. "Mine now. Brett, rack out for a while."

Yawning, Brett nodded and scooted back in their blind and found a damp spot beside Lucas. Dog-tired from boredom, Brett said, "Max, you should sleep more."

"I'll sleep when I'm dead," Max quipped.

Lucas cracked open his eyes. "Long dirt nap won't be much different than where we're at now." The ground squelched below him as he crawled forward, motioning to Caleb to switch places. Settling in next to Max, he handed over an MRE. "You might not need sleep, but you gotta eat."

Max took the offered bag and ripped it open. He spared a glance at Tanner before refocusing on the night vision scope. He and Lucas clicked from the first day, and Max enjoyed the budding friendship … something unique in his life. But a piece of his mind held gloomy thoughts and waited for the proverbial shoe to drop. Every time he began to believe he made a true friend, something happened to ruin it.

He and Jerry could've been friends, but his uncle forbade him from playing with him. The first boy who accepted him at Fairwinds didn't come back the following year. And after the ambush when he was twelve, he shied away from trying to make friends. Though he participated and excelled in all the team sports, his love of academics and a desire to achieve straight A's in his honors classes didn't leave much time for socializing.

"Red One to Red Two, how copy?"

Max depressed his comms. "Good copy."

"Three vehicles moving toward the complex from the southeast. Should be in your line of vision in five mikes."

"Copy." Max switched his scope from night vision to a regular one since, by the time the convoy arrived, the sun would be over the horizon and it would allow him to obtain visuals of the people.

Ten minutes later, a man exited the middle truck and turned to the north as he spoke. Max grinned as he sighted Anwar Massi. "Red Two to Red One. Confirm visual on HVT. Sending photos."

Virginia – Jake's Home

The buzzing of his phone on the nightstand pulled Jake out of a light doze. He glanced at the clock and almost groaned, finding it was two in the morning. He had only gotten to bed an hour ago after a long evening dealing with his eldest. Where Jake was hyper-disciplined and stalwart in his own mind, James tended to be disorganized and influenced by his peers.

Tonight was one of those times, but at least his son called him for help when he got in over his head. He drove to Norfolk to pick Jamie up when the guys he hung out with decided to go bar hopping with fake IDs instead of the parent-approved art show. Jamie got drunk but not smashed enough to compound his stupidity by getting into the car with his inebriated friends.

Jake squinted as he peered at the text and pushed up.

His motion woke Val. She rolled over and placed a hand on his back as she asked, "You gotta go?"

"Yeah. Sorry." He turned and planted a kiss on her. "Jamie's gonna be feeling quite hung-over when he wakes. Make sure you give him aspirin and then work his butt off with chores. I want him to experience the full misery of his decision."

Val chuckled. "Got it. But he did call. He gets brownie points for that … he's not in some hospital or jail."

Jake stood and pulled on his jeans. "True, but I want James thinking twice next time. If it doesn't hurt a bit, he won't learn to make the right choice even if it means going against what his friends are doing."

Valarie gave Jake a small salute. "Yes, Chief."

Pulling a shirt over his head, Jake grinned. He leaned over and gave her another kiss. "Love ya."

"Love you too." Val pulled Jake's pillow to her as the man who captured her heart more than twenty years ago picked up his wallet and keys and headed out the door to save the world. She squeezed the pillow and inhaled his masculine scent. Loving a team guy would never be easy, but she couldn't envision her life without him and hoped she never faced that reality.

Zulu Plane En Route to Algeria

Having gone straight to the tarmac, the members of Zulu and their support team, plus Lockwood, Farris, and Draper, gathered around the gear in the center of the aircraft for the briefing. Most sipped coffee, courtesy of Kira, who always had what they needed before they realized they did.

Nicole smiled at the guys as she said, "Found Anwar Massi."

"HOT DAMN!" Finn pumped his fist in the air. "About time for payback."

"Are you certain it's him?" Dave viewed the grainy photo.

"Yes. A recon team has been in place for almost two weeks. This locale was a long shot, but three hours ago, we received these photos, and this is Massi. The information the team provided will be useful in planning your assault.

"They gathered intel on building layout, size of the enemy force, guard rotation timings, and analyzed the perimeter. Their second-in-command also sent a recommendation for your entry point, which he indicates provides the best coverage."

Farris brought up another photo. "We need Anwar alive. Chatter indicates he is planning something big in retaliation for his brother's capture and detainment. It may be in motion as we speak. And one more thing. The last transmission from the scout team was a large shipment of arms arrived with Anwar."

She pointed to one of the five buildings. "The weapons cache is stored here." Her finger tapped a multi-story building on the other side of the compound. "Massi is in this house, though we are unsure of his location inside. Red Team will maintain a visual on both, and if either moves before you arrive, they will update us." Nicole passed out folders that contained all the data amassed. "Zulu and Sierra will execute the assault while Red keeps the compound's perimeter secure."

Jake nodded, and they began to dive into the materials to devise their plan. He reviewed the breach point suggestion and agreed with the detailed analysis. He liked how the guy's mind worked, and when they finished this mission, he would tell him.

Algeria – Woods North of Massi's Compound

"So, we do all the work, sit in mud for two weeks, and some other team gets to swoop in and bag Massi? That's not fair!" Brett groused after finding out from Gabe another team was flying in to snatch the HVT and blow the munitions.

As Caleb nodded in vehement agreement with his best bud, Lucas shrugged and said, "Them's the breaks for being on a support team. Glory goeth to the tip of the spear, but realize they couldn't do what they do without us and all other support roles."

"Still not happy!" Brett ripped open an MRE and pulled out the crackers as he silently fumed.

Caleb turned to Max, who remained quiet. "Doesn't this bother you? I mean, it might be Foxtrot coming, and you should be with them. Ridgeway's an ass for demoting you."

Max glanced over at Caleb. "Doesn't matter. As Lucas says, support is important, and I don't do this for the glory. Just want to make the world a better place."

"I still think Ridgeway is a jackass. I like Anderson, but he doesn't possess half the skills you do. He doesn't speak multiple languages, he's slower than Lucas," Caleb ducked the water bottle Lucas threw at him, "and well, the way you analyzed the layout and found the weak points ... don't think he can assess a target like you either."

At ease with the guys, Max lowered his shields a bit and revealed, "Ridgeway only demoted me because of the AAR. Zulu placed all the blame on me for things going sideways."

Lucas scrunched his face. "No way. That blows. Why the hell would they do that?"

"Not sure. A one-eighty of how they acted at the hospital. Anyway, it's in the past, I'm here, and we still have a job to do. Whoever is going in is relying on us to keep track of Massi and report any changes." Max refocused on the building with the weaponry, noting the guard rotation. The terrorists unloaded a boatload of ammunition and AK47s in addition to several RPGs. When the place blew, it would be one hell of a fireworks show.

Near Massi's Compound

In the dim light of a partial moon, Zulu and Sierra teams rolled their parachutes after a HAHO infil. Jake keyed his comms and reported, "Zulu One to TOC. Passing Wakefield."

"Passing Wakefield. Copy. ISR over the target, but in those trees, we have no visibility until you break cover." Lockwood responded from the aircraft. He checked off the mission step on the whiteboard before returning to view the video footage. Bryan would never lose the knots in his stomach as he observed his team from afar.

As the last man finished with his chute, Jake communicated with Red Team's leader. "Zulu One to Red One."

"Red One, go ahead."

"We're moving. Coming in from the southwest, using the breach point you recommended."

"Copy." Gabe would ensure Stirling got the credit he deserved later, but now was not the time to correct Master Chief Marshall.

Woods North of Massi's Compound

When Marshall signed off, Lucas unclenched his jaw. "So, the infamous Zulu is running this mission. When this is over, we're gonna have some words with them."

"Damn straight!" Brett and Caleb said in unison, ready for a little payback for what they did to Stirling.

"No. You're going to drop it." Max clenched his fist.

"Why?" Lucas stared at Max, not comprehending. "They can't get away with throwing you under the bus."

"Yes, they can, and they did. Anything you do will only bite me in the ass. I'm already on Ridgeway's shit list. Let's do our jobs and let sleeping dogs lie." Max took Ridgeway's threat seriously, and if an altercation with Zulu crossed his desk, the captain would likely deem it sufficient reason to boot him out of the SEALs.

Lucas frowned as he nodded. He wouldn't rock the boat now, but somehow, he would make this right for his new friend.

Outside Massi's Compound

As he trekked through the humid night, his boots sinking into thick muck, Axel Chase strove to contain his ever-present and annoying cough. He began sucking on hard mints in the past few weeks, which seemed to help some, but not entirely.

He couldn't figure out what caused his constant hacking. Axel rarely got sick. He didn't feel ill, and he didn't have a fever. He was not and never had been a smoker, so dust appeared the most likely culprit, but there was no dust here. His next cough resulted in uncomfortable stares from his teammates, and Axel decided he would do as his wife suggested and visit the team doctor after this mission, though he was loathed to do so.

Axel attempted to stifle yet another short coughing spell as the strike force reached the perimeter. Jake eyed him and whispered, "Put a lid on it, or you're gonna give us away."

As Finn prepared to pry open the service door, Axel reached into his pocket, for another mint to stifle his hacking. However, he discovered he was out of lozenges. Swallowing hard, by sheer force of will, Axel determined not to cough again.

Inside Massi's Compound

Upon breaching the walled compound, the combined teams split into two groups. Finn, Axel, and Babcox moved towards the north building, tasked with destroying the arsenal. The remaining ten men headed for the three-story abode to locate and snatch Anwar Massi.

Things went smooth as glass as they stealthily made their way through the quiet compound, and thanks to the excellent intel they received from Red Team, they avoided detection. Arriving at the target house, the group divided again into five-man teams.

Jake and Grant, with two Sierra members, would enter the front, leaving Sierra One to guard the exterior. Dave and Zach, with Rocketeer and two more support teammates, would go in through the rear with Sierra Two standing watch.

Both quartettes slipped in noiselessly and cleared all rooms on the ground floor. They met at the only staircase and moved upward, with Jake's team breaking off on the second deck and Dave's continuing to the third.

Massi's Compound – Munitions Building

At the arms depot, Finn and Axel, using suppressed weapons, quietly took out the two sentries. Stewart Babcox opened the door, and the three men moved inside. After clearing the first room, encountering no tangos, Sierra Seven stayed at the portal to provide coverage as Zulu Three and Six moved deeper into the structure to set the charges, which would destroy the munitions.

Entering the last room, a massive one at the back of the building, they found the cache. Boxes, crates, and long metal containers formed several aisles and lined two walls. Axel kept watch out a small window with limited visibility as Finn knelt and reached into his leg pocket for charges.

The tickle in Axel's throat became overpowering, and try as he might, he couldn't halt the lung-rattling coughs that came out. Axel dragged in a hitching breath and wiped at blurry, watery eyes when he finished hacking.

Finn turned to peer at Axel. "Damn, you okay?"

"Yeah," Axel answered as he glanced in Finn's direction. The timing was calamitous as he didn't notice the back door opening and one of Massi's men entering to check out the noise. A scraping sound alerted Axel, and he pivoted in time to catch a glimpse of a tango taking a bead on Finn's back.

Axel fired, the bullet going through the terrorist's head, but the man's finger still squeezed the trigger as he dropped dead. Multiple armor-piercing projectiles ejected from the submachine gun, none hitting Finn, but unfortunately, one struck a box of grenades.

The resulting blast wave picked up and slammed Axel against a free-standing metal shelving unit on the far wall. His body crumpled in a heap on the floor right before the shelves fell on him, pinning his legs.

Finn, semi-protected from the explosion by a stack of wooden crates on top of several metal strongboxes, got his bell rung twice. First, by the detonation knocking him down, and second, when one of the full containers toppled over and bounced on his helmet as he lay on the bare concrete.

At the front of the house, Stewart Babcox threw himself down, seeking cover as the walls shook with the forceful blast. It took him a moment to figure out something went terribly wrong. He regained his feet and moved through the smoky hall to the building's rear in search of Chase and McBride.

Inhaling a bit of smoke, Babcox coughed as he keyed his comms when TOC called for Zulu Three to give a sitrep. Finding both on the ground, Stewart fought the little voice in his head, which rejoiced, believing a position on Zulu might be opening if either or both of them died.

Babcox clamped down on his ambitions and reported, "Sierra Seven to TOC. Two men are down, not sure what happened, but something exploded." He checked McBride first and noted the burly, red-haired breacher beginning to stir. "Zulu Three's alive and dazed but coming around. He took a hard hit to the head based on the resultant laceration."

Rising, he went to Chase next, noting the massive storage shelf on his lower half. Babcox took a knee and yanked off a glove to check for a pulse. "Zulu Six is alive but pinned. I need assistance to free him."

11

No Man Left Behind

Woods North of Massi's Compound

BLINDED for a moment by the bright flash of light in the darkness from the explosion, Max blinked to clear his vision. With bated breath, he waited to find out the status of the three men. As soon as the request for help came over the headset, he was on his feet and running as he called out, "Cover me," to his teammates.

Lucas scrambled up and followed. "Got your six."

Max glanced back. "Stay high with the others."

"No way. Not letting you go alone."

"Red One to Red Two. Can you—"

"On our way. Red Four and Five are on overwatch. Three is with me." Max headed for a part of the wall he would be able to scale with little difficulty.

"Roger." Gabe communicated with TOC, informing them two of his men were on their way to lend a hand. He listened as Zulu One reported the blast woke the household, and they were taking heavy fire, so they couldn't assist their injured men.

Max reached the barrier, turned, squatted with his back against the adobe wall, linked his hands, creating a cup, and prepared to boost Lucas up. "You first."

"How? Never mind." Lucas didn't need to ask how the human spider would follow him without a foot up.

After heaving Lucas upward, Max trotted a few feet back to make a running start. He leapt and grasped a tiny handhold. Using his upper body strength, he pulled himself up until his fingers caught hold of the wall's top edge. Lucas's hand gripped his wrist and assisted him.

They took a moment to assess the interior of the complex, noting insurgents spilling out of the barracks closer to the house containing Massi. Time would be short, so they needed to sprint across an open expanse before anyone detected their presence or noticed the dead sentries outside the munition depot. Dropping to the ground, they raced for the front door.

Massi's Compound – House

Jake glanced out of the window, which gave him a view of the armory, and his gut turned. If he lost Three and Six to another Massi raid, he would ... well, he didn't know how he would finish the thought, but it would piss him off.

Unfamiliar with the west coast recon team and their leader, Senior Chief Miller, Jake hoped Red Team knew what the hell they were doing because, with the number of insurgents converging on his location, he wouldn't be able to help them if they got their asses in the fire. Refocusing on his situation, preparing for one hell of a firefight with his ten men against an amassing force woken by the blast. "Zulu One to Zulu Two. HVT isn't on the second floor. You find him?"

Dave halted near the last door after he and his team dispatched the ten insurgents who tried to prevent them from reaching the final compartment. "Negative. One room to check."

"Copy. Company knocking at the door in seconds. Be ready." Jake replied and motioned for Grant to join him. "Save the smoke for exfil. Let's reduce the numbers before they reach us."

Grant nodded, and both men pulled frag grenades and tossed them into the middle of the group rushing for the house. They turned their eyes away to protect them from the explosions, then returned to the window and began sending men to their maker.

Massi's Compound – Munitions Building

"Red Two to Sierra Seven, incoming from the front." Max halted at the portal of the building, took a breath, and caught Lucas's eye. They grinned at each other, adrenaline rushing through their veins, glad to be in the fight rather than sitting on the sidelines as spectators. Their muzzles lifted and lowered in unison as they entered, ensuring the area remained clear.

With quick, quiet strides, they moved to the rear and stepped over a dead body in the hall. Not taking the time for introductions, Max and Lucas headed straight to the pinned SEAL. Max released his Colt M4A1 to grab the shelving, and Lucas went to the other side to do the same. "Seven, pull him out when we lift."

"Roger." Stewart crouched and slid his hands under Axel's armpits, tugging when the massive frame rose several inches.

Pain ripped through Axels' leg, and he couldn't stop the groan as he was dragged a short distance.

Lucas took a knee. "Damn, he's got a compound fracture. This isn't pretty. We need to stabilize his leg before we move him." He glanced up at Max. "Find me something."

"Are you a medic?" Stewart asked.

"Yeah."

Max peered at Seven before his eyes went to McBride, noting the dazed expression as he sat with his head leaning against one of the crates. *Just my luck. The guy on their team who hates my guts the most.* Turning back to Seven, he said, "Help Lucas, then keep watch out the back. I'm going to make us a hole. No way are we getting over the wall with them in this condition."

"We're going out the front. Join with our teams for exfil," Stewart retorted, not liking the man dictating orders to him.

Max snorted. "Best way to end up dead. Look." Max pointed to the window, where chaos reigned as grenades exploded. He keyed his comms and said, "Red Two to Red One. Gonna send an RPG through the back wall to create an exit. Need coverage when we make a break for it cause the fireworks will bring unwanted guests to the party."

"Copy. Moving to provide cover." Gabe spoke with TOC, conveying Max's plan. He rallied his men, and the four began to move to a position from which they could pick off anyone wanting to crash Max's party.

Opening several containers, Max located a shoulder-held launcher and a missile. As he started to exit, McBride grabbed his pants. He stopped and stared down. "What?"

In a world of pain, his head throbbing and making thinking challenging and standing without assistance impossible, Finn mumbled, "Set charges first." Finn patted his leg pouch. "In here."

Max nodded. "Copy." Setting down the grenade launcher, he removed the explosives. Max met the moss-green eyes, and although a part of him remained angry for what Zulu did to his career, he strove to rise above negative emotions and be the better man. "We'll have you out of here soon."

Though it cost him in pain, Finn chuckled. "Least I don't have an arrow in my ass." He squeezed his eyes shut as the samba in his skull reached a crescendo, and relief came as he passed out.

Not willing to cede command, Babcox stepped away from the window. "You set the damned charges. I'll make the hole."

Lucas glanced up as Babcox left them uncovered. He spoke with Chase and learned the other's names as he created a makeshift splint. Nothing fancy, any doctor would cringe, but battlefield medicine must be fast and only sufficient to save a life. "Babcox, Stirling knows where to fire."

"I said I'll do it. Place the charges and be ready to move on my signal." Babcox grabbed the RPG and strode down the hall.

"Aim to the left of the truck. Will put us closer to the rest of Red Team." Max pivoted and flashed a grin at Lucas. "So long as we all get outta here, don't give a damn who shoots. Wanna watch our backside while I take care of this?"

"Sure, brother." Lucas grinned, grabbed his HK, and stood.

His body hit the floor a second later, a fine, pink mist floating down. Max's shocked eyes locked on his new friend. Only a tiny hole marred his forehead, but the back of his head was now gone.

Frozen in place for a millisecond, recognizing Lucas was dead, Max took cover and inched to the window. He peeked out the corner and spotted five tangos moving their way. Drawing on his training, he became emotionless, took aim, and fired two shots, but five bastards fell.

"Red One to Two. Status?" Gabe asked as he and his men eliminated three tangos approaching the munitions building.

Max inhaled sharply through his nose and exhaled gradually through his mouth as he turned to view his brother as an explosion indicated Babcox fired the RPG. "Fallen Eagle. Red Three KIA." He fought to control the anger rising as he realized if Babcox had stayed where he put him, they would've been alerted to the damned tangos … but Babcox didn't, and Lucas paid the price for the man's ambitions.

Stewart rushed into the room. "Ready to go?"

"YOU FUCKING BASTARD!" Max blurted out.

"WHAT THE HELL?" Stewart noted the charges lying on the floor and moved his gaze to the upstart who tried to take over. "WHY DIDN'T YOU DO AS I ORDERED?"

Axel's eyes rounded with disbelief as a member of Sierra appeared to wholly disregard a fallen brother. Never in all his years as an operator had he witnessed anyone behave so indifferently … not even the most callous officer he ever met. *How, in God's name, did Babcox manage to be selected for Sierra?*

"LUCAS IS DEAD BECAUSE YOU LEFT YOUR POST," Max bit out with venom.

Stewart turned to where Stirling pointed, and he swallowed hard. Later, he would figure out a way to spin things, as he always did. For now, he countered with force, "TIME TO GO. YOU GRAB CHASE. I GOT MCBRIDE."

"I'M NOT LEAVING LUCAS!"

"I SAID WE'RE GOING. If we stay here any longer, we'll be as dead as him. Someone can come back for him later." Stewart shifted, intending to crouch to lift an unconscious Finn.

"I WON'T LEAVE A BROTHER. NO MAN LEFT BEHIND."

Standing again, Stewart got in Stirling's face. A bit of spittle came out as he barked, "I'M SENIOR OPERATOR! YOU'RE JUST A PEON SUPPORT MEMBER."

Unflinching, not batting an eye, Max took full measure of the man before him and found him lacking in honor, compassion, and leadership ability. He held his tongue and fists, which itched to lay into the asshat. However, with his luck, even if he didn't strike out verbally or physically, Ridgeway would twist this to be his failure, and he would be out of the SEALs.

Max decided if this was to be his last act as a SEAL, he would go out with integrity. "I refuse to exfil without Lucas. My brother deserves to be taken home and not left to be desecrated and put on display by the terrorists. Lucas's family doesn't need those images in their memories. So, go if you must, but I'm staying until backup arrives."

Axel agreed with Stirling whole-heartedly, and he had the power to cut Babcox off at the knees. Although he was Zulu's rookie, he still outranked Babcox. "Zulu Six to TOC. Two men can't carry three. Need additional help for exfil."

Lockwood responded, "Hold what you got. Red Team already inbound." He monitored it all, and his stomach dropped upon hearing they had lost a man. He had ordered the remainder of the recon team to assist.

Peering up at the two SEALs still locked in a glaring match, Axel ordered, "Babcox, set the goddamned charges, then guard the front entrance. Stirling, cover our six."

Pissed off but needing to toe the line when Zulu gave an order, Stewart pivoted and placed the charges where they would do the most damage before stomping out of the room.

Appreciating the assistance, Max only nodded and assumed his position. He noted the firefight at the house appeared to be going in their favor as many of Massi's men ran in the opposite direction and towards the compound's front gate. He stole another glance at Lucas, and his heart cracked. The proverbial shoe didn't only drop … the steel-toed boot kicked him in the gut.

Massi's Compound – House

It burned Jake's gut to lose a man. He lost too many in his years, and his phone still contained the numbers of the fallen. But now was not the time to mourn. He had a job to do. "Zulu Two, status?"

"Jackpot. HVT bagged alive, though he's got a few bite marks. Coming to you." Dave aimed his weapon at Anwar, who had been taken down by Rocketeer in one hell of a flying jump as the fleeing terrorist tried to slip out a window with a fire escape.

Zach cinched the plastic cuffs tighter than he should, but one of their own had fallen while capturing this piece of shit. Though he had no clue who Red Three was, he was nonetheless a brother. Taking his knee off the small of Anwar's back, Zach rose and yanked the turd up with him. He peered at his dog and said, "Good boy. Bet you need a drink to rinse the foul taste from your mouth."

A snicker emitted from Sierra Six. "Rocky looks proud."

"Should be. Anwar almost got away. We would've lost him in the chaos below." Zach pushed their stinking HVT to Dave to lead downstairs. He sobered, recognizing they weren't done yet. They still had to haul their asses to exfil alive.

On the second floor, Grant picked off several more die-hard believers who continued attempting to reach the house. "Like shooting fish in a barrel."

"Piranha ... don't mind sending them to their seventy-two virgins," Sierra One said as he did the same as Zulu Four. Rob had no qualms about wiping terrorists, who sought to harm innocent people, off the face of the earth.

Grant quipped, "Something was lost in translation. It is actually one seventy-two-year-old virgin."

"Shut it and concentrate. We're not out of the woods yet," Jake admonished but realized humor helped them all cope.

Sharing a silent glance, Grant and Rob nodded and resumed clearing a path for them to get the hell out of this place. Hopefully, with no more brothers injured or killed. Both took solace in the bit of payback they were getting for Red Three.

12

Things Don't Add Up

GRANT and Scott, Sierra's medic, did what they could to make Finn and Axel as comfortable as possible for the flight back home. They positioned Axel's gurney at the front of the aircraft, but Finn insisted on lying in his hammock, so Grant acquiesced.

Taking a seat, Grant raked his fingers through his hair, blew out a breath, and glanced to the rear. The flag-draped box created a somber atmosphere. No one spoke more than a few words, and they came out hushed. Losing a fellow SEAL touched them all.

He shifted his focus to Stirling. Discovering he was Red Two shocked everyone on Zulu. Though they didn't say anything or ask, they all wondered how he ended up in a support role instead of being with his tier-one team. Their curiosity would wait for another time because Red Team deserved space to be together and work through their grief.

Returning his gaze to Axel, Grant sighed again. Before Red Three died, he properly stabilized the break, giving the Navy's surgeons the time necessary to repair the damage. Although the fracture would take time to heal, Chase would most likely operate again. The broken leg was not a career-ending injury. But the continued coughing and diminished breath sounds worried Grant. He didn't understand what caused the issue.

At times, Grant wished he possessed more medical knowledge and perhaps followed his mother's dreams for him to become a doctor, but he aspired to serve his country from a young age. And eight to ten years of college was something he could never afford. When Axel began hacking again, Grant rose to attend to his teammate.

Axel accepted the offered water when his coughing spell ended. With heavy-duty meds on board, he felt floaty and not in much pain for the first time since the blast. Resting his head on the pillow, he eyed Grant. His voice came out soft as he admitted, "This is my fault."

"What?"

"Me, Finn, and Tanner … I coughed."

"Huh?" Grant wondered if morphine caused Axel's confusion.

Axel lifted his head to peer at the back, then dropped it again. "Not entirely to blame, but I set things in motion."

Jake overheard, stood, and moved to the gurney. Due to the death, he and Lockwood decided to delay the debrief until after they returned to Virginia, but with Axel speaking, his desire to comprehend the chain of events in the munitions building needed to be sated. "Tell me what occurred."

As Axel began his hushed report to Jake and Grant, Stewart Babcox started relaying his version to Sierra One, placing the blame for Tanner's death squarely on Stirling's shoulders. Once Stewart realized Red Two was Preston Stirling's son, he figured it would be a slam dunk. He would paint Stirling as reckless as his father, and people would believe him.

Striking first, taking a strong offensive position, he conveyed to Rob that Stirling disobeyed orders, and if he had not, Tanner would still be alive. Stewart believed he would be able to counter any conflicting reports from McBride or Chase by indicating their head wounds could've skewed their perceptions. Though, he doubted either SEAL would support Stirling after overhearing some of McBride's jokes about Stirling getting lost, drugged, and shot in the ass a few months ago.

Rob listened to Babcox with half an ear, his gaze remaining on the members of Red Team. He focused on the young blond who took a knee, bowed his head, and placed a hand on the flag covering his teammate. He noted the voices of two members rising, and although they sounded irate, he couldn't make out their words over the engine noise.

He attributed their heightened emotional state to grief. Often, operators skipped denial and went straight to anger when a brother fell. Rob wondered how close Red Two had been with Red Three. His posture and the way his hand lay on the casket indicated he shared a bond likely as tight as his with Scott, his 2IC. Though appearances could be deceiving, and he might be viewing something else ... guilt perhaps.

Leaders carried a heavy load when it came to men relying on them to ensure they came home. When one of them paid the ultimate price, the weight of leadership often bowed a man in the manner of Stirling's body. He turned away, giving Stirling privacy, tuning back into Babble-cox, having missed most of what he said. Rob sighed when he realized it was some of the same shit he often heard from his rookie, stuff which made him question what the hell he thought when he selected Babcox.

After providing Gabe a concise report of what occurred, Max knelt next to Lucas's casket, sadness filling him. As his teammates continued to talk, he paid no attention. His thoughts centered on Lucas. *I'm sorry. I should've reminded you to check for tangos before standing. You'd still be alive if I had.*

The Grim Reaper dealt him another blow by killing his new friend, but his pain would be less than Lucas's family. Though he had only met Lucas three weeks ago, Max learned a lot about him. Lucas came from a tight-knit, loving family. Something Max longed for with a passion. Tanner's parents and siblings would be devastated, but at least they had his body to bury.

Another thing Max didn't have—his dad's coffin was empty, except for a pair of melted dog tags. Nothing of him or the others remained after the explosion.

Max fought the prickle of hot tears, not wanting to embarrass himself in front of everyone. He would cry later, in private, possibly in the shower, where his weeping would be concealed.

Raised, angry voices drew Max from his musings. He pivoted in time to witness Brett yank Babcox to his feet as he yelled, "YOU FUCKING SON OF A BITCH! YOU'RE THE REASON LUCAS IS DEAD!"

Caleb, hot on Brett's heels, swung at Babcox, intending on knocking the friggin' idiot's lights out, but Sierra One blocked the strike before it landed.

Max gaped as all hell broke loose when members of Sierra, Zulu, and Red engaged in a shoving match and verbal volley so loud most words became indistinguishable. Lockwood's voice reigned supreme after a shrill whistle caused most to cover their ears and grimace.

"ENOUGH! STAND DOWN. BEHAVIOR SUCH AS THIS IS UNACCEPTABLE AND UNBECOMING. Now, if you will all be calm, let's sort out the issue." Lockwood eyed the instigators. "What is the problem?"

Brett snorted, and in a disrespectful tone, he said, "Like you give a flying fuck. You and Zulu already threw Stirling under the bus once. You're probably going to try and do it again. But I'm telling you now, Red Team won't allow that to happen."

Jake stepped forward, his face set in a grim line as he demanded, "What the hell do you mean?"

"I thought the great Master Chief Marshall possessed a brain, but I guess I'm wrong," Caleb added fuel to the fire, not giving a damn what repercussions might come his way.

Lockwood put a hand to Jake's chest to hold him back as he assumed a hard-edged mantle he didn't usually need but could pull out whenever necessary. "Explain yourselves fully and civilly."

Gabe placed a hand on each of his men's shoulders, indicating for them to back off and he would take over. Keeping his tone respectful but hard, Gabe replied, "Stirling was a member of Foxtrot, a tier-one team. A spot he earned like all operators.

"He does one mission with Zulu, you lose him, he is injured, and finds the senator's son. He arrives home three days later, still on crutches, and is called into Captain Ridgeway's office to be raked over the coals, blamed for everything that went wrong and demoted to a support role.

"We won't allow you to make Stirling the scapegoat again. You might have a problem with who his father is, but we don't. He is one hell of a capable operator with a solid head on his shoulders." Gabe's eyes landed on Babcox. "Unlike some. If this moron had stayed at the window to cover their six, Tanner would be alive."

Jake's glare shifted between Babcox and Miller before settling back on Red One. "I don't know where you got the idea that we blamed the errors of the Argentina mission on Stirling, but you're dead wrong. As for this mission, I spoke to Chase, and he told us what occurred."

"And?" Gabe challenged.

"We'll be doing a full debrief in Virginia before any accusations are made or corrective actions are taken." Jake looked past Miller to Stirling, who still knelt beside the casket. Something churned in his gut, and the claim he laid his failures at Stirling's feet didn't sit well. He would need to talk to Lockwood and find out what kind of bullshit was going on.

"Gents, I believe everyone is overtired. Separate for now, and we will hash things out when we get home, and clearer heads prevail." Lockwood's demeanor brooked no dissent, and Jake ushered Zulu to the front while Miller motioned for his men to return to the rear, leaving Sierra in the middle.

Rob pointed to the seat from which Babcox had been yanked. "Sit. You'll begin again with your report, and I don't want any of your bullshit this time, or you'll be off this team before we land. You have one chance to save your hide. It better be the full and ugly truth of what transpired in that damned building."

Stewart swallowed the lump of fear, but it only fueled hatred for Stirling. Carefully modulating his tone and choosing his words to diminish his errors, Babcox began his report again.

As his teammates gathered around him, Max met Gabe's gaze. "You shouldn't have done that. Thanks, though."

"Why?" Gabe asked.

"Huh?"

"Why shouldn't I have backed up one of my men?"

"They're Zulu. I'm nothing." The slap to the back of his head surprised Max, and he turned to peer at Brett.

Brett's eyes narrowed, utterly serious as he stated, "Never say that again. You're *not* nothing. And I don't give a rat's ass if they are Zulu. What they did isn't right, and they need to be called on the carpet for that shit."

Max dropped to his butt and crossed his legs as he blew out a breath. "Been nice running with you. I might catch you in the head from time to time."

"What the hell's that supposed to mean?" Gabe joined Max on the floor and waited for him to answer.

Caleb and Brett dropped down too, concern written on their features as Max remained quiet for several more minutes.

Max breathed in and out to calm himself. His soulful blue eyes met Gabe's brown ones. "Thanks for the privilege of working with teammates who can see beyond what my father supposedly did. Ridgeway said the next time I screwed up, I'd be out of the SEALs and scrubbing the latrines for the rest of my enlistment. Lucas is dead. I think that qualifies as one hell of one."

The opposite side of his skull stung with a slap, this time from Caleb. "Quit hitting me."

"Quit being an ass. You. Did. Not. Screw. The. Pooch." Caleb enunciated every word, and then his shoulders drooped as he sighed. "As much as I want to blame Badcock … Lucas died because, sadly, Lucas made a horrible mistake. He forgot to check before lifting his head into view."

"I told him to take watch."

"Okay," Gabe agreed before making his opinion known, "but how he got there isn't on you. He made one mistake, and we will drill until no one on this team ever makes the same error."

Max couldn't believe his ears. "You don't blame me?"

"What the fuck? Why the hell would we?" Brett gawked at Max like he possessed two heads.

Gabe noticed the emotion flitter across Max's face before a stoic mask clamped down. He wore a similar expression on the day the Millers adopted him and witnessed it on each of his siblings' faces the moment they learned they had a forever family. Someone who grew up with a loving and caring family always around to support them would never comprehend the longing orphans experienced, especially those tagged as 'too old to adopt.'

The last thing Max needed now was anyone gaping at him or tossing twenty questions his way. Clearing his throat to gain the attention of his men, Gabe said, "Time to rack out. Max, come with me." He stood and offered a hand to Stirling, drawing him to his feet and steering him to the farthest corner at the rear of the plane, away from everyone else.

He sat and patted the seat next to him. When Max lowered himself and peered at him quizzically, Gabe squeezed Max's shoulder. "Time to rest, kid. Today, put you in an emotional blender. I meant what I said to Lockwood and Marshall. I'll go above Ridgeway ... all the way to Admiral Droit, if they try to pin this on you or if Ridgeway tries to kick you out. You are part of my team, and I watch out for my guys."

Max shook his head. "Don't ruin your career over me."

"Not going to, but not letting them railroad you out. You're too damned good. Hell, I think you have the makings to be Zulu's leader someday with some seasoning and training." Gabe went out on a limb and said, "Would be one way to honor your father and perhaps rewrite history."

Again, Max gaped.

"Get some sleep." Gabe crossed his arms and leaned back, achieving a semi-comfortable position. Sleeping upright for ten hours wouldn't be any fun for him or his team, but after two weeks in mud and rain, at least here, it was dry. Tomorrow, he would do whatever necessary to protect a young man he came to admire.

As Max prepared to grab some shut-eye, hoping sleep wouldn't bring nightmares, he didn't notice the assessing gazes of Marshall or Lockwood on him nor the concerned glances of his teammates as they resumed their seats near Lucas.

At the front of the plane, Jake stood with Bryan in quiet contemplation as they both observed Red Team interact with Stirling. When Miller took the young SEAL to the back, Jake released a long sigh and stared a moment longer before turning his gaze to Lockwood. "I need to find out a few things. First, why the hell was my AAR changed? I didn't place any blame on Stirling. The failings were on me.

"My op, my failure. I damn near got that kid killed. If not for Rocketeer's ability to track him once Draper found the smoke, we might never have found him, and his headless, arrow-filled body would be hanging from a tree."

The awful imagery in Jake's mind caused him to pause. "And two, how did this Captain Ridgeway obtain a copy of a classified AAR? Something stinks here."

Lockwood nodded. "I agree. I signed the report you submitted. I changed nothing. I'll speak with Captain Kendrick tomorrow. This will be investigated." A hint of a grin played on Bryan's face. "Intriguing watching his new team go to bat for him."

"They shouldn't have to. Hell, Stirling should still be with Foxtrot. I don't like this one damned bit." Jake squeezed the back of his neck.

"Having a change of heart regarding Preston's son?" Bryan arched his brows.

Unwilling to admit he might be wrong to Lockwood, Jake said, "Don't like when things don't add up. And the kid didn't deserve to be demoted. He did his job well." To deflect from conflicting emotions, Jake changed the subject. "We need to speak to Rob too. Based on Axel's brief report, Babcox needs an attitude adjustment."

Weary, Bryan gave Jake a nod. "Grab some sleep. Tomorrow will be a long day."

13

Many Questions, Few Answers

Virginia - Tarmac

CROUCHING, Max gripped a casket handhold, preparing to rise and carry Special Warfare Operator Lucas Tanner from the plane. To his left knelt Gabe, and behind them were Brett and Caleb, with two other members of Red Team. When the ramp finished lowering, Zulu minus their two injured guys, all of Sierra, and the lieutenant commander exited and formed two lines, coming to attention and holding a salute.

On Gabe's signal, they lifted their fallen brother's flag-draped box and began a slow cadence down, walking between the honor guard to the medical examiner's van. After sliding the coffin in, Max stepped back and offered his salute. He lowered his hand gradually as the van pulled away, but his eyes never left the vehicle until it turned a corner.

Gabe patted Max on the back, causing dust to waft off. Though Draper provided them wet wipes to clean their faces and hands during the flight, unlike Zulu and Sierra, who traveled with extra apparel, he and his guys still wore uniforms caked in dried mud. "Time to shower at the gym and grab chow before debrief."

Max turned red eyes to Gabe. Nightmares prevented him from sleeping for more than about twenty minutes. He tried for normalcy, though nothing about a dead brother was normal to him. "After weeks in the field, we all stink."

Kira Draper approached Red One and smiled. "Senior Chief Miller, I arranged for a room with sufficient bunks for you and your team to rest and clean clothing. If you leave your dirty uniforms in the hamper in the shower area, someone will launder and return them to you before the debrief. I'll swing by and escort you into the secure area in about four hours." She then gave Miller directions to their quarters and the mess.

Appreciative of Draper's actions once again, Max half-listened as he observed Zulu Six being wheeled out of the plane and into an awaiting ambulance. McBride followed under his own power, though Zulu's dog handler matched his steps, close at hand in case his teammate wavered.

As McBride stood beside the ambulance while they put Chase inside, Max's gaze locked with the moss-green eyes. He didn't understand the expression that crossed the breacher's face, though he didn't think it held quite as much venom and perhaps a hint of a thank you. He gave McBride a curt nod and pivoted to follow Gabe but halted when Lieutenant Farris called his name.

Turning back to the C17, Max noted two men leading the hooded HVT toward a smaller aircraft and the Naval Intelligence Officer hurrying to him. Gabe motioned to Brett for him and the guys to continue as he stopped to find out what Farris wanted with his second-in-command.

Closing the distance, Nicole said, "You speak Berber, correct?"

"Yes, Ma'am." Max ran a hand through his greasy locks, wanting nothing more at this moment than a hot shower to wash away two weeks' worth of grime, but the question portended something he wouldn't like.

"Perfect. You're coming with me." Nicole pointed to the plane where Anwar Massi was being loaded.

"Why?" Gabe demanded, prepared to back up his man again.

"I need an interpreter. Time is of the essence, and the one who should've been here by now is stuck in a massive traffic jam in the middle of the Hampton tunnel due to an accident. We can't wait for her to arrive or for Langley to send someone else."

Nicole took in Stirling's disheveled state, and her nose twitched at his ripe body odor. Although she felt terrible that he couldn't at least wash up and change, in her haste, she chose words which, combined with her facial expression, communicated disgust. "I'm no happier about this than you are, Stirling. Let's go."

"He's not in your chain of command. You have no authority to order Max anywhere, and he is needed for debriefing." Gabe didn't care for her tone or words.

"My CO cleared it with Ridgeway, and Stirling already gave you his report. That should be sufficient, and if questions for him arise, Lockwood can ask when I'm done with him. We're leaving now," Nicole ordered before pivoting and striding away.

"Yes, Ma'am." Max took a step, paused, and turned to Gabe. "Thanks again. Hopefully, I'll be back before the funeral. Raise a glass to Lucas for me if I'm not."

Gabe nodded and remained in place as Max trotted to catch up to the rapidly moving lieutenant. He grinned when Draper tossed Max a backpack and said, "Nothing fancy, but the clothes should fit. Included some snacks and water too."

Three Hours Later – Hospital – Finn's Room

"I don't need to stay." Finn swung his feet off the mattress, but he moved too fast and swayed as he sat up. He would've pitched forward to the floor if not for Grant gripping his shoulder.

"Yeah, right," Dave scoffed from his position on an uncomfortable plastic chair.

"You're not going anywhere. I agree with the doctor keeping you overnight for observation. Your bell got rung. Twice." Grant maintained a firm grip on Finn.

"I'm braw. Only a few wee stitches." Finn tried to pull out of Grant's grasp, determined to leave.

Appearing in the doorway, Jake crossed his arms and scrutinized his ginger-haired, stubborn breacher. "Might as well lie back and relax someplace comfortable. We'll be here waiting for word on Axel for several hours anyway."

"If you put it that way … okay." Little spots danced in Finn's vision as he gruffly acquiesced. Scooting back, he rested his aching head on the stiff pillow as he closed his eyes. The ringing in his ears had stopped hours ago, but the jackhammer in his skull persisted despite the pain medication.

Dave hid his smile. Jake's method for dealing with Finn usually worked, but on rare occasions, it didn't, so Jake ordered him. "Where's Zach? I thought he would be here by now."

Jake entered and headed for the recliner. "He's giving Rocky a bath and having the vet give him a once over. Never know what diseases he might pick up by sinking his teeth into the scum of the earth. He'll stop by when he's done at the kennels."

"Any word on Axel?" Grant sat on the foot of Finn's bed.

"Not yet, but Lockwood said he would pop up after the surgeon gives him an update."

"Why'd Stirling go with Farris?" Dave inquired as he reached for the paper coffee cup below his seat.

"Stirling went with the lieutenant?" Finn lifted his eyelids. "When?"

"Didn't make it off the tarmac … so about three hours ago." Jake settled in, understanding he, Grant, and Dave had about a half-hour before they needed to head to the base for debrief.

"According to Lester, Stirling is multilingual," Grant offered.

Jake nodded. "Yep. Lockwood overheard Farris on the phone during the flight arranging for an interpreter, but she didn't arrive, and with the approaching storm, they had no window to wait. Plus, if you recall from the briefing, Farris believes Anwar planned something to retaliate for his brother's detention."

Feeling like the host of twenty questions, Dave changed the subject as he asked, "Any idea how Ridgeway got a copy of our Argentina AAR?"

"Or why Stirling was demoted?" Grant added.

"No, but we're going to find out." Jake squeezed the back of his neck. "Also, figure out who altered it."

"Whoa, what'd ya mean, altered?" Finn eyed Jake.

"Right, you were in la-la-land when things got heated on the plane." Dave recounted the altercation for Finn and ended with, "So Ridgeway demoted him, and that's why he is on Red Team. His teammates went to bat for him. Apparently, not everyone wears blinders and judges him by his father's actions."

Grant sighed. "Twice now, he's saved a member of our team. We owe him a case or two of beer."

Guantanamo Bay Naval Base – Visitor Annex

After arriving at the detention center an hour ago, guards took Massi to be processed while a corporal drove Max and Nicole to the visitor's annex outside the secured sections where they could wait more comfortably. In addition to the breakroom with a table, chairs, coffee maker, fridge, and microwave, the small building contained six bedrooms with private showers.

Max didn't hesitate to make use of the facilities. Usually, he would speed through the task of showering, but he took extra time as the hot water cascaded over him to finally release the tightly held tears for Lucas. When spent, he scrubbed weeks' worth of grime off, but dirt and possibly dried blood still persisted under his nails.

After dressing in the loaned clothing, he towel-dried his hair as he sat on the bed. He then combed his fingers through his unruly locks, attempting to achieve some semblance of order. Tired yet happy to be clean, he pulled on the fresh, dry socks and peered down at his boots. He did his best to knock off the mud, but they wouldn't be inspection-worthy without a thorough scouring. However, he would wear them because they were the only footwear he had here.

Shoving a foot in, Max figured he owed a six-pack at least to Draper and whoever she scrounged this apparel from. After he tied the second boot, he rested his forearms on his thighs and let his head drop, wishing for a few hours of sleep and something substantial to eat. He didn't have a chance to consume any of the snacks Draper included in the bag.

The two-hour flight over had been a bust. For as much as Farris indicated it to be urgent to speak with Anwar, the man refused to acknowledge them or respond to any questions presented. Regardless of the languages used, Max tried several, in addition to those considered prevalent in Algeria, Anwar still remained as tight as a drum, wearing an annoying smirk on his face the entire time.

Max mulled over Anwar's behavior, and an idea began to form as he thought more about the man's expression. Rising, Max tossed the wet towel in the hamper and snagged the backpack, which now contained his dirty uniform. He headed for the breakroom, where Farris said she'd be waiting.

As luck would have it, the aroma of coffee greeted Max, and he found Farris at the table. He allowed his annoyance at being tasked with this job to fade away as he noted a sandwich and a full coffee mug across from her. "Lieutenant, I've been thinking."

Nicole lifted her weary eyes to the SEAL, pleased to find him washed. With all the dirt gone and his damp, curly hair tousled, he indeed appeared younger than twenty-four. "How about you eat while you tell me what you're thinking?" She motioned to the food. "Hope you like bologna," she teased.

"Starving. I'll eat almost anything." Max set his rucksack down and lowered himself into the chair, noting roast beef piled high on a French roll. He took several bites to sate his hunger as he studied the intelligence officer. Her questions for Massi had been relevant and probing. She was no slacker and appeared to take her job as seriously as he did his.

After taking a gulp of his coffee to wash the dry bread down, Max kept one hand wrapped around his cup. "I might be wrong. It wouldn't be the first time, but something is bothering me."

"What?" Nicole blew on the hot liquid in her mug.

"You're concerned Anwar picked a target, and things are in motion as retaliation for Sayed's detention, right?"

"Yes."

"But he only smirked at us on the plane."

"Right." Nicole took a sip and wondered where Stirling's train of thought would take them. Though she knew he spoke multiple languages, witnessing him switch from one to another with ease impressed her. She spoke Spanish and a bit of French, perhaps enough to order food or obtain directions, but she had never met anyone with his linguistic command. He could be quite useful in a support capacity, as Lester suggested.

"This is probably out there, but that smirk and his continued silence, well, what if he is planning an assault on Guantanamo to break his brother out? Given what is known about the Massis, they don't tend to hang out where they store their munitions. Not their MO, yet Anwar was in Algeria."

Nicole pursed her lips in thought. "Escape from here? Are you serious?"

"Yeah. A long shot and difficult, but with enough money and the right connections, which I wager they have, it wouldn't be out of the question."

"But why allow himself to be captured? And, if, as you suggest, they could buy his way out, why would Anwar risk exposing himself? Also, there is the fact they are never in the same location, which is one way they controlled so much of the arms traffic," Nicole countered.

Taking another drink, Max considered her questions. "Can't answer those, but my gut tells me something isn't what it seems on the surface ..." he trailed off as Farris arched her brow. *Should've kept my mouth shut.*

Her mind reviewing all the intel collected on the Massi network, Nicole's intuition niggled at her too. Though highly unlikely they'd attempt an escape or could pull one off if they tried, Stirling did have a valid point. She sensed she might be missing something and didn't want to be blindsided now, like when Zulu ended up in the trap while snatching Sayed.

She rose. "Let's go. I have a few more questions for the brothers. The guards took Anwar to Sayed's cell, and I ordered their conversation to be monitored while we freshened up."

Max slugged back the remainder of the coffee, and after grabbing his sandwich and pack, he hurried after Farris into the bright afternoon. The lieutenant flagged down the corporal, who drove them to the visitor annex and requested to be taken to the maximum-security cell block, which housed the highest-value and most dangerous detainees.

Virginia – Zulu Team Room

Men filed into the room and took seats or stood, waiting for Lieutenant Commander Lockwood to arrive and convene the debrief. Jake lowered himself into his chair and pinched the bridge of his nose. Many things swirled in his mind, though he needed to focus on the op review for now, so he tabled the things with Stirling and the health status of his teammates for later.

Bryan strode in, noting everyone who would be here was in attendance, and since he came directly from the hospital, he started the meeting with an update on Axel. "You'll be happy to learn that Axel is in recovery now, and the orthopedic surgeon gave a favorable prognosis on his leg."

"What about his persistent coughing?" Grant asked.

"No word on that yet. Okay, let's get down to business."

Zach zoned out as the teams reviewed the chain of events, dissecting and studying each step. He typically focused intently on this activity because he always learned something, but today, he couldn't stop thinking about Axel's cough. His fingers continued to run through Rocky's fur when his dog lay his head in his lap, as he realized the hacking reminded him of his grandmother's coughing fits before she died.

His attention was brought back as Dave said, "Without Rocketeer, we would've lost the HVT out the window. Our furry rocket bagged another scumbag."

Zach tuned in for the remainder of the debriefing, which didn't become as acrimonious as he believed it might've, mostly because Lockwood kept a tight rein on everyone.

14

Eye for Details

Guantanamo Bay Naval Base – Maximum Security Wing

MAX scanned the area as they rode the short distance in the dual-cab truck, hoping to detect anything amiss, but as far as he determined, everything appeared to be routine. Nothing stuck out, though he did note four men smoking next to a van near the max-wing. When they arrived at the gate, a guard escorted them through after verifying their IDs.

Upon entering the observation room, Nicole warmly greeted an interpreter she worked with previously. "Farid, such a pleasure to see you again."

Farid smiled. "And you, Lieutenant."

Max slipped in behind Farris as he finished chewing the last of his sandwich. His eyes moved to the monitors of various cells and found the Massis rapidly since every other room only contained one person. Both men sat on the single bed but remained silent.

"Have they spoken at all?" Nicole inquired.

"Other than greeting one another, no," Farid answered.

"I want both moved into an interrogation room."

Farid shifted uncomfortably in his seat. "Why? I mean, okay." He picked up a radio and relayed the request before rising. "They don't speak English. I'll accompany you."

"No need. I brought an interpreter with me." Nicole motioned to Stirling.

Farid scanned the young man wearing dirty boots, ill-fitting sweatpants, and an oversized t-shirt with *Arizona* printed above an image of a saguaro cactus and cow skull and the words, *It's a dry heat.* By appearance alone, Farid discounted the man's ability. "Are you certain? Berber has many dialects."

"I'm sure. His skills are excellent." Farris glanced at Stirling but didn't offer an introduction, knowing SEALs needed to keep a low profile.

"As you wish." Farid fidgeted a little, his smile becoming forced as he glanced at his watch. "I'll escort you to the room."

Bringing up the rear, Max noticed the four men from outside reentering and striding down the hall. *The smoke break must be over. You couldn't pay me enough to sit around all day on guard duty … worse than spending two weeks in a muddy pit doing recon.*

Max stood in the far corner near the observation mirror while Farris donned a headscarf and spoke with the unarmed interpreter. A short time later, two armed soldiers led the brothers in, and Max noted chains linked their wrist and ankle manacles to a belt around their waists, limiting their ability to move.

While one guard remained at the entry, the other unlocked the wrist chain to secure it to the tabletop. As Farris sat, Max studied both men. Anwar, now dressed in an orange jumpsuit, maintained his annoying smirk as his eyes burned with contempt for Farris. The expression set Max on edge, and his body tensed.

A tingling sensation ran down his back as his gaze landed on Anwar's hands. Until this point, he had not laid eyes on his fingers since black mitts covered them on the plane. He noted the partial ring finger on the right hand, which aligned with the description he received. However, the scar tissue over the decade-old injury contradicted its supposed age. The stump appeared pinkish and smooth when it should have faded and calloused.

Shifting his focus to Anwar's face, the man appeared to match the photo given to them for the recon, but the discrepancy of the missing finger told him this person couldn't be the real Anwar. "Ma'am, a word, please," he said, moving towards the door.

Nicole switched her gaze from Farid to Stirling, and although his face appeared placid, she perceived a wariness in his eyes. As she started to rise, an explosion set the overhead lighting to swaying, and in the next moment, she found herself on the ground underneath Stirling, his body shielding hers.

Three more blasts sounded in the distance as someone pulled Stirling off her. Nicole stared up into the apologetic face of Farid as the SEAL's limp body was dumped beside her. She spotted the trickle of blood running down Stirling's cheek, and it took a moment for her to register that one of them must've struck him with the butt-end of a weapon.

Her eyes whipped to Sayed when he spoke heavily accented but perfect English.

"We need to move. We will take her as insurance. Stupid Americans place a high value on women."

Yanked to her feet, Nicole spared a glance at Max, wondering if the blow to his head killed him. Anger welled inside, but she controlled herself, stating the obvious, "You speak English."

Sayed laughed. "Women are so gullible." He focused on the guard unlocking his restraints. "We must move before the soldiers lock this area down."

"You're not going to make it out." Nicole's mind whirled at the thought Stirling had been right. Clearly, Farid and the guards here had been bought or coerced into helping Sayed and Anwar escape. Comprehending she needed to stall for time, Nicole said, "Rather a risky plan to allow us to capture Anwar just to break you out of here."

Anwar chuckled, which drew Nicole's scrutiny. His smirk persisted, and that is when she realized his countenance was unnatural, as if his face was permanently set in that position. Her eyes went to his right hand, and she recognized the truth. "You're not Anwar."

Loosed from his chains, Sayed sneered at the woman. "The plastic surgeon did a wonderful job, don't you think?"

"Except for the nerve damage, I suppose," Nicole replied.

"Ah, yes, an unfortunate side-effect." Sayed moved towards the exit, only to end up on his knees in a chokehold.

Playing possum until Massi came close enough, Max made his move, tripping Sayed and lunging upward to encircle the terrorist's neck from behind. Overpowering the leader would be the only way to control the peons in the room.

Max commanded, "Drop your weapons, or I snap his neck. You get him killed, and Anwar will chop you into little pieces, one joint at a time, prolonging your misery for as long as possible. Give up now, and you'll spend the rest of your natural life in prison."

"KILL HIM!" Sayed raged until his air was painfully cut off by the arm around his throat.

Both armed guards hesitated, and one flicked his eyes to the female lieutenant. He was in so deep he didn't see a way out, and neither option appealed to him. He lifted his gun and sent a bullet through his own brain.

Fake Anwar grabbed for the gun as the man's body slumped to the ground. He aimed the pistol at the woman and demanded, "Let Sayed go, or I kill her."

At this point, the imposter speaking English surprised neither Nicole nor Max. Although frightened, having never had a gun aimed at her face before, Nicole managed to keep her voice level, "Escape is impossible. Guards are swarming the area, and all exits will be locked tight. It is daylight, and you are highly visible. You can't possibly believe they'll let you walk out of here with or without hostages as shields."

Max loosened his hold on Sayed's airway to ensure he remained alive. He hissed, "Tell them to stand down."

"Kill the bitch!" Sayed rasped.

At the same time Max dove for Farris, he shoved Sayed at the bogus Anwar. A burning sensation crossed his bicep as he once again protected the lieutenant. Several more shots rang out. Shattered glass from the one-way mirror separating this room from the viewing area tinkled to the cement floor as three lifeless bodies dropped around them.

Boots and voices swirled as the interrogation room filled with guards. A pair of hands were offered to assist both Nicole and Max up after he rolled off her. They gained their feet and found the second guard, Sayed, and whoever pretended to be Anwar dead. When the tremors got the better of her, Nicole appreciated Stirling's steadying grip on her elbow.

"Coming down from adrenaline can cause the shakes. Let's find you a place where you can sit down." Max then addressed the senior soldier, "I'm taking her out of here."

Receiving a nod, Max helped Farris step over the dead bodies and into the hall. He guided her fifty feet away before assisting her to the floor so she could rest against the wall. Staying alert for any latent threats, Max ignored his throbbing head and stinging arm.

After gathering her composure, Nicole peered up at Stirling. "How's your head?"

"Fine," he lied.

Nicole noted the blood on his arm. "Your bicep's bleeding."

"Only a graze. Nothing to worry about."

"You saved my life." Nicole caught his blue eyes. "Thanks."

"Welcome." Max flashed a grin.

Inhaling deeply through her nose, Nicole exhaled gradually as she closed her eyes to ground herself. Opening them again, she queried, "What did you want to tell me in there?"

"What you figured out. We didn't capture the real Anwar."

"How'd you realize?"

"Scar tissue on his finger was too recent. Shouldn't have been pinkish." Refusing to display the effects of his adrenaline crash, Max leaned on the wall, hiding his shaking hands behind him.

Noting the mass of armed soldiers in the hallway and Farid in handcuffs, Nicole said, "Sit. The wing is secure."

Max slid down and wrapped a hand around his still oozing bicep, needing to stem the flow. "Well, this didn't go as planned."

Nicole shook her head slowly as she released a short chuckle. "No, it didn't. However, I do believe we discovered the intended target anyway. Guantanamo."

"Yeah. Wonder how the real Massi will react when he finds out his plans got his brother killed." Max closed his eyes as the pounding in his head continued.

"A bridge to cross for another day." Nicole rested her head on the cement wall, too tired to plan and strategize. For now, glad to be alive ... thanks to Stirling's actions.

The more she interacted with her CO's nephew, the less Captain Athole's opinion of Stirling seemed to fit. Today, she found his actions to be anything but reckless or foolhardy. Stirling had an eye for details, assessed evolving situations fast, and responded accordingly.

"How long do you think we'll be here?" Max broke the silence which descended on them.

"A few days. I expect they'll need to debrief us. Why?"

"Want to make it home for Lucas's funeral."

Taken aback by the answer, Nicole stared at the young, blond SEAL, having almost forgotten he lost a teammate. "I'll do what I can to ensure you arrive in time."

"Thanks." Silence shrouded them again as they waited for the lockdown to be canceled.

Virginia – Zulu Team Room

When debrief concluded, Jake remained in his seat as everyone except Lockwood began to disperse. He noted Rob conversing with Gabe as the team leaders strode out. Most likely, discussing how many days of running the hills would result in an appropriate attitude adjustment for Babcox.

The man certainly needed one since his poor judgment and actions contributed to a man's death. Although there was enough blame to toss around when they examined the sequence of events, none of it landed at Stirling's feet.

"You planning on visiting Axel today?" Dave lingered, too, with no desire to rush home to an empty house.

"Yeah. I'll stop by later." Jake's hand fisted and released several times, still angry with aspects of the last mission.

"J, you're not gonna read him the riot act today."

Jake shook his head. "No, but we are going to have a long talk about his role in this debacle."

"A cough isn't within his control."

"Perhaps not, but he's been coughing for weeks and claiming it to be dust-related. The first rule of Zulu—"

"Don't lie to the team leader. We're all aware. I don't think Axel lied. Maybe he developed an allergy but thought it was related to all the dust. You have to admit, he looked like Pig-Pen after every drill you put us through."

Jake cracked a grin at the reference to the amiable yet filthy Peanuts cartoon character who attracted a permanent cloud of dust. "True. I guess I'll wait until Doc figures out the cause."

"Want to grab a beer? Cathy and the kids are at her parents' house in Richmond until tomorrow."

"No. I told Valarie I'd be home for dinner. You're welcome to come."

"Wouldn't pass up one of her meals. You ready to go?"

"Not yet. Want to find out if Lockwood will allow me to go with him to speak with Kendrick." Jake leaned back in the chair, waiting for Lockwood to finish the phone call that came in as the meeting ended.

"Alright. I'll swing by the hospital to check on the guys and wait for you there." When Jake nodded, Dave rose as Lockwood hung up and turned to them. Upon viewing his expression, Dave sat again.

"We spinning up?" Jake straightened his posture.

"On standby. The situation is evolving." Bryan reached for his coffee mug and set it down when he found it empty.

"And?" Jake prompted.

"Details are scarce at the moment, but it appears there's been an attempted escape from Gitmo. Four explosions occurred. One took out a watchtower, another blew a hole in the exterior wall of the maximum-security wing, and two detonated in the medium and low-security areas, resulting in chaos and several deaths."

"Anyone succeed?" Jake asked.

"It doesn't appear so, and the facility is in lockdown. But if they determine anyone did succeed, Zulu is on tap to hunt them down and retrieve them."

"We're down two men," Dave said.

"Sierra One and Two can fill out your ranks if necessary." Bryan raked a hand through his hair. "Farris was certain Anwar Massi was planning an attack soon. I wonder if this is related or only a coincidence."

"Don't believe in coincidences. Farris is there. Call her. She probably has useful details." Jake pushed out of the chair and began to pace.

"I can't. All communication is being funneled through secure channels. They don't want the media to get wind of this until the situation is contained. For explosives to be planted in those places, they had to have inside help. NCIS is en route to investigate." Bryan grabbed his cup and strode to the coffee pot.

As he poured the last dredges of lukewarm liquid, Bryan said, "Hope Farris and Stirling are alright."

Next Day – Guantanamo Bay Naval Base – Visitor Annex

A soft knock at his door pulled Max from the final vestiges of an unexpectedly pleasant dream. He cracked his eyes open as he sat and shifted his feet to the floor. Only a slight headache remained, and luckily didn't amp up as he called out, "Come in."

Nicole pushed open the door and kept her voice soft. "How are you feeling?"

"Fine."

She snorted. "You said that yesterday. Are you still lying?"

Max eyed the lieutenant, haloed by light from the hall. He would've never believed anyone if they told him he would be on friendly terms with someone who worked for his uncle. But Lieutenant Farris was a unique woman. Though she kept a stoic and controlled façade locked in place most times, she possessed a wicked wit. "Head only hurts a little."

"Okay. I got ibuprofen and lunch in the breakroom."

"Lunch?" Max moved his eyes to his Luminox wristwatch, noting it to be after thirteen hundred. A bit confused, he scanned the darkened room.

Nicole pointed to the windows. "Blackout shades. I figured you needed the sleep, so I pulled them this morning when I popped in to check on you."

Her words about checking on him and the fact he slept so long shocked Max. After being treated in the infirmary and interviewed by an NCIS agent, he hit his rack around eight-thirty last night. "Um, thanks. Guess I did."

"You took a hard blow to your head. The doctor said you might need more rest. How's your arm?"

"Fi …" Her gaze pinned him, and Max faltered a moment. "Fine. Really. A little sore, but no real damage."

"Okay. Well, your cleaned uniform is hanging in the closet. I'll leave you to dress." Nicole shut the door and headed for the breakroom.

Ten minutes later, after a quick shower and wrapping his bicep in a clean bandage, Max joined Farris at the table. Today's lunch consisted of a bowl of soup, turkey on rye, a bag of potato chips, and a slice of strawberry cheesecake. His drink selection included coffee, bottled water, and a shot glass filled with whiskey.

Nicole lifted her glass. "Thanks for what you did yesterday."

Though he wanted to discount his actions, Max only nodded and clinked his glass with hers before slamming the alcohol down in one gulp. "The good stuff."

"Yep. Figured we deserved it after yesterday." She took a spoonful of minestrone soup as Max started in on his sandwich. "I arranged a flight home for you. It leaves in forty minutes."

Max barely kept his jaw from gapping. "California?"

"Yes. You'll be there in plenty of time for the funeral."

"Thank you." When she smiled and nodded at him, Max asked, "Did they determine if more than those four guards and Farid are involved, and did anyone else die or escape in the havoc?"

"Yes and no. Fortunately, all detainees are accounted for and locked up. In the melee, the three Marines in the watchtower sustained minor cuts from flying debris, and two medium-security prisoners suffered second-degree burns. The explosives weren't placed to kill, only to cause diversions and create a fast route out of the maximum wing.

"Unfortunately, the prison's commander will be dealing with a colossal mess as he re-vets all his personnel. Farid confessed to his involvement and spilled the beans on the others in a plea deal. Two sailors in the processing center will be charged. They were tasked with fingerprinting and verifying Anwar's identity. They've admitted to falsifying the paperwork.

"Beyond them, a lack of adherence to proper procedures and some bribes appear to be how the guards smuggled in the plastic explosive." Nicole stopped for a drink of water.

"How did they plan to get off the island?"

"Farid indicated they had a series of vehicles stashed along the roads and planned to fly out of Aeroporto di Holguín. It is believed Massi had contacts with a Columbian drug lord, and in exchange for helping him escape, the brothers would provide him a shipment of assault weapons."

Max digested the information. "Wonder if Anwar will follow through or if the cartel boss is now on his hit list for failing."

"Either is a possibility. And given Anwar's bloodthirsty and vengeful nature, our names will be redacted from the reports. Now, eat up. You have a plane to catch."

15

Brothers to Count On

F INN tossed his rucksack on the floor near his black leather couch and his keys on the metal side table. He stood in the middle of his sparsely decorated apartment and stared out the mini-blinds for several minutes at the parking lot below before reaching for his TV remote, needing any noise to break the stark silence.

Striding to his fridge, he didn't give a damn Doc said no alcohol and pulled out a beer. Well, he cared a bit about what Grant said, so he didn't grab the entire six-pack or his bottle of Scotch whiskey, though getting sloshed tonight sounded like a perfect plan. He popped the lid off, sauntered to the sofa, and plunked down. Taking a swig, he stared at the seventy-inch flat screen, but he didn't see the image displayed.

His own movie ran on a loop. Though he had not been conscious when Special Warfare Operator Tanner died, Jake explained what transpired. It was a preventable death as far as Finn was concerned. An ill-timed cough from Chase, compounded by Babcox's arrogance and Tanner's rookie mistake. If any one of those had not occurred, a young sailor would still be alive.

But they did, and Tanner paid the ultimate price for absolutely fucking nothing. The man they bagged was not Anwar Massi, only a planted double.

So much shit went sideways recently. Anger welled deep in the pit of his stomach, and Finn didn't have an outlet since he couldn't go beat the crap out of a heavy bag, lift weights, or drink his feelings away. He squeezed his eyes shut as he took a long swig but opened them when Stirling's blue eyes haunted him again.

When he met Stirling's gaze on the tarmac, something caused a gut-twisting reaction he didn't understand. And frankly, didn't want to either because the Mighty Finn did *not* do touchy-feely emotions. Sure, he had them, but he never conveyed his deepest ones to anyone. Except for the manly expression of rage. The softer stuff, the hurt, the grief, the sorrow, the longing, the loneliness, those he kept under lock and key.

Finn mastered covering and deflecting the missing pieces of his life with booze, meaningless sex, and his job. He would never be a family man like Jake, Dave, and Grant. Little rug rats were not in his future … though he enjoyed being Uncle Finn.

He vowed years ago he would never marry. Finn refused to put a woman through raising kids all on her own, like his mother. In truth, she had help from her parents, but after his father died, his mom struggled to come to grips with the fact the love of her life passed away. She planned to raise her family and grow old with Patrick, but life was fickle, and laughed at her plans.

Banging on his apartment door drew Finn out of his stupor. He rose and moved to the entrance, wondering who the hell was bothering him. If his crabby neighbor came to complain about the volume again, he might end up doing something he would later regret. Yanking the door open, he growled, "What do you want?"

"You greet everyone bearing pizza so nicely?" Zach smiled as Rocky rushed in and circled Finn's legs.

"Sorry. Not in the best mood." Finn stepped back, swinging his door wider for Zach to enter. He pushed it closed and returned to his seat. Rocky hopped up beside him and lay his head in his lap to be petted as Zach set the pizza on the coffee table.

"Figured. None of us are." Zach opened the box, withdrew a slice, and sat in a chair. He noted the half-consumed beer.

The aroma of his favorite pie finally won, and Finn leaned forward to snag a gooey piece. "Why are you here?"

"Grant."

A typical response from the man of few words. Their dog handler didn't elaborate without a prompt. "If Grant thought I couldn't be on my own, why'd he drop me off and leave?"

"Said he had things to take care of, asked me to make sure you ate something, and," Zach reached for the beer, "didn't drink. I'll finish this for you."

"What the fuck?" Finn frowned.

"Only following orders." Zach chuckled.

Finn bit into his pizza and chewed, trying to come up with a retort, but his thinking remained a bit slow. He settled for, "Go grab me water if you're gonna drink *my* beer."

Rising, Zach went to the fridge, snagged a bottle, and stopped to fill the spare water dish Finn kept for Rocky. Returning to the main area, he spotted Finn feeding his dog bits of crust. "Don't spoil his dinner and ruin all my training. He's not a house puppy."

Finn smirked as he gave Rocky another little treat and quipped, "He deserves it for putting up with you."

Grinning, Zach tossed the bottle at Finn and plopped into a chair. "If we're going that route, we all deserve a keg for having you on this team."

"Ha-ha." Finn unscrewed the top and gulped down a quarter of the water before grabbing another slice as they descended into a comfortable silence.

Once he finished the last slice, Finn rested his head on the back of the couch. Staring at his ceiling, his thoughts centered on the bombshell Axel dropped on them this afternoon. "We're back to finding a new guy. Damn, this sucks for Axel."

Zach nodded. "I didn't realize until after the mission his cough sounded like my grandmother's before she died."

Finn shifted to peer at Zach. On the rare occasion he spoke without prompting, they usually gained some insight into the quiet man. He waited to see if Zach would continue.

Toying with the label on the empty beer bottle, tearing it at the edges, Zach said, "She was a lifetime smoker, so it came as no surprise she ended up with lung cancer." He lifted his eyes and met Finn's gaze. "But Axel? Hell, he never smoked a day in his life, and his parents didn't either. His diagnosis is out of the blue."

"Aye." Axel's situation contributed to Finn's bad mood. The doctors knew about the cancer before Chase went into surgery for his leg but chose to tell Axel privately afterward. Axel broke the news to his wife before informing them. "He's going to beat this. They only need to remove part of his lung."

Zach grimaced. "Still ending his career, and he will be going through chemo. No fun. I watched my grandma suffer all the side effects, and she still died."

"Axel isn't your grandma. He will fight and win. You heard him yourself. He's got a wife and kids to live for, and they're more important to him than this job."

Silence reigned again as both men became lost in their thoughts of how they might react to finding out a simple cough signaled the end of their time on Zulu.

Zach ended their reflection when he asked, "So, do you think Jake's going to offer the position to Hector Morales?"

"Probably. He was our second choice, and it doesn't make sense to do a full deliberation again. Won't be any other reasonable candidates to assess." Exhausted, Finn yawed.

The yawn cued Zach to follow the rest of Grant's instructions. He stood and picked up the empty box to toss in the trash. "Time for your meds and to grab some shut-eye. I'll swing by tomorrow morning and give you a lift to the base."

Finn eyed Zach. "Why?"

"Well, I won't if you're not interested in heckling Babcox as he runs the hills. Rob's putting Sierra Seven through the wringer, trying to knock some arrogance out of him."

A harrumph emitted from Finn. "The cocky turd won't ever change. I'm not sure why Rob selected him for the support team in the first place. But aye, I'll come ... nothing better to do."

Grant's House

Pulling to a stop in the driveway, Grant bowed his head and took several long breaths, exhaling gradually with each one, preparing to go inside. A technique he perfected years ago to separate his worlds. He compartmentalized his home life from Zulu as seamlessly as he switched into medic mode.

He became so skilled at keeping the wall between them that no one except Jake was aware his personal life had been blown to hell in the past few months and that had been out of necessity. The slow spiral down began over a year ago but reached the bottom the day after Axel's welcome barbeque.

Grant turned off the ignition, realizing his transition routine was unnecessary today. Lifting his head, he glanced at the brochures in the passenger seat. After dropping Finn off and calling Zach to check on their errant hothead, who often drank more than he should, he began the process of touring apartment complexes.

A sigh escaped as Grant's gaze landed on the lease agreement that he signed only thirty minutes ago. He now had a new place. Turning his head, he stared at the dark windows of what used to be his welcoming home. So much changed in the blink of an eye. Hopes and dreams had been dashed for so many lately.

With sluggish movements, Grant exited his truck and headed for the front door for the last time. Tomorrow, he would load up his boxes and move. Sliding the key in and turning, he listened for the familiar click before gripping the knob. He pushed the door open and realized the squeaky hinge he intended to oil would now be the problem for the next occupants.

He sped through the living room, not wanting to meet the ghosts of the worst day of his life. Grant ended up in the kitchen, and he flicked on the lights. An envelope on the counter caught his attention. It had not been there when he left this morning.

Making his way through the maze of boxes, his hand hovered over the package. He recognized Lindsey's handwriting, and his stomach flipped. "I damn well don't need this today."

Whether he needed it or not, Grant ripped open the envelope with viciousness and glared at the handwritten letter and official documents he found within. Mixed emotions fought an ugly battle, leaving him battered on the inside.

Grant didn't think this day would come for him … he would beat the odds. He believed he would be in the ten percent, but he turned out to be no different than ninety percent of SEALs … at least in terms of marriage.

He read her sickeningly simple message. **Signed the divorce papers. The paternity test confirms the baby isn't yours, so I'm not going to fight for child support.**

"NO SHIT, SHERLOCK!" Grant yelled, crumpled the note, and threw it at the wall.

A myriad of memories assaulted him. The first few years had been bliss. Then, her nagging began. She wanted him to leave Zulu … not something he would do until he could no longer fight alongside his brothers. Lindsey didn't grasp the concept of loyalty. She fucking did not understand. As evidenced by her betrayal of their wedding vows.

The night of Axel's barbeque, she donned her false mask and chatted with Val and Cathy like good friends, but once home, Lindsey's venom reigned supreme as she trashed Jake's and Dave's wives for everything from their cooking to the clothes they wore, and how they handled their kids. Lindsey claimed she would be a much better mother than them.

Competitive and materialistic didn't begin to describe Lindsey, and Grant often wondered why she married an enlisted sailor since his pay would never give her the things she desired. He tried hard to be an attentive and caring husband. Spent as much time with her as possible, but he never seemed to be enough for her.

The last straw came the day following the party. They went to Lindsey's first ultrasound, and he discovered the fetus was three months older than she claimed. He couldn't be the father. He had been deployed at the time she became pregnant. She betrayed him, and he couldn't forgive her, so he filed for divorce.

Grant drew in a ragged breath and sat on a carton. As he blew it out, interestingly enough, some of the weight he carried in the past few months lifted. Though a slight tinge of sorrow for what might've been … a child to love … still lingered.

Using his well-honed skills, he shoved the thought in a box, acknowledging one day, he might meet an honest, loving woman, and they could bring a baby into this world to cherish.

He smiled. "I'm free of the lying, cheating bitch." His emotions swung like a pendulum, and his grin faded. *Crap. Now, I need to tell the team Lindsey is out of my life. Shit. I should've clued them in when I filed the paperwork. Axel's bombshell sent them reeling this afternoon. Now I gotta tell them the baby isn't mine, and I kicked Lindsey to the curb.*

Rising, Grant went to his fridge, sighed when he recalled it would be empty, and then groaned when he realized he let Lindsey take all the furniture. He wanted a fresh start with no reminders of her in his new place.

Grant pulled out his cell phone and dialed. When the call connected, he said, "Mind if I crash at your place tonight?"

Dave's Home

Hanging up the phone, Dave turned to Cathy. "Grant's going to stay the night. I hope that is alright."

Cathy smiled. "No problem. Did he say why?"

"No. But I figure it must be something significant if he isn't staying with Lindsey tonight."

Cathy's expression soured. "She can be a bit much to handle."

Dave laughed. "That's a massive understatement. She'd give the Wicked Witch of the West a run for her money. Though I would never tell Grant."

"I tried to engage with her, but she is stand-offish unless it's at a team function. Then she's sugary sweet like we're bosom buddies. Never quite understood what attracted Grant to her. Thought he had more sense and better taste in women."

"Careful, honey. That's his wife, and he's about to have a kid."

Cathy rolled her eyes. "Like your witch remark, I'll keep those comments between us. I haven't even shared them with Val, and we are besties."

Dave pulled his lovely wife to him and kissed her gently. "God blessed me with a beautiful soulmate."

The timer beeped, and Cathy stepped back. "Want to corral the twins and wash them up while I pull out the roast?"

"Um, no. I'll handle the oven."

"Chicken," Cathy teased.

"Bwaaak, bwak-bwak. I'm wholly aware of my limitations." Dave snatched the mitts from Cathy.

"They're not so bad." Cathy giggled.

"Says the woman who can tangle with a tiger and have it purring in two seconds. Terrible three-year-old tantrums in double form need the right wrangler." Dave chuckled as he moved toward the stove.

"Alright, but you're putting them to bed tonight." She grinned when Dave paled. She headed for the family room, "Oh, and put another place at the table for Grant. Even if Lindsey made dinner, which I doubt, Grant's gonna need something edible. I swear that woman can burn water."

Dave only nodded as he removed the pot roast, the aromas tantalizing his palate, unlike Lindsey's unappetizing contribution to the barbeque. Usually, he shied away from her food, but he forgot to ask who made the dish. He gagged on the first bite and had to spit it out. What he tasted could truly be classified as a crime against potato salad.

As he went to grab another plate, the screams of his fraternal twins rent the air. They hated washing up almost as much as going to sleep. He traded the lesser of the two evils with his wife without realizing it. Though, depending on what brought Grant to his place tonight, he might be able to dodge that bullet too.

If he did, he would owe Cathy big time. Perhaps a date night, dinner, and a movie of her choice if Jake's daughter agreed to babysit Aidan and Nadia.

Fifteen minutes later, two kids with clean hands sat in their booster seats while Cathy cut up their vegetables, and her husband went to answer the door. Dave returned with Grant in tow.

"Uncle Grant," screeched from both kids.

"Hey, kiddos." Grant tousled their hair before taking a seat across from them. "Cathy, this smells delicious. Thanks for allowing me to barge in on short notice."

"You are family. No thanks are necessary. Now set an example for the little ones and eat up." Cathy placed the plastic animal plates in front of her children.

The meal passed with pleasant conversation and minimal food being dropped by the twins, who almost nodded off at the table. Dave excused himself to help carry his kids to their room, glad for an easy bedtime, but he would still take Cathy out soon. She deserved it for all the wonderful things she did.

When Dave re-entered the kitchen, he found Grant washing the dishes. "You didn't need to do this." Dave snatched a towel off the rung to begin drying.

"I'm family, right? Everyone pitched in when I grew up."

Dave nodded. During dinner, he avoided prying, but Cathy said she would give them time alone so he could figure out what brought Grant here. The only thing he came up with was Grant might be upset about Axel's diagnosis, and Lindsey was not the most compassionate woman. "I'm not going to force you, but if you want to talk about what's bothering you, I'm listening."

"Who says anything is bothering me?" Grant washed a glass, keeping his focus on the water.

"Well, you're here for one thing. Not that I'm complaining. You're always welcome, but a call out of the blue is unlike you."

Grant rinsed and handed the glass to Dave. "Yeah, a bit out of character for me, huh?"

"Yes, but we're brothers. I've got you covered here and on the field." They finished the washing without speaking another word. After hanging the dish towel to dry, Dave grabbed two beers and said, "Let's go out back," as he handed over a bottle.

The balmy, light breeze wafted around them as they sat in the lawn chairs on the patio. Grant released a sigh. "I should've told you guys something a while back."

Dave stiffened. "You're not leaving the team, are you?"

Grant's eyes whipped to Dave. "HELL NO!"

"Then, whatever it is, we can handle." Dave took a sip and waited for Grant to continue, relieved they wouldn't be losing the best-damned medic in the Navy.

Grant stared at the gathering condensation on his bottle. "I need your help telling the guys. Finn can be a jerk. Zach, hell, sometimes it is hard to tell what he's thinking."

"And Jake?" Dave prompted.

Turning his gaze to his second-in-command, Grant confessed, "He's already aware. I had to make some changes to my CACO form, plus he needed to know where my head was at in my personal life. Though I don't allow it to bleed into my job."

"Okay."

After taking a swig, Grant laid it all out. "Lindsey cheated on me. The baby isn't mine. I filed for divorce when I found out a few months ago, and she signed the papers today. Left them in my old place. I gave her all the furniture. I didn't want it, and she moved everything out this morning. Kept my books and personal stuff. I'm moving into my new apartment tomorrow."

Staggered by Grant's disclosure, Dave drew in a breath and released it slowly. "Whoa, brother. That is a heavy load to carry. I'm so sorry you went through that all alone."

"Yeah, well, walls between worlds, you know." The weight on his shoulders lifted a bit more after sharing with his teammate. "So, will you help me if Finn and Zach freak?"

"Yes. I got your six." Dave pulled out his cell and began a text.

"What are you doing?"

"Inviting them to brunch, and afterward, we're all helping you move into your new digs."

Grant leaned back and relaxed, glad he called Dave on the spur of the moment. "Thanks, brother."

16

Par for the Course

Virginia – Lockwood's Office

JAKE had been at the training grounds with Zach and Finn since daybreak, watching Rob put Babcox through his paces. Typically, Jake deferred to Rob when it came to disciplining Sierra members. But wanted to impress upon Babcox that his attitude wouldn't fly as a member of Zulu's support team.

Lives depended on everyone being a team player. With the shit Babcox pulled in Algeria directly contributing to Tanner's death, he needed a reminder Jake didn't tolerate egotistical behavior. So, in addition to running the hills, Babcox would be grounded from several missions and received a formal written reprimand.

He left the others when Lockwood requested his presence in his office. Halting at the entry, Jake rapped and waited for Lockwood to grant him entry.

"Enter." Bryan motioned to the chair as Jake came in and shut the door behind him. "Take a seat. We need to talk."

"Did Kendrick get back to you yet?" Jake asked as he sat.

"Partially, but we've got a few things to discuss before we broach that topic."

Jake nodded and let Bryan take the lead.

"First order of business. Axel will be moved to Bethesda tomorrow. He'll remain on Zulu's roster as inactive until he is medically retired."

"Do they have any idea how he ended up with cancer?"

"Unclear. It might be exposure to radon, asbestos, or other factors. So, your team needs a sixth member."

"I discussed this with Dave yesterday. Hector Morales was our second choice. Makes sense to offer the position to him." Jake leaned back. "Going to check with the others this afternoon as we help Grant move."

Bryan sighed. "Hate to break this to you, but Morales has been selected for the Warrant Officer Program. He won't be transferring to Zulu."

"Damn. Okay. Guess we need to do a full round again."

"Perhaps, and perhaps not." Bryan slid an unmarked, sealed envelope toward Jake. "I want you to read the contents of this with an open mind after I share something else." Jake reached for the packet, but Bryan kept hold. "After."

Jake sat back. "I'm listening."

"This brings us to your question about Kendrick's response."

"Okay." Jake had been a bit miffed that Lockwood had met with Captain Kendrick without him.

"Kendrick contacted the Naval Criminal Investigative Service to open an inquiry into how Ridgeway obtained a classified AAR. Ridgeway claims the report came with other documents prepared for his review. The clerk in his office, Yeoman Hayden, claims no knowledge of the specific file and presumed it must've been with the stack of files he put on the captain's desk."

"Claims? Can they be substantiated one way or the other?"

Bryan nodded. "Yes and no. NCIS analyzed the fingerprints on the papers and envelope. They only found Ridgeway's."

"So, he hacked the system and altered the AAR?"

"No. This is where things become complicated. A search of his computer revealed no access to the document, and the barely perceptible tracking dots indicate it was printed in Virginia."

"What?" Jake's brows drew together.

"As to the alterations, they were done with finesse and made Stirling appear to be wholly inept in all aspects of the mission."

"In what way?" Jake needed details.

After blowing out an irritated breath, Bryan shared, "It indicated Stirling consumed too much alcohol and was too busy partying to identify potential targets, deliberately discarded the GPS trackers, and if not for Zulu arriving, the senator's son would've been killed because Stirling ran to save himself."

"Shit! No wonder Red Team wanted to hang us by the balls." Jake rose and began to pace. He stopped and peered at Lockwood. "This isn't right. Someone is out to ruin his career. Any idea who?"

Bryan shook his head. "The printer lead is a bust. It's a high-volume, common area machine with unmonitored access. Though they can pinpoint the date and time the file printed, there is no way to determine who sent or picked it up."

Jake's gut twisted. "So, it's a cold case that will be shelved?"

"No, the investigation is a priority and will remain active, but with no leads, well, not much they can do at this point."

Placing his hands on the back of the chair, Jake eyed the plain envelope. "What's in there? The falsified report?"

Bryan stood and rounded his desk as he snagged the thick package. "No. Read it tonight, and we'll talk again tomorrow. I have something I want to run past you, but you need to read this thoroughly beforehand."

Jake took the white envelope. "Being a bit vague here, Lockwood. We don't operate well without a solid plan."

Laughing, Bryan sat on the edge of the desk. "Remember to keep an open mind, Jake, and all will be revealed."

"My mind is always open."

"Except when it is closed," Bryan quipped before changing the subject. "So, Beckett got a new apartment?"

"Yeah. Lindsey finally signed the divorce papers so that messy chapter of Grant's life is over. Val and Cathy made some calls and scrounged up some furniture for him ... he gave all he owned to that witch. And Val's sister got him a smoking deal on a bedroom set. It will be delivered later this afternoon."

"Any worries about where his head is at?"

"None. He's as solid as ever. Grant's going to tell Finn and Zach at brunch today." He checked his watch. "If there's nothing else, Sir, I need to be running."

Bryan pointed to the envelope. "That is for your eyes only … for now."

"Copy." Jake pivoted and exited, itching to find out what Lockwood wanted him to read.

Returning to his chair, Bryan sighed. The idea he and Kendrick cooked up had merit but would only work if Marshall came on board with no reservations. He had been Jake's CO for several years, and he put his trust in the man, as did Kendrick.

In fact, Kendrick perceived something in Marshall years ago and believed the master chief to be one of the rare team leaders. A one-percenter, for lack of a better term. One of the reasons why Kendrick granted Zulu Team a vast amount of leeway in how they operated. He didn't want to mess with a well-oiled machine.

Dave's Home

Grant now understood why Dave invited the team to brunch. He grinned as Aidan sat in Finn's lap, feeding his uncle French toast sticks, dripping tons of syrup in their breacher's dark red beard. A similar scenario played out with Nadia and Zach, though Dave's daughter *accidentally* dropped many pieces on the floor for Rocketeer to gobble up.

With the kids in their laps, neither man would be inclined to go off the deep end when he came clean with what he had been dealing with for months … and hiding from them. Grant inhaled and set his fork down. "Guys. Need to tell you something."

Finn turned to look at Grant and ended up with a piece of toast planted in his beard. He pulled it off and, with a smirk, tossed it to Rocky, earning a glare from Zach.

Into the silence afforded him, Grant said, "Lindsey cheated when we were in the Philippines. Baby's not mine. I'm divorced."

Zach's eyes rounded, shocked by what Grant shared. "Holy sh…" Cathy eyed him, and he changed shit to "shucks!"

Finn's jaw dropped, and Aidan promptly shoved another syrupy morsel into his mouth. Taking time to chew and swallow, Finn was hurt that Grant didn't come to them sooner. "Got a few things to say. One, good riddance to a bad penny. Two, why the fu," he got Cathy's evil eye and switched his words, "fudge, didn't you say something about this before. Shucks, we're your brothers. You didn't have to go through that alone."

"Jake said the same thing when I filed the paperwork." Grant peered at his team leader, who only nodded.

Paying no attention to how much French toast Nadia gave to Rocky, Zach concentrated on his friend. "Some friend I am. I should've noticed. How do you feel?"

Wanting to ease the tension, Grant grinned. "With my fingers."

"Me too," Aidan innocently joined the conversation and rubbed his sticky fingers on Rocky's head. "Furry. Soft."

The guys chuckled as Zach groaned, knowing their team dog would be getting a bath in Dave's backyard after brunch.

Cathy and Dave shared a grin. The twins would love to help wash the pup and wouldn't realize they were getting clean too, with no screeching or tantrums.

"One more thing," Grant said when the chuckling died down.

"Better not be leaving the team. That isn't allowed, and if you try, I'm locking you in your cage," Finn stated.

"No. I need help moving. Got a new place yesterday. Gotta have all my stuff out of the old place by tonight."

"When did you have time to apartment hunt?" Zach asked.

"Yesterday. That's why I sent you to babysit Finn."

"Hey, I didn't need a sitter," Finn groused to more chuckling.

After discussing what needed moving, they decided to leave Zach at Dave's to wash Rocky. Zach would meet them at Grant's new apartment when he finished.

As they headed out the door, Finn swung an arm over Grant's shoulders. "You're coming with me to Glitter Girls tonight to celebrate the reinstatement of your bachelor status."

"Sure." Grant grinned, glad to have his brothers.

San Diego, CA – First Presbyterian Church

Max sat stiffly in the pew beside Gabe as Lucas's sister spoke about her older brother. The picture she painted was of a man who went out of his way to help others. He had been an Eagle Scout, an avid baseball fan, and a member of a thespian group that put on plays at the children's hospital. The world lost a kind man and an excellent son and brother.

He shifted slightly when Gabe rose to speak, and his mind wandered. He was not allowed to tell the team they snagged the wrong guy or about the escape attempt, which was a need-to-know situation, and Red Team was out of the loop. His teammates and Lucas's family would never be told Lucas died a senseless death, but the reality gnawed on Max's heart.

After Gabe finished and pounded his SEAL trident on the top of Lucas's coffin, Max rose with the rest of the team and filed to the front to do the same. Placing his Special Warfare insignia below Caleb's, Max formed a fist and hammered in the pin, which consisted of a golden eagle clutching a U.S. Navy anchor, trident, and pistol. Then he moved to stand beside Brett as Captain Ridgeway and other officers added their Budweisers.

When the service ended, Max wanted nothing more than to drown himself in a few beers. He started for the exit but stopped when a soft woman's voice from behind him inquired, "Are you Max?" He turned and found Lucas's mother standing there.

"Yes, Mrs. Tanner, I am." Max tensed, uncertain of what she wanted from him.

Reba reached out and clasped the young man's hand as she noted the bruising near his temple. "Thank you for coming today. Lucas spoke so highly of you. He was happy to find someone who enjoyed mythology as much as he did. The last time I talked with him, he said he wanted to invite you to dinner and introduce you to us." Her voice wobbled as tears slipped out and streaked down her cheeks.

Unsure how to respond, Max remained silent but gave her hand a slight squeeze.

Reba's gaze briefly shifted to Lucas's team leader as she said, "Rob told us you were with Lucas when he died."

Max swallowed the lump forming in his throat. "Yes, ma'am."

"Did he suffer? Was he in pain?"

The grief and anguish on her face nearly undid Max, and he struggled to keep his voice from cracking. "No. It happened too fast for him to suffer."

Mr. Tanner approached and wrapped his arm around his wife. "Dear, time to go." Directing a small, sad grin at Stirling, he said, "Thanks for being here. It means a lot to have Lucas's teammates and friends here to say goodbye to our boy."

Max nodded.

Reba started to turn away but halted and dug into her purse. She reached for Max, pressing a dog-eared, well-loved book into his palm. "I want a fellow Greek mythology enthusiast to have this. It is ... was Lucas's favorite collection of myths."

"Ma'am, I couldn't take something so precious from you." Max tried to give it back, but she wouldn't take it.

Tears fell freely as Reba said, "Please. Read it from time to time, and think of Lucas. He continues to live on, so long as he is in our hearts and minds."

Max fought against the hot prickle, but his eyes still welled with liquid. Blinking caused a tear to escape. "I will. Thank you." He clutched the book tightly as the Tanners exited the church.

Rob swung an arm over Max's shoulders. "Come on. Time to lift a glass to our fallen brother."

Coronado, CA – Pirate's Cove Pub

Four beers and three shots into his night, Max slid off the stool at the high-top table where Red Team gathered to drink and reminisce about Lucas. Although not entirely sloshed since he could hold his liquor, Max staggered a bit as he made his way to the bar to buy the next round. Along the way, Max bumped into a few people and mumbled apologies. He placed the order and waited for it to be filled as he stared at Lucas's photo on the wall.

The new addition was courtesy of Brett. The guy was forever taking photos in his off time. Lost in his thoughts, not enough booze in him to deaden the grief, Max didn't pay attention to those around him. This bar was close to the base and, as such, a favorite hangout for all Navy personnel, not only SEALs. And where SEALs gathered, so did frog-hogs ... women who wanted to say they slept with a SEAL.

In his dress blues, having come straight from the funeral, Max cut a fine figure, especially with his trimmed hair and clean-shaven face. He attracted the eye of many women, but at the moment, he was not interested in hopping in the sack with anyone.

Sure, he did on occasion, but after Lacey's death, he tended to compare all women to her and found them lacking in qualities Lacey had possessed. A one-night-stand here and there was all he managed, mostly because he focused on his career and making it to a tier-one team in record time.

He accomplished his goal, and Foxtrot drafted him, or more fittingly, got stuck with him. They were the last team to pick that year, and the surname Stirling meant more to the team leaders than his stellar performance. Although in the top three, team after team bypassed him in the selection, and he ended up on Foxtrot.

Though last to be assigned a team, Max concentrated on the positive side—making lemonade again—and savored the thought his achievements would've made his father proud. It put him one step closer to restoring his dad's honor. But then Argentina and Zulu happened, and he got pushed ten steps backward.

Although, if honest, being on Red Team, the camaraderie he developed in a short time with four of the seven guys was a cooling balm on a burn and gave him hope he might someday return to being a top-tier operator. Then Lucas died.

This time, he struggled to find the silver lining. He doubted any elite team would ever add him to their roster again, particularly if Ridgeway had a voice in the matter, and he did. The captain, like so many others, couldn't look beyond his last name and judged him for actions they believed Preston did, which he didn't.

The pitchers were set in front of him, bringing Max out of his morose reflections. He paid, shoved his wallet in his pocket, grabbed both, and pivoted. Max squeezed his way through the crowd to Red Team's table, where Gabe enthralled the guys with another humorous anecdote about Lucas.

Though he tried to laugh along, he was not ready for the lighthearted celebration of a life cut way too damned short. He set the beer on the tabletop and caught Gabe's eye as he said, "I'm gonna be going."

"I'll go with you," Gabe offered since they lived at the same apartment complex only a few blocks away, which made this a convenient watering hole for them.

"Nah, you stay."

Caleb gripped his bicep, wanting to gain his attention. Max let out a hiss as the excessive pressure caused pain to spike where fake Anwar grazed him. The wound didn't require stitches, but if touched, it still burned as if a dozen hornets stung him.

"Hey, why ya hissing at me? Just want you to stay." Having consumed enough beer to sink a battleship tonight, Caleb misread Max's expression as anger.

Gabe's gaze returned to the bruise on Max's face, one Stirling refused to explain, and he correctly identified pain in Max's scrunched eyes. Something went down at Guantanamo, but apparently, Max wouldn't or couldn't share. "Let go, Caleb. Max is likely tired from all his travels."

Caleb released his hold. "Fine! Pretty boy should go home so the ladies will start looking at the rest of us."

"Speak for yourself. I don't have no problem getting women," Brett slurred and launched into an argument with Caleb.

As Max snagged the book Mrs. Tanner gave him from the table, he recognized Frick and Frack typically argued about inconsequential stuff, seeming to enjoy their banter. However, when it came to something significant, like missions and confronting Zulu for him, Brett and Caleb stood firmly rooted as one brother with the power and conviction of two.

Max's heart twisted as he realized his budding friendship with Lucas might've developed that kind of brotherhood, given time. He shelved his gloomy thoughts, said, "Night," and headed out of the pub for the short walk home.

Near Max's Apartment

Gabe strolled down the sidewalk, taking his time, in no rush to return to his apartment. After Max left a half-hour ago, the others began dispersing, and a few of the guys exited with frog hogs. With Brett's assistance, he poured Caleb into the cab and, although not necessary, instructed Brett to ensure their plastered brother made it home okay.

With his mind on Lucas, still dealing with losing a man under his command, Gabe didn't pay much attention to the often-traveled yet dim path he walked. Several streetlights had gone out months ago, and the city had not gotten around to replacing them.

As he passed an alleyway, a flash of light tawny color caused him to grin, believing it must be the tomcat who claimed this area as his own. Gabe caught the feisty furball once and tried to give him a home, but the feline preferred to live life on its terms and bolted at the first opportunity. Now Gabe only set out cat food near his place.

A soft groan reaching his ears caused Gabe to halt and turn around. He couldn't see anything in the narrow, dark alley, so he pulled out his phone when another moan sounded and switched on his flashlight app. For one second, he couldn't believe the sight before his eyes. "Max?" In the next, Gabe moved forward with true concern for his teammate.

Struggling to his knees, Max wrapped one arm around his ribs and panted after spitting out coppery saliva. A bright light flashed on him, and he moaned again, trying but failing to prepare for a second round. When he recognized Gabe's voice, he collapsed to the trash-strewn ground with a grunt.

Gabe crouched, put a hand on Max's shoulder, and cautiously rolled him on his back while using his cell for illumination.

Biting his lip as pain rippled through him, Max peered at Gabe, unsure how long he had been lying next to the dumpster like discarded trash.

"My God, what happened?" Gabe took in the bloody nose, split lip, and abrasions on the bruised side of Max's face.

"Got jumped." Embarrassed by his inability to fight off the attackers, Max said, "Came at me from behind. Rammed my head into the wall ... got me to the ground ... more than one."

"Can you walk if I help, or should I call 911?" Gabe waited for an answer, aware all SEALs had some medical training and would realize if they sustained severe injuries.

"Yeah."

"Which one?" Gabe noted the confusion, began to rethink his earlier assumption, and juggled the phone to dial.

"Don't call." Max spat more blood-speckled spit. "Get me home. I'll be fine."

Gabe snorted. "Says the man spitting blood."

"Inside cheek cut ... minor." Max steeled himself and only let out one or two soft moans as Gabe helped him to his feet.

Once he had Max's arm around his neck and they took a few shuffling steps, Gabe asked, "Did you recognize them?"

Max's mind was elsewhere, and he halted. "Book."

"Book, who?"

"Lucas's book," Max clarified.

Gabe shone his light around until he found the mythology book and then propped Max against the brick wall while he went to retrieve it. Returning, Gabe slung his teammate's arm over him again and gripped his wrist before encircling Max's waist with his other arm. "No worse for wear. Now, do you know who beat the shit out of you?"

Max shook his head and stumbled forward with Gabe's help. Although he never saw faces, he suspected they were SEALs. Fueled by the false bravado of alcohol, one spewed antagonistic vitriol disparaging his father as they kicked him.

17

Emotional Blender

Coronado, CA – Max's Apartment

MAX stood in his shower, letting the hot water massage his aching back as he leaned his forearms on the tiles. He hurt everywhere still, but at least today, he could move without wanting to howl. Yesterday had totally sucked, and he only forced himself out of bed to pee.

Damned-good thing Red Team was off rotation for the next two weeks. Ridgeway told Gabe he wanted to wait to review the AAR before putting them back in the field. By the time the team re-activated, Max would be in shape to do whatever a mission might require from him. But today, showering and ordering a pizza would be the extent of his activities.

He appreciated Gabe helping him home the other night. He probably wouldn't have made it on his own. His team leader cleaned him up, put him to bed, brought him two bags of frozen peas, which worked well as malleable icepacks, and spent the rest of the night on the floor keeping watch over him.

The caring actions surprised Max. When he woke yesterday morning to find Gabe crashed out near his door, Max didn't quite know what to say. He opted for a quick thanks and assurance he was okay. To which Gabe laughed and told him he needed to look in a mirror before he tried to claim he was alright. Gabe had been annoyingly right.

When Max went to the bathroom for the first time, shortly after waking, he witnessed his less-than-stellar state. The bruising from the rifle butt at Gitmo now had friends. He received a black eye and abrasions on his cheek where his face kissed the asphalt. His lips were a bit swollen, and the split on the bottom one turned an angry red.

Fortunately, his face escaped further injury, and he marveled at the fact his nose had not busted, considering how hard they slammed him into the wall. Unfortunately, the same couldn't be said for the rest of his body. His torso, arms, and legs took the brunt of the abuse as he attempted to protect his ribs, which resulted in significant bruising to his limbs.

At some point, his arms moved away from his chest, either by force or incapacity on his part, and they went to town on his back and ribs. He lucked out. None of the bones snapped with all their vicious kicks, and when Gabe probed his abdomen, he found no signs of rigidity, so thankfully, no internal bleeding either.

However, the bone-deep bruising hurt like hell, and he may have sustained a few hairline fractures but refused to go to the infirmary for x-rays. Nothing would come of reporting the assault to the police since he had no clue who jumped him. He also didn't want to be humiliated by revealing he couldn't defend himself. Instead, Max decided to lick his wounds, move on, and be much more aware of his surroundings at all times.

When the water became cool, Max shut off the tap and rested a moment in the steamy sauna he created. With a suppressed groan, he reached for the towel and stepped on the bathmat. Once dry, Max tugged on his boxers and decided they would be the extent of his clothing today.

Shuffling to his kitchenette to grab a glass of milk, Max hoped it was not out-of-date since he hadn't done any grocery shopping before going to Algeria. Opening the fridge, he gaped in surprise. He must've been in worse shape than he thought yesterday because he didn't recall Gabe coming back after dinner, but the food in his fridge indicated otherwise.

He selected a bottle of iced mocha and yogurt since they wouldn't require cooking or aggravate the cuts in his mouth. He wandered back to his bed, gingerly lowered himself, and placed the bottle on his nightstand, which was an upturned crate.

Pulling the foil cover off his peach yogurt, Max noted Gabe plugged his phone into the charger for him. He pressed the button to check for any missed calls or texts, not expecting any since no one ever called him. The one-hundred-plus messages, mostly from Brett and Caleb, dumbfounded him. Max realized his cell must be set to silent mode because he never heard it buzz.

After changing the setting so he wouldn't miss any calls, Max flipped through the messages as he spooned in a bite of his breakfast. Frick and Frack appeared to be on a rampage, declaring when they found out who waylaid him, the idiots wouldn't need coffins because no one would find their bodies … something about them becoming shark food.

A little light shone behind Max's gray cloud, creating the silver lining he searched for and couldn't find for many days. Red Team might not be tier-one, but he was still a SEAL, and if he kept his nose clean and did his job, he would go a long way in restoring honor to the Stirling name. Having three teammates who judged him for himself felt damned good.

Virginia – Training Grounds

Jake strolled up to Dave, halted, lifted his foot to the bottom rung of the fence, and followed his second-in-command's gaze to the tire flip zone of the obstacle course. "Thought Finn would be out here with you?"

Dave didn't take his eyes off a sweat-drenched Babcox as he replied, "Nah. He, Zach, and Grant are chilling at the pool in Grant's complex. Finn said something about a bunch of hot babes, and he'd rather chase tail than heckle Babcox."

Recalling being out here two days ago before meeting with Lockwood, Jake nodded. "Finn did enough the other day. I swear Babcox wanted to punch him. The guy is thin-skinned."

Turning away from Babcox, Dave agreed. "Better toughen up because Finn isn't going to let up anytime soon. He's still pissed off at Babcox."

"Aren't we all?" Jake sighed, dropped his boot to the ground, and pivoted to lean against the fencing. The subsequent discussion with Bryan, after reading the material with an open mind, ran through his head. "Made a decision without consulting the team."

His curiosity piqued, Dave shifted his stance and studied Jake's posture. Something substantial weighed on him. "About a sixth man? If you did, that won't go over well. There's a reason we all provide input. Remember Cummings?"

"Yeah, something I'm not likely to forget." Jake paused to consider his words. "Nothing set in stone, but yeah, it is about a replacement. Something Lockwood presented to me yesterday, and I agreed to give it a shot, see where it goes."

Dave's brows rose. "Gonna enlighten me, brother?"

Loud cussing broke the moment, and both men turned as Babcox unloaded all his frustration on a teammate. Rob had to separate two of his men before they came to blows. Dave and Jake shared a version of the same thought. *How the hell did Babcox get this far with his attitude?*

Coronado, CA – Captain Ridgeway's Office

Despite the loud, angry complaints his muscles delivered to his brain, Max remained at attention as he faced the captain because Ridgeway had not permitted him to be at ease. The summons to report to his office came after lunch, and Max managed to dress and arrive on time ... barely.

Yesterday, Gabe shared with him the full details of the debrief session with Zulu and Sierra and how no errors were laid at his feet. The news was welcome, but Max wouldn't be surprised if Ridgeway still considered Lucas's death his fault and ended his career anyway, citing some trivial technicality. And even if he filed an appeal for reinstatement based on the after-action report, it would likely fall on deaf ears and be shit-canned.

Ridgeway eyed the SEAL, still seething over the shadow Stirling cast on his previously spotless career. Being a suspect in an NCIS investigation, which implied he purloined a classified AAR and, worse, modified said paperwork, fueled his enmity of Stirling and turned it to outright hatred.

The verbal thrashing and written censor his superior added to his jacket for not reporting the classified document landing on his desk still chapped his ass. Ridgeway wanted Stirling to pay for the disparagement of his honor and loyalty. He spent hours reviewing the Algeria AAR, which he was provided legally, picking out things he could use to kick Stirling out of the teams.

Then, late yesterday, the phone rang, and his world brightened. He was assured Stirling would no longer be his problem and would get what he deserved. But that didn't mean Ridgeway couldn't inflict some retribution before Stirling left.

Keeping Stirling at attention might be petty, but given his appearance when he entered, Ridgeway came up with some parting potshots. "What do you have to say for yourself?"

"Sir, I don't understand the question?"

"Fighting." He waved a hand at Stirling's face. "Your teammate is killed, and a few days later, you dishonor him and disgrace the uniform by engaging in a brawl."

Max blinked at the cold comment. He wondered how to respond and decided to reveal the humiliating truth. "I didn't fight, Sir. I got jumped when I left the bar."

Ridgeway sneered. "Unlikely story. Not believable. Unless you were three sheets to the wind and couldn't stand properly, which sounds more plausible."

"I drank, Sir, but wasn't drunk. A group of men caught me by surprise from the rear as I walked home, Sir."

"More reason you're not fit to be on any SEAL team. Just like your father." His gaze shifted to the sealed envelope on his desk, which had been delivered by overnight courier this morning. He picked it up, rose from his chair, and moved to stand eye-to-eye with Stirling.

Suppressing all emotion, Max adopted a stoic expression and locked his steely gaze on Ridgeway. The narrow-minded idiot might be his commanding officer but in no way his superior. The best way to handle a man like this was to keep his mouth shut. He learned this lesson early.

Uncle Athole had been a splendid teacher in how to deal with self-important assholes. Max perfected the emotionless mask at fourteen years old. The more emotion he revealed, the meaner his uncle had become. Dick Asshole's hits also became harder ... both the verbal and physical ones.

At fifteen, he broke and refused to take anymore. The punch came with a price, unleashing years of pent-up rage. Max had to learn to control his fury and direct it into positive things, which made him ultra-competitive in school. The success he achieved in his rage-fueled late teens also demanded a ransom ... a cocky bravado that was backed by ability.

He had to rein that in when he joined the Navy, but it lurked in the recesses of his mind, and in situations such as now, he tapped into it, refusing to be the one to break eye contact first. It would be a small victory, but nonetheless, it would be a win for Ridgeway to blink first.

The intensity in the blue eyes locked with his brown ones unnerved Ridgeway, and he took a step backward, his gaze darting down to the envelope in his hand. He held it out, and in his harshest tone, he said, "You are not my problem anymore. You've been transferred. Present these sealed orders to the Officer of the Day when you arrive at your new duty station."

When Stirling took the white envelope, Ridgeway moved back to his chair and added, "You have three days to organize your move. Hayden has your travel details. Dismissed."

So many questions swirled in Max's head, but he only pivoted and marched out, not knowing where Ridgeway transferred him or what his position would be. Hayden handed him a package as he stopped at his desk. If the clerk said anything, Max wouldn't recall ... his world just got deep-sixed ... again.

Max's Apartment

Less than six hours after making his vow to be vigilant of his surroundings, Max walked down the hallway to his apartment in a haze, unaware of Gabe, Brett, and Caleb standing at his door. How he got from Ridgeway's office to here would remain a blur. Again, Gabe's voice sliced through his pain.

"Max, where the hell did you go? You shouldn't be out of bed. I filled your fridge." He halted, noting Max wore his working uniform.

Renewed anger welled in Caleb and Brett when they viewed the state of Max's face. They sorely wanted to pound the responsible parties into the ground and make them wish they never touched their teammate.

Focusing on Gabe, Max's shoulders slumped. He found a team that gave a damn about him, and now all was lost. "Ridgeway called me into his office." Max fished out his keys and unlocked the door, leaving it open for the others to follow him inside.

"What did he want?" Gabe noted Max's defeated expression mixed with a grimace as he slowly lowered himself to the mattress.

Max took a moment to study the three men peering at him. Concern played on Gabe's face. Frick and Frack displayed both worry and disgust. Max was aware they disliked Ridgeway, and his news would cement their opinion of the captain. "Ridgeway transferred me again."

"NO WAY!"

"FUCKING ASSHOLE!"

"WHY?"

Max stared as Caleb, Brett, and Gabe shouted and answered, "Yes, way. I agree. I don't know."

Putting up a hand to silence his men, Gabe took the lead. "He didn't tell you why?"

"Not in so many words. Accused me of fighting and lying when I told him I got jumped. Handed me sealed transfer orders." Max dropped both envelopes on his bed. "Told me I have only seventy-two hours to arrange my affairs. Pack and stuff."

Brett couldn't keep quiet. "We'll appeal. He can't do this. He has no cause to demote you."

Fists clenched, Caleb grumbled, "Damned cake-eater! What team did he transfer you to?"

"What part of sealed orders didn't you hear?" Brett eyed his friend.

Gabe focused on Max's last statement. "So, you're moving duty stations. Where?"

Exhausted, aching, and not wanting to have this conversation, Max flopped himself on his back and immediately regretted his move as pain spiked in his ribs. "Not sure. Hayden gave me travel vouchers. Didn't look at them."

"Want me to?" Gabe offered.

"Yeah, sure." Max closed his eyes and tried to breathe through the pain he caused himself.

Brett spotted a bottle of ibuprofen on the little counter and went to retrieve it as Gabe picked up the packet labeled Travel. He returned with two tablets and water. "Here, Max. You need a couple of these."

Raising his lids, Max eyed the pills before reaching for them. After popping them in his mouth, he lifted his head enough to wash them down with a swig of water, then laid back and rubbed his sore neck.

Flipping through the documents, Gabe's gut twisted as he stopped and peered at Max. "Dam Neck."

"Hurts a bit, not too bad," Max said, misunderstanding Gabe's remark.

"Dam Neck, Virginia. You're being sent to DEVGRU's base," Gabe clarified.

Max's eyes whipped open. "DEVGRU?"

"Holy shit!" Caleb's jaw dropped.

Brett laughed. "This isn't Ridgeway's doing. You must have a guardian angel who worked a miracle to get you back into DEVGRU. You're gonna kick some ass, but I'm sure gonna miss having you as Two-IC."

Sitting up, Max took the papers from Gabe and stared at the location where he was to report. A bittersweet smile grew along with apprehension. "Who? How? Why?"

Gabe sat next to Max. "I told you all about the debrief. I also spent some time talking with Rob Powers, who is Sierra One. He said the members of Zulu were shocked to find out you were demoted after Argentina and ticked off someone altered the AAR. Perhaps someone there wanted to right a wrong and pushed this transfer through."

"Man, we gotta get you packed. I'll call the guys. We'll knock this out in a few hours, then we can go celebrate your transfer." Caleb pulled out his phone and started to type a group message.

"Hold up. Tomorrow is soon enough. Max isn't up to partying yet. He needs to rest today." Gabe peered around at Max's sparse belongings. The three of us can handle this, but everyone can meet at the Pirate's Cove tomorrow night at seven."

Caleb nodded and changed the message.

His head spinning with the news, Max let the documents slip out of his hands as he whispered, "Thanks, Dad."

Gabe, the only one to catch what Max said, grinned as he laid a light hand on Max's shoulder. "Your father is peering down from Heaven and smiling with pride."

Max grinned and sighed. The emotional rollercoaster of today exhausted him. A transfer to the east coast, back to DEVGRU headquarters, could mean many things. Though Caleb and Brett assumed he had been assigned to a team, his orders were sealed, so Max couldn't verify if they were good or bad. For all he knew, his new position might be refilling magazines for operators since they fired an average of 2,500 to 3,000 rounds per week in training.

With his mind still in a whirl with many questions, at Gabe's prompting, Max shed his boots, found a semi-comfortable position on his bed, and closed his eyes. Within ten minutes, he was asleep, even with the internal turmoil and Frick and Frack arguing about the best way to pack up his stuff.

18

Righting a Wrong

RELIEVED that the Officer of the Day didn't request an explanation for the blue and purple around his eye or the sickly mixture of greenish-yellow on his cheek, Max stood at attention as Captain Pascal opened the sealed envelope and reviewed the documents. The captain's countenance didn't display any emotion as he refolded the papers, rang for his clerk, and instructed Yeoman Bushnell to escort him to another building.

Pascal dismissed him without providing any information as to his assignment, which somewhat worried Max, but he figured his fate would be revealed soon enough. For now, Max was grateful Bushnell appeared to be in no hurry to return to his desk and chose to walk at a leisurely pace to their destination. Although his body had started to heal in the past three days, Max still ached something fierce after a long cross-country military flight, sitting on a hard, cramped seat.

Max followed the yeoman, but his mind went back to two nights ago. Red Team sent him off in style, and he appreciated the friends he made in the short time he spent on the team. What he didn't expect was Gabe to enter his sister's number in his phone contacts and make him promise to give her a call after he got settled. His former team leader only grinned and shook his head as Caleb and Brett begged for Cali's number.

The fellowship he found with them helped move him into a positive headspace, and hope yet again flickered to life. If they could see beyond his last name, perhaps his new team would too. And if they didn't, well, it would be old hat, and he knew how to operate in a hostile environment.

Max put his musings aside when he and Bushnell stopped at DEVGRU's restricted area security checkpoint. He handed his ID to the gate guard to be validated and then waited for a new escort when Bushnell pivoted to return to his post. Ten minutes later, Max stood at parade rest in front of Captain Kendrick.

Seth Kendrick kept his expression neutral but couldn't help comparing the young man before him to the little boy who would run and jump into Preston's arms when they returned from deployment. Maxwell grew into an interesting mix of Preston and Lois. He possessed his mother's wavy, light blond hair and ocean-blue eyes. Preston's eyes had been a paler blue, and his hair a darker blond. From his father, Max inherited his chiseled facial features, height, and robust physique.

Noting the black eye and abrasions, Kendrick wondered if Farris left those injuries out of her report but concluded by their coloring they appeared more recent. Though a bit curious, he didn't inquire as to the source since SEALs trained as they fought, and as such, sometimes they sported various contusions.

Part of Seth wished he had taken a more active role in Maxwell's career, but until recently, he didn't realize how many of Preston's detractors rose to positions of power in the last eighteen years. The kid shouldn't be paying for Preston's mistake, but based on several of the reviews he read from Max's COs, that usually proved to be the case. Some were fair-minded, but many used the kid's parentage against him … Captain Ridgeway being the latest.

It didn't take much to leave the captain with the impression Max would be demoted when he called him to initiate the transfer. All he said was Stirling would receive what he deserved. And he would! Kendrick would do his best to restore everything Maxwell earned, which Ridgeway unjustly stripped from him.

Choosing to take an informal approach, Kendrick said, "Take a seat. We have a few things to discuss."

Nervous but not about to show it, a bit of Max's cocky bravado eked out in his body posture as he sat. He waited for Kendrick to continue as he wondered what a DEVGRU captain would want to talk to him about.

Seth repressed the smile that wanted to burst out. *Jesus, his mannerisms are so like Preston's. I'm going to have to guard against becoming too friendly with him ... he isn't Preston.*

Clearing his throat, Kendrick decided to modify what he originally planned to share. It wouldn't be smart to reveal he pulled strings to right a wrong, and a hurdle remained. Marshall still had the last say in this matter ... a promise Seth made to gain Jake's agreement.

"Let me be frank and crystal clear. Every operator under my command earns the right to be here. I do not grant favors, and I base all disciplinary action on verified performance issues or lack of adherence to our ethos."

Kendrick tapped a file on his desk. "After the Algeria mission, Lieutenant Commander Lockwood brought to my attention a serious matter concerning you."

Max braced himself for a hammering and fought not to lose all hope again.

"As a result, I opened an investigation, which is ongoing, and I can't discuss it in detail other than Ridgeway demoted you based on a falsified report. The bottom line is you got more than the tip of the arrow in your ass after Argentina. You got the shaft."

Max snorted. "Yes, Sir."

Kendrick's lip curled in a half-smile before he suppressed it. "The reason you were given sealed transfer orders is you will be given a say in the matter."

Intrigued, Max sat straighter, and an old image flashed in his mind. The captain seemed vaguely familiar.

"I'm unable to reinstate you on Foxtrot since they are outside my purview, and all my assault teams are at full strength."

A lead stone landed in Max's gut. *So, not returning to a top-tier team. Foolish to allow my hopes to rise.*

Kendrick rose and moved around to the other side of his desk and sat on the edge. "I'm going to offer you two options. One, you may choose to go back to Red Team, which will put you under Ridgeway's thumb. Two, you can opt to join a support team within my command, and when an opening on a tier-one team becomes available, you will be placed with them.

"I'll give you a day to consider which alternative best suits your goals. Any questions?" Kendrick studied Max's reaction.

Max reeled at the fact the captain gave him a choice. As much as he liked running with Gabe, Brett, and Caleb, they would flay him alive if he didn't grab the opportunity to return to DEVGRU with both hands. "Sir, I don't need time. I accept your offer of a path back to a team. Thank you, Sir."

Seth flashed a broad grin. "Excellent." He reached for the folder on the desk. "Only need you to sign the paperwork to make it official. My clerk arranged for base housing in anticipation of your acceptance. You can stay there until you make other arrangements if you prefer to live off base."

He handed a pen to Max and tapped on the paper. "Sign here, and afterward, Smith will ensure you are provided proper credentials and take you to your quarters. You will report to your team tomorrow at zero-eight hundred."

Max signed, set the pen down, and stepped back when a critical question came to mind. "Sir, which team am I assigned to, and what is the name of the CO?"

"Senior Chief Powers. Sierra Team. They have cages in the Zulu complex. You have been there once before, but if you need a reminder where, ask Smith, and he will direct you."

"Sierra?" Max failed at keeping the surprise from his tone. He never expected to be part of Zulu's support team.

Kendrick extended his right hand to Maxwell. "Yes. You possess exceptional skills, Stirling. I don't plan on wasting them. Your father would be proud of the man you've become."

A vague image of a man handing him a folded flag flashed as the firm handshake ended. "Did you know my dad, Sir?"

Seth nodded. "We were friends. I was his CO when he led Zulu. Wish I had not been ill during his last mission. He might still be with us. My coverage pressured him into leading the op, though he already filed his paperwork to stand down." Seth cleared his throat, having said much more than he intended.

Max blinked. "He planned to leave the team?"

In for a penny, in for a pound. Kendrick stood as he said, "Yes. After Lois and your grandmother died, Preston ... well, you were his world, and he would do anything for you—one of the few men who managed not to build walls between home and team.

"He understood what was important, so he was willing to step down when you needed him more. I was absent from TOC, but some claim his headspace was off, and that's what got them killed. What I'm certain of is the man who I called a friend was human, and he should've never been vilified for one mistake."

Several thoughts whirled in Max's head, but he shelved all but one for now. He must be patient and take Kendrick's measure before broaching the subject of what he overheard as a child. Max couldn't risk stirring the pot at this point with accusations for which he had no proof. He got a second chance to follow in his dad's footsteps, so he posed a safe question. "Sir, did you hand me my father's flag at his funeral?"

"Yes." Emotion welled as Seth recalled the brave boy saluting his father but needed to reaffirm his position. "As I made clear when we started, in my command, men are judged on their performance. You earned this opportunity." Kendrick called in Smith, and when Maxwell left, he resumed his seat.

Seth withdrew a twenty-year-old photo of himself with Preston and Zulu Team from his top drawer. He still missed his friend and wondered if Preston might be alive today if he had been in TOC during that fateful mission. Seth couldn't change history, but perhaps he could influence the future. *Brother, I hope my plans for your boy work out ... time will tell.*

Zulu Equipment Cages

Dave stood in his cage, managing a deadpan expression, keeping his thoughts to himself while studying the reactions of his teammates. Jake dropped a bomb on them only moments ago. Zach now sat cross-legged on the floor, giving Rocky a belly rub. As always, he found the quiet man the most difficult to read, but Dave didn't perceive any irritation.

Grant smiled. So, Dave believed he would be all in. The medic would do his due diligence and ask when, not if, they would be reviewing all the details. Grant preferred to check all the boxes. Jake's answer had been preempted by Finn's gripping.

He shifted his gaze to Finn, who now verbally sparred with Jake, grousing up a storm. Zulu Three wanted absolutely nothing to do with what Jake proposed and made his opinion known … loud and clear. To Jake's credit, he allowed Finn to vent.

Dave himself was of two minds. He had been the first to speak up and defend Stirling, and he pushed Jake not to judge him by his father. However, he had reservations about Jake's plan or, more correctly, the scheme he agreed to.

Though Stirling possessed raw talent, Dave wondered if he might be too unseasoned for the role. Stirling was the youngest SEAL to make it through Green Team. Although they had seen him in action three times, Dave wanted to review his jacket as much as Grant did. Finn drew his attention with his latest complaint.

"I'm not babysitting a wet-behind-the-ears nerd boy." Finn crossed his arms and glared at Jake.

Reaching his limit of Finn's protests and belligerence, Jake replied, "Not asking you. He's on Sierra—"

Finn cut in, "But you said—"

"I SAID WE ARE GOING TO OBSERVE HIM. I MADE NO COMMITMENT BEYOND ASSESSING HIS SKILLS."

Zach chimed into the silence following Jake's outburst, "He's one helluva fast nerd. You do recall what he accomplished to rescue Levi. Doubt any of us could do that parkour stuff."

"We need to find another seasoned guy. Not some pretty boy who can climb. He needs to be able to shoot and a whole lot more," Finn retorted.

Leaning on the work table in the middle of their equipment room, Grant eyed the most outspoken member of the five strong-willed and opinionated operators of Zulu. "Finn, lest you forget, he saved your ass."

Finn huffed.

Despite his reservations, Dave added, "He's a team player. Refused to leave a brother behind. He also found Dexter."

"Luck, not skill. He wasn't searching for him. Stirling was drugged out of his mind and on the run," Finn countered.

"Jake, why would you agree to assess him?" Dave asked, curious about what would've compelled his friend to consider this in the first place.

Running a hand through his hair, Jake paced for a few moments before answering. "Kid got railroaded. Someone has it out for him. Ridgway couldn't care less and would prefer to kick him out altogether. The only thing Kendrick asked was if we'd take a look. If he isn't a right fit, it ends, and when a spot opens on another team, he will be placed."

"Well, I, for one, won't be wiping his ass and snotty nose!" Finn slammed his cage closed and stomped out of the room.

Jake eyed the others. "Stirling begins training with Sierra tomorrow. We'll give him several days to settle in before we start scrutinizing his abilities."

Grant nodded. "When do we get to review his jacket?"

"You don't."

"What? We always do." Grant stared at his team leader.

"Not this time. Lockwood allowed me to read Stirling's file but restricted me from sharing details with anyone."

"Why?" Dave inquired.

"He wants us to form our own opinions."

"Makes sense," Zach said as he rose to take Rocketeer outside, effectively ending the discussion.

19

Flight of Icarus

Sierra Equipment Cages

TAKING a breath to steady his resolve, and donning his confident mantle, Max gripped the knob and prepared to meet his new team. Entering, he recognized the faces but didn't have names to put with more than Powers and Babcox. The laughter in the room died as soon as they spotted him.

"Welcome to Sierra, Stirling. Glad you're onboard." Rob stepped forward with an outstretched hand.

"Thanks." Max firmly gripped his CO's hand and shook it.

"Let me introduce the guys." Rob began introductions in order of their call sign numbers. "Scott Holden, second-in-command, and our medic. Devlin Allard can drive anything under the sun. Rakeem Chambers, explosive expert. Orlando Tamayo, heavy weapons operator. Terrance Whitcomb, breacher extraordinaire. Stewart Babcox, sniper.

"Guys, this is Maxwell Stirling. His specialties include sniper, linguistics, and climbing." Rob pointed to the three empty cages. "Pick whichever one you want to store your stuff. We run with a standard set of weapons and gear, but if you have a preference for your sniper rifle and scope, tell Draper, and she will procure it. Any questions before we hit the hills for a warm-up run?"

Max shook his head as he selected a cage, dropped his bag, and hoped his aching muscles didn't impede his performance.

Training Grounds

Though Max possessed ample experience working through and hiding pain, as the day wore on, it became more difficult. Early on, he managed to ignore his misery, and the run loosened his tight muscles. By mid-afternoon, he dug deep into reserves to keep up with the grueling training. Now, besides being dog-tired, his chest burned with each lungful inhaled, but Max refused to allow his fatigue or discomfort to show.

Uncle Asshole taught him early to mask his pain. Discipline for any infraction started with open-handed swats to his bare butt when he was six but progressed to a belt and paddle by the time he turned seven. Max didn't think he would live past eight, almost didn't, and after the incident that nearly killed him, concealing his physical condition became a matter of survival.

Things might've changed when he went to Fairwinds Military Academy, except for the creepy male nurse who made his skin crawl every time the man touched him. He hated going to the infirmary and did everything in his power to avoid ending up there. This resulted in Max covering up his illnesses, injuries from sports, and the physical abuse he received at the hands of Athole during school breaks.

After joining the Navy and discovering many of his superiors wanted him to fail and hunted for reasons to eject him from the pipeline and teams, he mastered the ability to suck it up and plow through most non-life-threatening aches and pains. Today would be no different, though tonight he would crash as soon as he got to his room.

Max drank the last bit from his water bottle as they hiked to the obstacle course, which Rob declared would be the final task today. Rob also said he would be pushing them to improve their times, and the man who took the longest owed a case of beer.

Usually, Max enjoyed a challenge and didn't doubt he would come in first, but not today. Completing the O-course without his lungs bursting into flames, legs turning to rubber, and arms failing to haul him up the apparatuses currently seemed unlikely.

As Sierra gathered at the starting line, the members of Zulu converged near the fence, which provided a view of the entire course but was closest to the cargo net climb.

Dave spoke first as they all arrived from different directions, "So much for giving Stirling a few days to settle in."

Jake only shrugged as Finn groused, "No time like the present. The sooner you all realize he isn't right, the faster we can begin the real selection process again."

"Gonna eat your words," Zach muttered.

"What?" Finn challenged.

Zach's cobalt blue eyes zeroed in on Finn's moss green ones. "Watched him in the shoot house earlier. Though young, I think he has what it takes."

"Playing paintball isn't being under fire," Finn retorted. He wanted a seasoned guy so he didn't have to play nursemaid to the team rookie. He didn't with Axel and wouldn't have with Hector either. Finn believed there must be a better, older, more rounded candidate in one of the tier-one teams—anyone except the cocky, annoying, too-big-for-his-britches Stirling.

Rob shouted, "Go," to the newest Sierra member, drawing all their attention to Stirling as he sprinted toward the first obstacle.

"Still fast as a rabbit," Grant remarked as Stirling hit the parallel bars and used his upper body strength to quickly propel himself from one end to the other.

Max dropped to his feet at the end of the metal bars, his biceps singing a sad song, but he did his best to turn a deaf ear. He raced for the second hurdle, the tires, and moved through them slower than usual, his quads none too happy with the effort required. Clearing them, he hopped on the first and then second higher post, which put him closer to the top of the short wall.

Crouching, Max sprung upward, grabbed the edge of the wooden structure, and hauled himself up enough to use one leg to bring the rest of his body up before shifting his grip to extend both arms completely on the opposite side to reduce the distance to the ground before letting go.

Winded and in significant pain, things typically unfamiliar to him while running a course, Max groaned as he approached the tall wall. As if the eight-foot wall was not tall enough, he now must scale a twenty-foot one. He grasped the rope, planted a boot on the vertical surface, and began the hand-over-hand method to climb. Reaching the apex, Max placed his foot on the narrow horizontal ledge and swung a leg over to straddle the crossbar.

Unusual for him, he sat a moment to catch a breath, his chest heaving and lungs burning in their attempt to draw in enough air. A bit lightheaded from reduced oxygen, Max descended using a fast rope technique.

He jogged to the next obstacle instead of running and dropped to his knees. Flopping to his stomach for the barbed wire crawl, Max was half-tempted to find out what Senior Chief Powers would do if he simply laid there and rested. Stubbornness and pride made him move, albeit at a slower pace than usual.

At the other end, Max struggled to rise—his reserve tank near empty. Little speckles danced in his eyes as he staggered towards the sixty-foot-tall cargo net. *Pull it together, Stirling. You can't show your limitations on the first day. You need to prove you're worthy of being here. They'll eat you alive if you don't. Up, over, and down, just like hundreds of other times.*

Max began to climb, and every muscle shrieked for more oxygen and less movement. One hand, one foot, up and up he went until he reached the summit, which at this point might as well be Mount Everest. With sheer determination, he started down the other side, one step after another. He kept going, and no concept of time or distance registered as his vision tunneled.

Fingers grabbed. Missed. Boots slipped. The wind ruffled Max's hair as he sped downward. Arms flapped, seeking purchase as his mind screamed, *Men can't fly. Icarus tried and failed.*

The impact expelled all air from Max's lungs, ceasing his thoughts, and blackness engulfed him. Unconscious, he didn't hear the shouting nor witness the expressions of shock, panic, and concern as twelve SEALs rushed toward him.

Grant reached Stirling first, followed by Jake, Zach, Dave, and Finn. They skidded to a halt in a cloud of dust, and Grant went to his knees as the others waited for his directions. A fall from a height of ten feet could be deadly, so Stirling's twelve-foot swan dive to the sand base below almost certainly would result in a trip to the emergency room if it didn't kill him.

"He alive?" Jake asked as Grant's fingers searched for a pulse.

"Yeah, but he's not breathing," Grant replied as Scott dropped to the opposite side of Stirling.

"Impact most likely seized his lungs. Rob's calling it in," Scott said as his fellow medic rubbed hard on the kid's sternum.

With his phone to his ear, arranging for medevac helo to land near their location, Rob paced as both team medics assessed his rookie. He caught Jake's eye and glanced away. It would be too soon to lose another brother … and this one during training. A ragged gasp came from Stirling, dousing Rob with a wave of relief.

"WHAT THE HELL?" Jake yelled after Scott cut open Stirling's shirt with his tactical knife to search for injuries.

Everyone gaped at the deep purple and blueish black fringed by dark olive bruising all over Max's torso.

"This isn't from the fall. It's several days old." Scott peered up at Rob. "He shouldn't have been training in this condition."

In medic mode, Grant recognized the old contusions didn't matter at the moment. When Stirling started breathing again, he also began to move. Cognizant of the possibility of head, neck, or spine injuries, Grant needed him immobilized. "Finn, hold his head still. Zach, Jake, keep his legs from moving."

No one questioned Grant when it came to medical stuff, so they moved and did as told.

Dazed and in a world of agony, Max's eyelids lifted as a shadow fell over his face. With consciousness and a shallow breath came searing pain, causing him to whimper and try to curl up.

"STAY STILL," Finn barked to cover the tender emotion evoked by witnessing the sluggish, pain-filled blue orbs beneath him. A brother in agony always pierced Finn's heart.

"Chill! No need to yell at him," Dave instructed Finn.

"Max, hey, look at me." Grant snapped his fingers, wanting Stirling to reopen his eyes. He field-assessed his pupil response when they did. Shielding Max's eyes from the direct sun again, he said, "You hurt, but you must remain still. Can you do that?"

With no breath to answer, Max tried to nod, but McBride held his head in an unrelenting vice grip. He mouthed yes, with no sound, and squeezed his lids shut again as he struggled to breathe. The Zulu medic and Scott didn't ask him any more questions, but they began running hands up and down his limbs, checking for broken bones, and he wanted to blackout to escape the pain and humiliation of falling on his first day.

The helo landed, and personnel with supplies raced to them. With the assistance of the team medics, they put the fall victim in a cervical collar and secured him to a spine board. Through the ordeal, their patient remained conscious yet confused and only released a few quiet moans as they rolled him on the board.

Most of Sierra Team members stood by with concerned miens, though Babcox kept his face neutral because displaying joy over a teammate's suffering would not be in his best interests. Today, he successfully hid his disdain for Stirling. Necessary since Rob seemed to like the new guy, and it never paid to land on the wrong side of his team leader.

As Stirling was carried off toward the helicopter, Babcox did allow a slight grin to appear. Stirling's injuries would likely be severe enough he wouldn't be returning.

"What the hell are you grinning about?" Finn growled when he noticed Babcox's expression. The jerk would become the target of his ire because although he didn't much care for young Stirling, Finn would never wish him harm.

Babcox startled and sought an appropriate response. "He's alive. Thought for sure the fall killed him." He relaxed when his comeback appeared to appease McBride, and the burly man returned his gaze to those carrying Stirling.

"We need to talk," Jake directed at Rob.

"Yeah, later, though. I'm going to the hospital. Once Stirling is settled, he's got some explaining to do." Rob started to follow, intending to go with Stirling. He called over his shoulder, "We're done for today. Wrap it up, boys."

Zulu members remained in place, minus Grant, who helped carry Stirling, as Sierra dispersed, not needing a second invitation to go shower and relax after a grueling day of training.

Once they were alone, Dave voiced what each pondered. "One of those bruises was a distinct boot imprint. Who the hell beat the crap out of him?"

Jake raked a hand through his hair and came to a stop at the nape of his neck, where he squeezed. "Don't know, but I'm sure as hell going to find out. Rob's right, Stirling owes an explanation. He damn near killed himself. That shit doesn't fly at this level." Jake marched away, leaving his men staring at him.

Zach's quiet voice reflected on another side of the issue. "The bruising is deep, especially over his ribcage. With the way he performed in the shoot house, I never would've guessed he was nursing what must be painful ribs."

Finn groused, "He should've said something to Rob. Hiding shit like that will get someone killed in the field."

"Or save someone's life," Zach countered before striding off.

Dave arched a brow as Finn fumed. "You both have a point. But I believe the real question is ... why didn't Stirling tell Rob?" Dave followed Zach.

Peering up at the cargo net, a slight shudder ran through Finn as he recalled the moment Stirling lost his grip and plummeted like a stone to the ground. Like Babcox, he thought the blond puppy had bought the farm. Finn allowed rage to fill him to push away long-buried memories he didn't want to address.

His gaze dropped to where the kid landed as residual images of those dazed eyes and the colorful mottled skin on Stirling's chest and back came to mind. He noted Stirling's back was as bad as the front when they rolled him. Someone, probably more than one, beat the holy shit out of him, and he wanted to know why.

20

Operated In Worse Condition

ROB exited the emergency treatment area, still a bit shaken by the state of Stirling's body. Bruising didn't only exist on his torso but also included his arms, legs, and buttocks. He came to an abrupt halt upon spying Jake, Dave, Scott, Grant, and Lockwood. The first four, he expected to make the twenty-five-mile drive to the hospital, but not the lieutenant commander.

Bryan stepped forward upon spotting Rob. "How is he?"

His question claimed the attention of the others, and they all turned towards the door.

"Damned lucky to be alive. Must have a horseshoe stuck up his ass. Two broken ribs and a concussion to add to his list of injuries. Doc wants to keep him a day or two for observation but will release him if all goes well and there are no complications."

"And his other injuries?" Bryan questioned.

"He's covered head to toe in contusions. Took a hell of a beating about four to six days ago based on the discoloration."

"Did Stirling tell you what happened?" Dave asked.

"No. They dosed him up on painkillers. I've never seen ..." Rob trailed off and drew in a deep breath. "I'm going to contact his previous CO. Miller might know, and he seemed quite protective of the kid. And he is only a kid. How did he manage to make it to this level at twenty-four?"

"He's only twenty-four?" Grant wished he could read Stirling's jacket and wondered what it contained that prevented them from doing so.

"Yeah. Got a peek at his chart and noted his date of birth. Turned twenty-four about six months ago." Rob focused on Lockwood. "I understand the plan here, but I'm gonna tell you now if Zulu doesn't want Stirling, I do."

"Never said we don't want him. Need to do my due diligence," Jake interjected.

"What plan?" Scott turned a confused mien on Rob.

Bryan sighed. "Gentlemen, this is not the place or time to discuss the matter. Rob, call Miller. Find out if he can shed light on the beating and provide me with any details you uncover."

"Copy."

"What room are they moving him to?" Grant inquired.

"Not assigned yet. Doc said he'd send someone out to tell me once they did, but it would be at least an hour. I'm going to grab a coffee and call Gabe." Rob headed to the vending machines at the back of the waiting area, and Scott followed.

When Jake started for the ER entry, Lockwood stopped him. "Stay here."

Frustrated, Jake shook his head. "He needs to answer for why he deliberately hid injuries."

"You heard Rob, Stirling's unlikely to respond ... no matter how loudly or sternly you ask. There's time to address the issue, but first, we need to understand the full situation."

Dave leaned against the wall. "We're dealing with more than ambivalence to his last name, aren't we? Is that why we aren't allowed to review his file?"

Bryan turned to Dave, who possessed a level head and the ability to calm Jake. "Yes, but that is all I'm saying."

Allowing Lockwood's words to settle in his mind, Dave nodded. "Alright. Jake, Grant, let's grab a seat."

As his men sat in the plastic chairs, Bryan entered the treatment area, needing to speak with the doctor.

NMCP – Max's Room

In a slow rise to consciousness, Max first detected an antiseptic and pine odor and a soft beeping. Next came a dull ache of his entire body, along with something irritating under his nose. Lifting a hand to knock whatever it was away, someone prevented him from doing so.

"Leave it be. You still need oxygen." Rob gently pressed his rookie's hand into the mattress.

Squinting, the light overhead a bit too bright, Max recognized his team leader. His brain slowly caught up, and he recalled what happened. "I screwed up."

A snort from the other side of the room drew Max's eyes. They widened upon finding Master Chief Marshall sitting in a chair. He turned back to Senior Chief Powers when he spoke.

"Yeah, you did. And we're going to talk about why you hid your injuries. But before we do, you need to understand this can never happen again."

Unable to remain on the sidelines, Jake stood, his tone and expression unyielding as he asserted, "Never. Had we been spun up and required Sierra's assistance, and you went into the field in that condition, you would put everyone's lives at risk."

Rob eyed Jake with a silent, *'Back off, he's my man for the moment.'* Returning focus to Max, he said, "Want to explain why you didn't inform me?"

Not really. Max realized that response wouldn't go over too well, particularly with Marshall's harsh expression. In his still somewhat muddled state, he picked something equally imprudent. "Operated in worse condition. Nothing to tell." Though true, the flash of anger he received from both Powers and Marshall told him he screwed up again.

Rob tamped down hard on his fury. A conversation with Gabe Miller and one with Scott and Grant had infuriated him. Stirling had been treated like crap by many of his COs, so his comment held a ring of truth. It twisted Rob's gut, but Lockwood vowed to do what he could to investigate the assault.

Jake's reaction was less restrained. "WHAT PART OF NEVER DIDN'T YOU UNDERSTAND?"

Swallowing hard, Max averted his gaze.

"NOT NOW, JAKE," Rob bit out harshly. "In fact, Stirling is on my team, so I'm going to ask you to leave."

Arching a brow, Jake crossed his arms and stood his ground but lowered his voice a little. "And your team is MY support team. Anything to do with Sierra is MY business too."

"Enough!" Bryan ordered as he entered, having overheard both leaders when he was still two doors away. "This is a hospital, and you need to keep it down. Both of you go to the café for coffee, now! I want to speak with Stirling … privately."

Rob complied without complaint, but Jake required a second admonishment, which Bryan gladly offered, "What part of now, don't *you* comprehend?" Bryan waited until the door closed before he pivoted to face Stirling.

In the past few hours, Bryan grasped the young man had a challenging path, and men like Captain Ridgeway complicated things. Though he figured Stirling didn't trust many people, Bryan approached this situation with consideration as he would any other. He pulled the chair over, noting Stirling's squinted eyes. "Are you in significant pain? If so, we can speak later."

"I'm fine, Sir."

"Alright. If that changes, tell me." Receiving a slight nod, Bryan decided to not beat around the bush. "We are aware you were jumped outside a bar after Tanner's funeral. Miller supplied the details. He also informed us Ridgeway didn't believe you when you told him. I do." He paused to let that sink in.

Unsure how to respond, Max remained silent.

"Furthermore, we found proof. A store surveillance camera across from the alley captured a video of three sailors attacking you." The next part angered Bryan. It went against SEAL tenets. "Enhancement of the dark images didn't produce facial features, but in the light of a passing car, the glint of a trident pin can be seen. As a result, I must ask, do you know your attackers?"

Max maintained a steady gaze as conjecture became reality, and the betrayal of the brotherhood he valued sucker-punched him. "No, Sir, I do not."

Bryan leaned back. "Has anyone threatened or attacked you before? Honesty, please."

Closing his eyes, Max recalled several fights with guys on other teams because of his last name. "Usually gave as good as I got."

"So, I take it, a few one-on-one arguments?"

Max caught the change of term, which sent relief through him. Fights were not unheard of between men with aggressive natures, which most SEALs possessed, but if a commanding officer got involved, both would be punished. Lockwood's use of argument meant he wouldn't pursue disciplinary action. "Yes, Sir."

"And what prompted these arguments?"

Wincing, Max rubbed his aching head but refused to request a postponement of this questioning. He wanted to get it over and done. "Difference of opinion, Sir."

"In what regard?"

"The honor of my father and their opinion, I don't deserve to be a SEAL because of what they believe he did."

"Discord ever bleed into missions?"

Max shook his head. "No, Sir. Personal issues don't belong on missions and are checked at the door. None of them were on my team at the time."

"I see. I'm going to need their names to pass on to NCIS."

"Why?"

"The evidence found on the video requires a full investigation. Whoever attacked you doesn't deserve to wear the trident."

"Oh." Max closed his eyes as he supplied the four names.

Noting the fatigue and not wanting to tire Stirling, Bryan decided to let NCIS handle any additional questions. He stood and said, "Thank you for your candor. You're officially on medical leave until your ribs heal. If you had informed Powers of your condition, the same would be true, though it would've been only a couple of weeks, not the six or seven you are facing."

Bryan smiled. "Get some rest now because when you return, you're going to be running the hills from sunrise to sunset for failing to report an injury to your team leader."

"Yes, Sir." After Lockwood left, a slight grin came to Max's face as he drifted to sleep with the thought, *I'm not off the team.*

Twenty minutes later, Jake re-entered the room with Rob and resumed his seat. Scrutinizing Stirling, Jake made an enlightening remark. "He's so young. Damn, I'm old enough to be his father."

Rob chuckled. "But he's an exceptional shooter coupled with brains, Jake. I would love to keep him, but from what I saw today, he is a perfect fit for Zulu. Fresh blood will make you evolve."

The Barnacle

Finn downed the last of his beer. "Just because I don't think he is right for our team doesn't mean I'm okay with what happened to him. I'd be quite happy to fly to California and show the rotten shit-buckets exactly what I think about what they did to him. Give them a taste of my fists."

Grant tossed his dart at the board. "We have no idea who they are. The video Lester located doesn't show their faces."

"Oh, I have ways to find out." Finn grabbed Zach's beer and drank half. Their dog handler wouldn't realize when he came back from the head.

"And exactly how would you do that?" Dave probed.

"Bait and switch. Go in and talk shit about Stirling and wait for a bottom-feeder to bite. Someone's gonna brag about what they did. Though if they were real men, they wouldn't be bragging about three against one and attacking a brother right after a funeral. That's wrong, cowardly, and fucked-up." Finn took another drink from Zach's mug.

"Hey! Quit drinking my beers," Zach declared as he spotted Finn. "That is five you owe me."

"It was lonely. You shouldn't leave your drink alone so often." He chuckled and ducked Zach's half-hearted attempt to hit him. "Missed again."

"I'm sic'ing Rocky on you next time. He'll take a chunk outta your ass." Zach sat and eyed his near-empty mug.

"Nah, he likes me too much. I give him treats."

"And ruin his training." Zach sighed. "Your turn to buy."

Finn rose and went to the counter to order. As he waited for the beers, Finn leaned back on the bar and scanned the occupants. The Barnacle was the Pirate's Cove of the east coast. A SEAL hangout. A place for comradery.

He hated to think what likely went through Stirling's mind when he learned members of the brotherhood beat the shit out of him. What he discovered today made Finn ashamed for judging Stirling by name only. The kid earned the right to be here, the same as all of them, regardless of his father's actions.

As he paid, he spotted Jake entering and ordered one more. Grabbing three beers in one hand and two in the other, sloshing a bit on the floor as he walked, Finn returned to their table. He slid a mug to Jake. "Did Stirling tell you why he hid the injuries?"

Jake opted to hold back the full details for now. "No. But I got the impression this wasn't the first time it happened. Lockwood came by to talk to him about the security camera footage Lester discovered, and when he finished, Stirling was sleeping, so I left."

"Did he know them?" Grant hoped he did so they could be held accountable for their actions.

"Lockwood said no but got names of four guys who had an issue with him in the past. Not sure if any of them are involved, but they will be questioned."

Dave took a sip and inserted his two cents, "I hope they identify the perps and charge them."

Toying this his glass, Zach said, "Whoever did this doesn't reflect our values and should be keel-hauled."

They all nodded, drinking for several minutes as they silently contemplated the issue until Finn spoke, "He needs protecting."

Dave snorted beer through his nose at Finn's remark. After coughing a few times, he said, "This from the man who is dead set against Stirling being on this team."

"It isn't because of his name. He is too damned young ... too green. I don't want to be babysitting a wee laddie who still needs his knickers changed. He was with Foxtrot for what, like, three or four months? He's still a rookie by any measure."

Jake eyed Finn. "And how did you come by that knowledge?"

A sheepish expression crossed Finn's face. "Have sources."

"And who are they?" Jake demanded.

"Not gonna say." Finn's gaze shifted to Dave for support.

"I'm not saving your ass, so don't look at me. Bossman asked you a question. It's best to answer straight up. The first rule of Zulu is don't lie to the boss."

"Don't want to get the person in trouble. I sorta sweet-talked my way into getting some basics. Not the full jacket, only things like what teams he's been on and his training evolutions. I had to find out when Grant told us he's only twenty-four."

Hoping to deflect from naming his source, Finn said, "He joined the Navy at seventeen. Went straight to BUDs after recruit training, bypassing prep school. He graduated from sniper school and was deployed for the first time when he was only twenty."

Finn held Dave's, Zach's, and Grant's full attention, so he continued, "He got selected for Green Team as soon as he met the requirements, finished in the top three, but was drafted last. Then Ridgeway demoted him based on a crock-of-shit AAR. Someone is gunning for him, and that shit isn't right."

Aware of all that and more, Jake only nodded. He would let Finn off the hook for digging because, as elite operators, they lived and died by intel, and one of their basic tenets was to adapt and overcome, which he did in this case. However, Jake wondered if the individual who supplied Finn with the information might be a security risk.

However, instead of drilling Finn for a name, Jake said, "Stirling's on six weeks medical leave. Afterward, we'll follow the same plan. He's sticking with Sierra for now, and we will continue to draw from Sierra if we require a sixth man for any mission."

21

A Place for the Kid

Four Days Later – Rob's Truck

LEANING against the headrest, Max stared out the window at the drizzling rain and traffic, still wondering if he had fallen down the rabbit hole. Except for Gabe's team, never once had teammates given a damn about him. Never before had anyone visited him in the hospital, offered him a place to stay, or gone out of their way to help him.

But Sierra appeared to be different. One of his teammates remained in his room the entire time, but mostly, it was Rob or Scott. They let him sleep or entertained him, whichever he was up to at the moment.

Devlin, the team driver, claimed his wife made the fancy fruit tarts he brought in, but Terrance ratted him out. Max laughed, much to his ribs' displeasure, when the guys razzed Devlin for his hobby. Devlin's threat to stop sharing his creations with them shut everyone up quick. Based on the tarts and other treats Devlin brought him, the man was a damned-fine baker.

Yesterday, the aroma of pizza drew him from his slumber, and he found Scott and Grant in his room. Curious as to why Zulu's medic visited, Scott explained that, as team medics, they would be his first contacts if he experienced any unexpected pain or shortness of breath after being released. As they ate dinner, Scott entered both their numbers into his phone.

When the doctor kept him hospitalized for an additional two days because his headache persisted and he lived alone, Scott, Rob, and Terrance each asked if he wanted to spend a few days at their homes. He politely declined, in part because he didn't want to be a burden and partly because he didn't know them well enough to fully trust them yet.

Life and Athole taught him well that if something seemed too good to be true, it never lasted. So, Max justified his refusal of their kind offers by telling himself that investing in them and becoming closer would cause him more hurt when everything went to shit again.

However, he did accept a ride back to base when Rob insisted. A wise choice, given they'd been stuck in a traffic jam for an hour so far. He could only imagine how much a cab ride would've cost him since they were still at least twenty minutes from base.

The rain increased, creating a mesmerizing pitter-patter pinging on the roof of Rob's truck, and Max found it harder to keep his eyes open. The heavy-duty meds were part of the reason he slept so much in the past four days. Broken ribs sucked, and although he usually shied away from painkillers, he diligently took the meds as prescribed so he could draw in deep breaths to prevent pneumonia.

He didn't need anything else to delay his return to operating. Facing another five or six weeks doing nothing might be enough to drive him crazy. Max didn't know how to chill for more than a few days. He supposed he could spend his time brushing up on languages he hadn't spoken in years. Losing the battle to stay awake, lulled to sleep by the soft music and rain, Max's head lolled to his shoulder and ended up against the cool window.

From the backseat on the driver's side, Scott noted Max's state and quietly said, "He's out."

Rob glanced over at his rookie. "Hope he won't be pissed off."

Scott chuckled. "Based on what we've learned in the last couple of days, I don't think he will be mad. Though, I do believe I might need to treat him for shock."

Outside Apartment Complex Near Base

Twenty minutes later, Rob came to a halt outside Devlin's place, glanced in the rearview mirror, and grinned. "Got your shock treatment kit?"

Scott snickered as he finished sending a text to Devlin. "Yeah. Dev says everything is ready. Time to wake the kid."

Focusing on the blond man in the front passenger seat, Rob said, "He is truly a kid in our line of work. He's only six years older than Jake's son Jamie."

Scott's grin faded. "Sometimes, the flashes in his eyes speak of an old soul in a kid's body. You think everything's gonna work out for him?"

Rob shut off the ignition and undid his seatbelt. "Only time will tell, but for now, let's get him inside."

Slipping out the crew cab, Scott went around the truck and rapped on the passenger side window. "Hey, Max, wake up."

Groggy, Max cracked open his eyes and peered at Scott. "Yeah, okay." His lids closed again as he shifted and stifled a groan. Days passed since his ungainly dismount from the cargo net, yet every muscle still ached. After opening the door, Max let Scott assist him out of the lifted truck to keep from jarring his ribs.

Once out of the vehicle, Max became aware they were not at his quarters. "Where are we?"

"Devlin lives here. Told him we would pop by on our way back to base. We won't stay long." Rob started for the entrance so Max wouldn't ask more questions.

Though wanting nothing more than to go to his place and crash in his bed, Max followed without complaint and decided to cover his exhausted state by behaving as if he were okay. "Wonder if he has any of those cookies left."

"Probably does," Scott responded as he brought up the rear. He stayed close to Max in case he slipped on the rain-soaked sidewalk. The kid didn't need to be falling again so soon, and he perceived Max's fatigue and the flicker of dismay at the thought of making a pitstop to visit a teammate.

Inside Apartment

Thankful Devlin lived on the second floor and not the fourth, the trip up the stairs winding him more than he would like and tiring him out. Max waited while Rob knocked on the door. He almost groaned when it opened to reveal the entire team, minus Babcox, who only stopped by his hospital room once. He didn't much care for Babcox, so it was no loss.

"Hey, you're a free bird now," Devlin said as Max entered.

"Needs to work on his flying. His flapping didn't save him before," Terrance quipped.

Max rolled his eyes and didn't comment. In the last few days, he heard about every joke imaginable about his fall, though all done in good-natured razzing. "Devlin, I need to piss, where's your head?"

"Door on the right." Devlin's grin was too bright for giving directions to the bathroom, but Max didn't notice.

Greeting the others as he made his way to the short hall, which had a door on the left and right, Max took in the layout of the apartment. Functional and more than double what he had in California. He wondered if there might be any open units and decided to ask Devlin when he returned.

Max chuckled as he spotted the gray and navy blue shower curtain. He owned the exact same design and a matching bathmat. The PX's choices were indeed limited. After taking care of business, he yawned as he washed his hands.

Taking a moment to assess his reflection, Max noted the bruising around his eye had changed to a light yellowish green and had faded significantly since the attack. Though not a vain man, Max determined to wait until his facial discoloration disappeared completely before calling Cali.

Explaining his stupidity and how he got them wouldn't impress the beautiful sister of his former leader. It was bad enough that he had to admit to Lockwood and, subsequently, the NCIS agent how he'd been caught unaware. Not one of his finer moments and one Max wished to forget.

Exiting, he found everyone lounging on comfortable furniture. Going to the island, which separated the family room area from the kitchen, Max eased himself onto one of the stools. The place was a decent size for two people, but if and when Devlin and his wife had kids, they would need more space.

"So, what do you think of the apartment?" Devlin asked as he handed Max a root beer since he couldn't have alcohol yet.

"Nice. I got the same bathroom accessories." Max paused as several of his teammates snickered. He refocused on Devlin, who grinned at him ... creepy. "Um, do you know if there is an available unit? I'm not too keen on living on base."

The guys erupting in full-blown laughter caused Max to glance around. He noted the coffeemaker, which was the same brand as his. The platter filled with cookies was too. When his eyes landed on the upturned wooden crate near the window, Max's jaw dropped. He would recognize it anywhere because he spent hours carving the detailed trident years ago.

Rob stood and made his way to Stirling. "A bit presumptuous on our part, but welcome home."

Max blinked and stated the obvious, "This isn't Devlin's?"

"I actually live in the building. Three doors down." Devlin patted Max's back a little too hard, forgetting about his ribs until glimpsing the wince. "Sorry."

Rob held out a set of keys. "Yours if you want it. The landlord is a friend of mine. Reasonable rent and the furniture is included."

"Yeah, um, thanks." Flabbergasted, Max opened his palm, and the keys jingled as they landed.

Scott sidled up to Max. "We're gonna get out of your hair and let you take a nap. Remember to call Grant or me if you need anything." He motioned for the others it was time to leave.

Max thanked them as they exited, still stunned they did this for him. It was not until he sat on his bed Max wondered how they got his things from storage. He spied and reached for a note on his nightstand, a real one, and grinned. *Enjoy your new place. Draper.* He likely owed the logistics specialist another beer.

San Diego – NCIS Interview Room

Special Warfare Operator Dwayne Pipe studied his hands as they rested on the table. He had been sitting in this tiny room for an hour, stewing. For days, he debated with himself whether to play innocent and go about his life or to come clean and accept the consequences. His family would not be proud of his actions, and for the most part, he was not either.

Dwayne tensed when the door opened, and his stomach turned to lead as the NCIS agent entered. This morning, he made a decision and drove straight to the field office. Once there, he told them he must speak with an agent.

Taking a seat, Bill Walters kept his face neutral. He wondered what this SEAL needed to say. "Sorry for the wait. What brought you in today?"

Gathering the courage he should've tapped into last week, Dwayne said, "I'm here to confess to a crime."

Bill's brows arched. "And what crime is that?"

"I took part in an unprovoked assault on a fellow SEAL. I didn't want to, but my CO kinda ordered me."

"Kind of? Explain."

Dwayne rubbed his sweaty palms on his pants. "It wasn't a direct order, but my CO's always been a bit of a hardass, and if you cross him … well, recently, it's gotten to the point he will make your life hell on earth. Saying no isn't much of an option."

"Who did you assault, and why?"

"Maxwell Stirling. My team leader has had a beef with him for years. I'm not certain of the details. It happened before my time. Although my teammates wouldn't elaborate, they said something occurred during deployment, and Stirling got transferred.

"Then, when we learned Tanner died." Dwayne glanced down as memories of Lucas, the friend he made in BUDs, flowed through his mind. Putting them away for now, he lifted his gaze again. "I found out Stirling was with my friend when it occurred. I told Massey, and he went off the deep end."

"How did you find out?"

"I overheard Mrs. Tanner speaking with Stirling at the funeral."

"Okay, what happened next?"

"We drank quite a bit, and with each round, Massey became more agitated. He insisted we teach Stirling a lesson. When Stirling left by himself, we followed him out of the bar." He dried his hands again. "I'm sorry I didn't stop them earlier."

"What do you mean earlier?"

"Shit, I screwed up big time. My career is over for participating, but when Massey talked about getting payback, I thought it would be a few punches, make him hurt a little … but the three of us damned-near killed him. Massey rammed Stirling's head into a wall so damned hard he dropped to the sidewalk like a rock."

Bill put up a hand. "When you refer to Massey, I presume you are talking about Senior Chief Gavin Massey."

"Yes."

"Who else is involved?"

"Special Warfare Operator Paul Fawn. He's also on my team."

"Okay. What happened after Stirling was on the ground?"

"Massey and Fawn dragged him into the alley. We all kicked him as he curled into a ball to protect his chest and head. I stopped after a couple of kicks, but the other two kept going. When I yelled at them to stop, Fawn backed off, but Massey kept kicking and kicking while he accused Stirling of being just like his father. Massey was possessed or something. Never seen …" Dwayne inhaled sharply and blew out a long breath.

"After Massey stomped on Stirling's torso and said, 'I'm going to fucking kill you,' I tackled Massey. He was so enraged I couldn't hold him, and when he got away, he went back to Stirling. Both Fawn and I were stunned by Massey's savagery. I told Fawn I didn't want to be a party to cold-blooded murder. Neither did he. It took both of us to drag Massey away from Stirling."

Dwayne removed his trident pin and laid it on the table. "I left Stirling in that alley, not knowing if he was dead or alive. I broke faith with my brothers and will plead guilty to whatever charges are brought against me."

Dam Neck – Captain Kendrick's Office

Jake and Bryan entered and took a seat when the captain motioned to the chairs. Neither understood the summons, but both came promptly.

"I'll come right to the point. Senior Field Agent Campbell, who is handling the investigation into the falsified AAR and the assault on Stirling, received a call about an hour ago from their San Diego field office. One of the SEALs involved in the attack came forward of his own volition and confessed. He named the other two. All three are in custody, and the case is now with JAG."

Jake frowned as he processed the unfathomable news. *SEALs don't attack their brothers.* "Why?"

Seth recognized the disbelief in both Jake's and Bryan's expressions. "This is where it becomes messy, so bear with me as I try to summarize the details Campbell uncovered. When SWO Pipe confessed to his part, he indicated his team leader, Senior Chief Massey—"

Jake interrupted, "Massey? Gavin Massey?"

"Yes."

"One of Stirling's former CO's who wrote a scathing review," Bryan interjected.

Kendrick nodded. "Yes, one of his previous team leaders. An interesting piece of information Campbell discovered is that Massey's uncle was Blake Smith."

"I know that name but can't recall from where." Jake snapped his fingers as the cog fell into place, and his disbelief increased. "Smith was Zulu Six when Preston Stirling ran the team."

Bryan let out a low whistle. "Did he blame Maxwell for his uncle's death?"

Kendrick leaned forward and rested his forearms on the desk. "Quite possibly based on things he said during the attack. But when Stirling was placed on Massey's team, no one realized the connection. According to the other attacker, SWO Fawn, discord between Massey and Stirling became visible to him and grew during deployment.

"Fawn said his CO rode them all hard, but Stirling hardest of all. They all believed, in the beginning, it was a rookie thing, and Massey wanted to whip Stirling into shape. But it started to go beyond acceptable limits after an incident.

"Stirling had been assigned overwatch as the rest of the men moved to a building to snag the HVT. He took out a military-aged male wearing an S-vest, but from his position, he didn't spot the woman. Her proximity to the team, when she set off hers, rang their bells and peppered them with shrapnel.

"Afterwards, Massey became ruthless in his treatment of Stirling, assigning him every shit job imaginable. The lieutenant commander noted the change and the effect on team dynamics, so he transferred Stirling, and things settled back into a groove."

Jake ran his fingers through his hair, frustrated by the whole situation. "This is a fucking mess. I assume Massey is going to be charged with attempted murder and the others with assault."

Kendrick sighed. "In JAG's hands. There is one other detail that might alter the outcome."

"They deserve to rot in jail. What could change the sentence?" Jake fought hard to remain in his seat and not pace.

"Two days ago, Massey had his annual physical, and he told the doctor he's been experiencing headaches and loss of control. They did an MRI, and it showed signs of prior traumatic brain injury in the frontal lobe, which controls decision-making in response to emotions. Massey's lawyer will likely argue the uncontrolled rage he exhibited is the result of the TBI."

Jake clenched his fist. Needing to focus on something else, he inquired about the progress on the fake AAR. The information relayed only amplified his concerns. NCIS was no closer to discovering the culprit, as the leads they followed all dead-ended.

When Kendrick dismissed him, Jake headed for the gym to use the heavy bag to relieve his tension and think through what it would mean to have Stirling as a member of his team. The kid had skills and needed a little protection, but would that put the rest of his men at risk if they accepted him and his additional baggage?

22

Breaking the Ice

Three Weeks Later – The Barnacle

FINISHING his shot of whiskey, Finn ruminated on recent events as Grant took his turn at the dartboard, and Zach went to the bar to order another round. Since coming clean about his divorce, Grant hung out with the team's bachelors more often and even humored Finn by going to Glitter Girls once.

To Finn, Grant appeared to only go through the motions without his usual zest for life. Finn was not sad the bitch Lindsey left. He only wished her cheating and trying to pass off another guy's spawn hadn't impacted Grant so hard. Finn wanted to help his buddy through this rough patch without getting all sappy and decided Grant needed to get laid.

When Zach returned, beer bottles in hand, Finn said, "We gotta find Grant a woman to put him back in the game."

Zach chuckled. "Don't think he needs any help in that department. Give him time."

"Nah, my dad used to say … best to hop right back in the saddle when the demon mare throws you. Time for him to play the field and sample a bevy of beauties."

Turning to his teammates, Grant eyed Finn. "I'm the one who did the throwing. And all I'll find in this place is a frog-hog, and I'm not interested in …" he trailed off as his eye caught a woman entering the bar.

Both Finn and Zach turned to find out what silenced Grant.

Zach let out a low whistle as he viewed a woman with all the right curves, chestnut hair, and striking blue eyes. "Wow. Not the typical frog-hog."

"The bonnie lassie is all mine, lads," Finn ratcheted up his affected Scottish brogue, one he brought out when he wanted. "Seeing as Grant isnae interested, and she is definitely out of dog boy's league." Finn set his bottle down, intending to ditch his brothers to engage with the stunning woman.

"If anyone's outta her league, you are," Zach retorted, ready to brush past Finn to reach her first. But all three halted when a familiar blond-headed man entered and put his hand on her back to guide her toward an empty table.

As he lifted his beer, Finn groused, "He sure is a pretty boy, isn't he? When she's ready for a brawny man, I'll be here."

Zach resumed his seat and studied Stirling for a moment. "Glad he's up and about." He turned to Grant and asked, "Did Scott give you any indication of how long he'll be out?"

"Last we spoke, about three more weeks before he is cleared for duty." Grant shifted his gaze away from Stirling and the gorgeous woman. "Who's up for a game of pool?"

Across the bar, Max found a table for himself and Cali, then went to order their drinks. He returned and took a seat. He said, "I'm still not sure why you wanted to come here. We could've gone someplace nicer."

Cali's lips turned upward in a flirty smile as she leaned forward to whisper, "Well, you see, I'm on a secret mission."

"Oh?" Max grinned.

"Yep."

"And what is that mission?" Max took a swig of his first beer in almost a month.

"Wouldn't be secret if I told you." Cali's blue eyes sparkled as she teased Max. She wrapped a hand around her bottle, lifted it, and took a sip as she relaxed and scanned the patrons. "Well, if you promise not to tell, I'll share with you."

Max placed his hand over his heart. "I'll take it to my grave."

"Gabe sent me to recon where you hang out. Make sure people play nice and set them straight if they dare bother you."

Max snorted.

"Hey, I can do it. I do have five brothers I kept in line."

"So, Gabe wants you to protect me?"

"Yeah." She flashed him a smile as she winked.

"What do you think of the local watering hole?"

"Truthfully?"

"Yes."

"I love it. I'm a beer and pretzels kinda girl, and the places I go after work with my colleagues are a bit pretentious for me. Though I like wine and those fancy hors d'oeuvres, some of the regulars can be so full of themselves. I prefer people who are real, honest, and down to earth."

Max agreed and gave her a slight nod. "What drew you to working in an art gallery?"

Cali's eyes lit up. "The sculptures. I'm fascinated by artists who find the inner beauty in a block of marble or slab of clay."

Max listened as Cali told him about many of the pieces in the gallery and how her passion evolved. He was aware from the first time they met that she and all her siblings were adopted, but her openly sharing her painful past surprised him.

Her life before being adopted by caring people seemed as lonely as his. She never knew her father, and he was not listed on her birth certificate. Cali spent her afternoons after school, and many nights, wandering the museum in her town when her junkie mother was too drugged out to care for her. At twelve years old, Cali entered the foster system after her mom overdosed, and the Millers adopted her a year later.

Cali halted and bit her lip, realizing she just dumped her life story on Max in the past fifteen minutes. It was not the smartest thing to do with a guy she was attracted to. "Sorry, bad habit. Most people hide their pasts when they're crappy. I tend to spill everything out, so there isn't an anvil over my head."

"No worries. I'm glad you found your passion. Some people never do." Then, to avoid reciprocating with his messed-up childhood, Max used deflection. "Wanna play pool?"

"Sure. Gotta warn ya. I'm a shark. Used to earn additional spending money from my brothers. They never learned when to quit." Cali hopped off the stool and followed Max to the tables.

"Hey, Pretty boy, how about a game of two-against-two?" Finn rested his hip on the pool table.

Max nearly groaned. One reason he had not wanted to come here is Rob indicated this is where Sierra and Zulu tended to hang out, and he didn't want to run into any of them tonight, but he couldn't deny Cali's request.

"Who's that?" Cali whispered.

Max desired to answer 'a jerk,' but he had to work with McBride in the future, so he opted for, "A guy I know."

"Well, yeah, I guessed that part."

Before Max could say anything else, Cali strode up to the ginger-haired man and introduced herself. "Hi, I'm Cali. What do you want to wager on the game?"

McBride grinned. "I'm Finn. How's about twenty … if that's not too steep for you?"

"Make it forty, and you have a game. You can break." Cali waited while Finn glanced at his dark-haired friends and got nods before going to select a stick.

Max followed suit as Grant racked the balls. Tonight was not turning out as he expected, but then again, Gabe told him Cali was a unique and special woman. Though uncertain about socializing with Zulu members, Cali effortlessly put everyone at ease, and soon he was on a first-name basis with Finn, Grant, and Zach … something he never envisioned happening.

As Cali lined up her shot to sink the final striped ball before tackling the eight ball, three phones buzzed, putting an end to the evening. No money exchanged hands for the double-or-nothing game as Finn insisted it technically was not over, but the guys did leave shy eighty dollars from the previous two games.

Outside the Barnacle

After one more beer and a bit of casual conversation, Max strolled beside Cali, escorting her to her car. He didn't want the night to end so soon but accepted she had an early morning meeting and needed to get home at a decent hour. Reaching their destination and coming to a halt, he said, "I enjoyed tonight."

"Me too. I'm glad Gabe sent me on this mission." Cali peered around the mostly empty lot. "Where's your car?"

"Sold it to Brett before I left Coronado. He needed a vehicle, and it would've cost me more than the car was worth to ship here. Been searching the ads for a replacement but haven't found anything I want yet."

"Want a lift home?" Cali offered, wondering why Gabe had left out that little detail. She assumed Max flew here because driving across the country would've been too difficult, given his physical state after being jumped.

"My place is only a short walk."

Cali cocked a brow. So had his apartment in California, and that had not worked out so well for him. "Hop in."

"No, really, there's no need."

"What if I just want to know where you live?" Cali smiled.

"You could ask," Max responded with a grin.

"What's the fun in that? And besides, I take my secret mission seriously. Gotta make sure you arrive home safe and sound." Cali unlocked the doors and pinned her gaze on the man who intrigued her. "Come on, humor me."

Max relented, chuckling as he opened the passenger door. After she got in, he provided directions, and as she pulled out of the parking lot, he said, "Perhaps next Friday, we can meet at one of the pretentious places you hang out with your coworkers?"

A thrill of electricity zinged through Cali. "Chesapeake is a long way from here, and you don't have a car."

"I'll prioritize finding one. Nothing else to do at the moment."

The electrical current thrummed again. "Okay. I'll text you the address during the week."

Zulu Plane En Route to Tunisia

Stewart Babcox lay across several seats, relaxing with his headphones on and listening to his favorite playlist. He was stoked to be running with Zulu on this mission, selected because they needed a second sniper. This would allow him to show them he would be the perfect replacement for Axel.

Zulu occasionally tapped men from Sierra, like Zach. The dog handler had been Sierra Four for a couple of years, but Marshall decided his skills and that of Rocketeer were needed on a more routine basis, so Zach got the offer to join Zulu when a spot opened. So, Stewart viewed his placement on Sierra as a proving ground of sorts and this op as his audition.

Loud laughter invaded his ears over and above his music, which caused Stewart to open his eyes and glance in the direction of the Zulu members as they hung their hammocks. He popped one earbud out, intending to eavesdrop on their conversation.

As the laughter ebbed, Zach continued his story. "Finn pulls out his Scottish brogue, thinking he'll impress Cali. He's all ayes and isnaes trying to sound like some Highlander but mixed in all his cowboy references. At one point, Cali pins him with a quizzical expression and says, 'Never met a Scottish cowboy before, but it suits you.'"

Not interested in their inane banter, Babcox put his earbud back in and increased the volume to drown them out. He heard it all before, and he didn't much care for McBride. When he joined Sierra, he learned McBride's grandparents and mother came directly from Scotland. His mother married a rancher in Montana, whose family also hailed from the old sod, but unlike his mom, his father was born in the USA. Stewart believed the flame-haired hothead didn't belong on the premiere strike force since he was only half-American.

Stewart dismissed those thoughts in favor of ones that painted him the hero of the day. Ones where he made a difficult shot taking out a scumbag, and Marshall praised him for his precision rifle skills, telling him he was better than Dave Katz.

The cherry on top of Stewart's daydream was when Marshall extended his hand and said, *'Babcox, we want you to be Zulu Six. When I retire, you'll become Zulu One. Welcome to the team.'*

While Babcox swam in his fantasy world, Dave settled in a seat beside Jake after the banter died down, and the other men climbed into their hammocks to catch some Zs before they had to rise and prepare for the HALO jump into Tunisia. "Interesting, they hung out with Stirling tonight."

Jake nodded, his eyes still on the map in his lap. "Yeah."

"Finn didn't have anything negative to say about him."

Closing the file, Jake turned to Dave. "And?"

"Might be a positive sign, brother."

"Not sure I would read that much into it. Finn had eyes on Stirling's woman, according to Zach."

Dave lifted a brow. "You know Finn better than that. He might chase after anything in a skirt, but he would never poach another brother's girl. Finn's positive interaction with him tonight might indicate he is willing to give Stirling a fair shake."

"Still need to observe him. There are things in his jacket that concern me, and he is young. Hell, he's only six years older than Jamie and likely still as immature—"

"Stop." Dave eyed Jake. "Stirling isn't Jamie. Although he is only slightly older, the fact Stirling achieved top-three in Green Team tells me he's mature enough to do this job. Nobody, and I mean nobody, comes that far without possessing the right stuff.

"Yes, he is still young, but imagine what he'll be like in a few years if he is mentored by the best." Dave cracked a smile as he said, "Might even be another Jake Marshall. Remember what Derek West did for you when you were a young gun? I think it is about time we start planning for Zulu's future."

Jake stared at Dave with a strong dose of skepticism. "And you believe Preston Stirling's son is the future of Zulu?"

Dave stared back with censure. "No. I believe Maxwell Stirling might possess what it takes to lead Zulu one day. He is his own man, and it's time for people to quit judging him by his father."

23

Unexpected Find

Five Days Later – The Barnacle

SCOTT leaned back, assessing their hopefully short-term rookie. Before Rob headed off with Zulu and Babcox for the mission, he shared the potential path for Stirling and asked him to keep an eye out for Max while he was gone.

So far, Max appeared to integrate well with everyone on Sierra. He perceived a budding friendship between their driver and new sniper as Devlin and Max discussed muscle cars. Regardless of Zulu's ultimate decision, the consensus of the men here was Max was likable and fit well on their team. When their conversation lulled, Scott inquired, "So you find a car you want yet?"

"No. Combed through the ads, but nothing is right. I'll probably be taking a cab to Chesapeake on Friday."

"You can borrow my truck if you want," Terrence offered.

"Not if he wants to guarantee his arrival." Devlin chuckled.

"What's wrong with Old Yeller?"

"The easier question to answer is, what isn't?" Devlin lifted his soda, choosing to be designated driver again because having the guys pick up his tab for beverages and food was a perk.

Scott snickered but then said, "I asked because my neighbor is selling her late husband's Mustang. Might be a bit out of your price range, but perhaps you want to take a look tomorrow."

"What year is it?"

"1969, I think. Though I could be wrong."

"Does it run?" Devlin asked.

"Yeah, sounds sweet. I'm not sure of the interior condition, but the paint job is decent. Though Mr. Filmore kept the vehicle in the garage and only drove it on occasion."

"Why is she selling?" Max's interest piqued upon learning the year and model.

"Mrs. Filmore decided to move closer to her granddaughters with the passing of her husband. How about you come by around two tomorrow?"

"Sure. Thanks."

"Hey, I'll give you a lift over. I can't pass up an opportunity to check out a Mustang. Maybe take it for a test drive." Devlin grinned when Max agreed.

Next Day – Outside Filmore Residence

Sitting in the driver's seat of the candy apple red Mustang, Max's heart pounded. Long-ago happy memories filtered in as his fingers brushed over the steering wheel. Though not in pristine condition, this was a well-maintained Mustang with a set of new tires. As Devlin examined the engine for him, Max indulged for a moment, closing his eyes.

A small boy's laughter filled the air as he sat on his father's lap and gripped the wheel. Exhilaration zinged through him as he steered the car around the empty parking lot and yelled with glee, *"Faster, Daddy. Faster."* The deeper tone of an adult male's laugh joined in as they flew at lightspeed ... or what passed as lightspeed for a five-year-old but was more like ten miles per hour.

The Mustang's hood dropping pulled Max from his daydream. Though he liked muscle cars and could change oil and such on his own, Max appreciated having a teammate who lived and breathed cars check it out for him. "So, what's the verdict?"

Devlin leaned on the door, moving closer to whisper, "If you don't buy this, I'm going to piss off my wife and use our house savings account to buy it."

Max chuckled. "That good?"

"Yeah. Time to talk turkey. I'll play up the few things I found wrong and bring her price down."

"Is what she's asking fair?" Max opened the door and slid out.

"Perhaps a little high, but everyone starts high and haggles over price. That's how cars are bought and sold."

Max peered at Mrs. Filmore, who appeared to be in her sixties. His walk down memory lane brought forth other images, including one of his grandma. If she were still alive, Max wouldn't like it if a young buck tried to take advantage. "She's only selling because she needs the money to move. I want to be fair to her."

"Suit yourself. But let me ask a few questions, please."

Max nodded, and they went around to the other side of the car, where Scott stood talking with his neighbor. Max overheard Scott thanking her for babysitting his kids last night.

"My pleasure. I can't wait to be closer to my grandbabies." Marigold turned to the young blond. "Are you interested?"

Devlin stepped in before Max could seal his fate of paying full price. "Seems to be sound, but do you know if it has received regular maintenance?"

"Absolutely. My dear Mark babied Red ever since he acquired her. She only had two owners before us. All the records are in the glovebox." After opening the passenger door, Marigold withdrew a pouch. "Here, you can see for yourself."

Max opened the folder and thumbed through the documents as Devlin posed another question to the seller, but he would never recall what his buddy asked. Max stopped when he came to a handwritten bill of sale, which listed the buyer as Mark Filmore and the name of the previous owner. His ears buzzed, causing him to waver and lean against the Mustang.

Scott noticed Max pale and sway. "Max, are you okay?" He didn't get a response, and when he called Max's name again, both Devlin and Marigold halted their conversation and turned.

Slowly, Max's gaze lifted and met Marigold's. "Whatever you're asking, I'll find a way to pay. I want this Mustang."

"Max!" Devlin's tone carried a bit of annoyance. The kid certainly didn't have a clue how to negotiate.

Marigold read something in the ocean-blue eyes, and her grandmotherly instinct came out in full force. "You need to sit." She gripped his arm and maneuvered him to the passenger seat without an ounce of resistance as his eyes moved back to the paperwork. "Now, I never heard of anyone buying a vehicle like that before, and I've been around the block a few times. How about you tell me why you want it so badly?"

Max swallowed the lump in his throat, his gaze returning to Mrs. Filmore as he pulled out a slip of paper and offered it to her. "I drove this car when I was five. My uncle sold it after my dad died. I'm Max Stirling, and Preston was my father."

Marigold's eyes shifted to the sale receipt, and her hand covered her mouth as she gasped upon reading, *Seller: Richard Athole, executor of Preston Stirling's estate.*

Scott peered over her shoulder, stunned. "What a small world."

Max gathered himself. "Name your price, and I'll come up with the funds."

A soft smile came to Marigold's face. "Come inside for some lemonade, and let's discuss a fair price."

An hour later, keys in hand, still flabbergasted, Max strode to his car, slipped into the driver's seat, and caressed the steering wheel. Max paid no attention to the three people standing on the porch. Scott and Devlin were still in awe at the turn of events, and Marigold was pleased to make the young man's life brighter.

Max inserted the key and turned over the ignition, bringing the Mustang to life. He never expected to set eyes on this car ever again. Uncle Asshole sold it even though Dad promised it would be his one day.

Depressing the clutch, he shifted into first gear and lifted his left foot as he gave it a bit of gas with his right. Exhilaration coursed through him as Max pulled away from the curb. His destination would be the parking lot where his dad let him sit on his lap and drive for the first time.

Zulu Plane En Route to Virginia

Stoked the mission went as planned, clean, smooth, the intel was correct down to the number of tangos to expect on target, and most importantly, they snatched their HVT with nary an issue, Zulu was in high spirits. Jake and Dave handed out beers, and Jake offered one to Farris. When she declined, preferring her iced mocha, he turned and held it out to Farris's techie, Lester, who grinned and accepted.

Dave gave a bottle to Babcox and said, "Excellent shot taking out the guy wearing the s-vest."

Stewart clinked bottles with Dave and silently preened at the rare praise from Zulu Two. Though he believed himself to be a better sniper than Katz, he would keep his mouth shut for now because, as far as auditions go, this one was perfect.

His shot saved McBride and Marshall, as well as the HVT, who Farris ordered taken alive. Barak Solal supposedly possessed information that would lead them to Anwar Massi, who still evaded all attempts to locate him.

Babcox took a seat on one of the crates in the middle of the aircraft and basked in the afterglow of a successful mission, with visions of becoming Zulu Six. When Marshall and Katz sat a short distance from him, he directed his gaze on McBride, who stood on the opposite side talking with Draper but attuned his ear to eavesdrop on Zulu One and Two.

Stewart's hopes increased as Katz said, "About criteria for the new guy, precision rifling needs to be high on the list."

"Agreed, but as I said, we're going to observe Sierra training for several weeks. We need to ensure team dynamics aren't thrown off, and I'm not sure he is the right fit. He must demonstrate he is a team guy. There are conflicting reports in his jacket."

Babcox frowned. He didn't realize his all-too-frequent headbutting with former teammates would be part of his file. But apparently, he would have an opportunity to rectify Marshall's impression. He only needed to bite his tongue and be a gung-ho team player while they assessed his performance.

He most definitely must keep his opinion of Stirling under lock and key. Stewart still wondered how Stirling landed a coveted spot on Sierra. His father's legacy alone should've prevented him from being anywhere near Zulu ... not even in a support capacity.

Deciding now would be a great time to begin displaying his team spirit, Babcox stood and wandered closer to McBride. He considered how best to ingratiate himself with number three since McBride would be tasked with mentoring the new teammate.

Though, in truth, Stewart didn't think Finn McBride had anything of value to teach him. The Montana hick with a big mouth, who complained about sea and jungle missions, and relied on a fake Scottish accent to try to get women to sleep with him, had nothing on Stewart except age. Babcox could run laps around anyone on Zulu, with the possible exclusion of Marshall.

As Babcox moved towards Finn, Dave glanced his way and lowered his voice. "When are we going to be able to review Stirling's jacket. I don't like being kept in the dark. It's like going on a mission with crap intel. The shit always hits the fan."

Jake settled back and lifted the beer to his lips. "I'll speak with Lockwood tomorrow but no promises. However, I did give some thought to your comment about choosing someone for Zulu's future. You have a valid point, and thus, I must do due diligence, no matter whether it is Stirling or someone else."

"Agreed." Dave let the matter drop and slumped in his seat to find a more comfortable position. With the mission complete, his mind wandered to his family. Aware he was only a few hours from being home with his wife, a grin appeared. As much as he wanted to spend time with his twins, he hoped they might be asleep, allowing him some time alone with Cathy.

Zach's Home

Glad to be home after almost six days away, Zach dropped his spare leash on the countertop and then filled Rocketeer's food dish. Picking up the water dish, he went to the sink and grinned as he stared at Rocky in the backyard.

Rocketeer rolled around in the grass like a puppy, and Zach figured he also preferred the cool, green lawn to the hot sand in Tunisia. Once he finished with his dog's needs, Zach went to the fridge and stood with the door open, pondering what to make.

Cooking would be too much effort, so he grabbed a canister of peanuts and the last banana before ambling into his living room. After plopping on the plush leather couch, selected because dog hair would be easier to clean off, Zach propped his feet on his coffee table and pulled the top off the nuts. He peeled his banana and dipped it into the peanuts before taking a bite.

Savoring the combination of flavors, Zach's body uncoiled, releasing his remaining post-mission tension. Everyone came home alive and unharmed—the best possible outcome—but the tango with the deadly s-vest could've changed everything.

Although Babcox took him out in time, in Zach's opinion, the suicide bomber got too damned close to Jake and Finn. He believed from Babcox's position that Sierra Seven should've spotted the threat sooner and dealt with it. His gut told him if Dave had been in that location, the jihadi would've never gotten so close. And though it still niggled at him, Zach held his tongue in debriefing because, without solid proof, Babcox deliberately waited his perception would only cause unnecessary friction.

The doggie door clanked, alerting him to Rocky coming in, and Zach hurried to eat the banana because his canine partner would beg for his share, and he only had one in the house. The patter of paws on the hardwood flooring indicated Rocky headed straight for him, bypassing his bowl of kibble.

Shoving the final bit into his mouth, Zach tried to be inconspicuous as he chewed, but his efforts didn't fool Rocky. The pup stood at his knee and peered at him with a sad expression, which conveyed, *"You didn't share with me."*

With regret, Zach said, "Sorry. I was hungry and too tired to cook. I'll buy more tomorrow." His offer of some peanuts resulted in Rocky forgiving him, hopping up beside him, and laying his head in his lap. Before long, the exhausted duo was snoozing.

24

A True Believer

Four Weeks Later – Training Grounds

MAX sprinted up the hill carrying a fully-loaded rucksack. His breathing remained well-modulated despite this being his tenth roundtrip. Though Sierra's team leader deemed running an appropriate disciplinary action for hiding his injuries from them on the first day with the team, Maxwell didn't view this as punishment.

In Max's mind, Rob afforded him the opportunity to regain his stamina and prior level of readiness. The extra running benefitted him physically and unexpectedly created cohesiveness within his new team. Max was prepared to run the hills solo, but each morning, when he arrived in the predawn to begin his required laps before the day's scheduled training session, every member of Sierra showed up and ran with him.

Their actions reminded Max of his BUDs days, where an entire team paid for one person's screw-up. After the third day, he asked Scott why they were running, and Sierra Two's answer astonished him. He said Babcox suggested doing so would be a show of faith in their new teammate and hasten integration.

Since Babcox had been standoffish on his very first day, Max assumed the guy disliked him merely because of his last name, like many others in his past. Max thought he must've misinterpreted Sierra Seven's deportment, so he readjusted his opinion.

Things were looking up for him, which put him slightly on edge. Experience told him this wouldn't last, but Max decided to seize the happy interlude and hold fast for as long as possible. Yes, he would hurt when he ended up in the shitter again, but at least for a brief moment, his life was almost all he desired.

Breathing hard as the crest of the hill loomed, Max grinned as Cali came to mind. In the past four weeks, they went out six times. For the first time since Lacey, a woman intrigued him, and he wanted to spend his off-hours with her. Although they lived vastly different lives, her world filled with refined parties, fine art, and snobbish intellectuals, whereas his consisted of dirt, bullets, and boisterous frogmen, he sensed a connection with her.

"Your grin tells me you got another date lined up with Cali," Devlin declared as he kept pace with Max.

Max chuckled, but his, Rob's, and Babcox's phones began buzzing, cutting off his reply as he pulled it out and read the text telling him to report to Zulu's briefing room.

Rob patted Max's shoulder. "Appears three of us have been spun up. We better hustle back. Scott, you're in charge of the boys while I'm gone. Stick with what we planned for today."

"Roger."

Scott clapped his hands. "Alright, boys, you heard the boss. Perhaps by the time they return, Rob will believe Max learned his lesson, and we won't be out here running the hills before dawn every day. Let's head for the gun range."

"Hopefully, but while they're gone, my wife will be happy I'm still in bed when she wakes," Devlin said.

Scott nodded in absolute agreement.

As he jogged beside Stirling, Babcox briefly wondered why Zulu tapped the new guy for the mission but focused mainly on the fact Marshall wanted him to join them. Stewart believed he did a superb job highlighting a team-first mentality in the past week, and his effort caught Zulu One's notice. More than once, he bit his tongue to keep his opinions of Stirling to himself, but this positive outcome made it worth his silence.

Zulu Team Room

Divested of his rucksack, Max grabbed a water bottle before sitting in the back with Rob and Stewart as Zulu gathered at the table for a briefing. A thrum of excitement coursed through him as this would be his first official mission as a member of Sierra.

Despite only a week of training with his team, Max found his groove faster than usual. He attributed this success to his six weeks of downtime, which allowed him to become familiar with each man, gauge team dynamics in a social setting, and apply what he learned while working with them.

As the men took their seats, Lieutenant Commander Bryan Lockwood said, "We're going after Anwar Massi again."

"Hot damn!" Finn blurted out.

Nicole strode to the front as she clicked the remote to display a map of the western part of Libya. "Barak Solal provided a possible location for Massi. His information correlates with intel intercepted by CIA assets regarding a potential arms deal going down in the northwestern region."

"Given the Massis' reputation for brutal violence, Libya requested our assistance in apprehending him. We'll fly into Ghadames East Airport under the guise of humanitarian aid, then Zulu will covertly forward position in the home of an asset, Nader Khames, to recon the suspected exchange location. Once Anwar is confirmed on-site, you will snatch him, and the Libyan military will secure the weapons stash."

Nicole's attention focused on Max, pleased to find him operational again. "Mr. Stirling, your linguistic skills will be useful as Mr. Khames speaks little English. How's your Ghadamès?"

Hating to be put on the spot, Max answered honestly, "Rusty."

"Okay." She turned to Kira. "Draper, can you round up a language program for him to review in flight?"

"Already done and on the plane." Wanting to be prepared, Kira included a laptop with a database of languages to Zulu's standard equipment list as soon as she learned Stirling would be working as their primary interpreter.

Once Farris provided a full mission briefing and Zulu made preliminary plans after reviewing aerial photographs of the small oasis town in the northwestern part of Libya, Bryan took over and said, "Wheels up in one hour."

Rob flashed a grin at Max as he stood. "At least we have time to shower before we go."

Max smiled. "True." He followed Rob out, glad for the opportunity to grab the man who he held responsible for Lucas's death. He also hoped this was not another trap since knowledge of Sayed Massi's death had been withheld from the public. Anwar must've discovered his first attempt failed and might try again.

Libya – Khames' Home

Sliding down the wall to the floor in the corner of the empty room in Khames' three-story abode, from which they would observe the target location, Max crossed his arms on top of his knees, lowered his forehead to them, and closed his eyes, thankful not to be taking first watch. He spent most of the flight brushing up on the Berber language of Ghadamès while the others slept, which left him exhausted now.

"Max, you okay?" Rob dropped beside his tired rookie.

"Yeah."

"Alright. You rack out." Rob glanced up at Jake and received a nod of agreement. Both leaders were aware Max pushed himself to prepare for this mission. A smart choice since their CIA asset barely spoke ten words of English. Communication with Nader Khames would've been impossible without Max translating for them when they met at the rendezvous point.

A soft snore beside him told Rob that Max had wasted no time falling asleep. He rose and strode across the room to assist with preparing the surveillance equipment. He hadn't gotten a chance to speak with Jake recently and, in a quiet voice, asked, "So what is your impression after watching us train?"

Jake took a brief scan of the sleeping blond. "Brash with rough edges, but a skilled shooter and team player."

Rob agreed with the assessment. "He's a true believer. How long did Lockwood give you to make a selection?"

"Not rushing. We'll pull from Sierra until we decide."

"He's been jerked around a lot. He fits well on my team, so be sure he's the right one before you offer him the position because if it doesn't work and you send him down again, well," Rob trailed off, unsure whether to share what he discovered about Max's need to belong and wished he had kept his mouth shut.

"I'll be certain. Once Zulu, always Zulu." Jake ended his chat with Rob as he said, "When Finn, Zach, and Babcox return from setting up the sneak cams, you guys all rack out. Dave, Grant, and I will take the first watch."

Jake moved to the side of the window and peered at the target building. He refused to fall into another Massi trap. They would wait until they confirmed that Anwar Massi was here without a doubt. As Dave and Grant took up positions behind the scopes, Jake once again turned his gaze on Stirling.

During the past week, he studied the self-confident SEAL as he trained with Sierra. Though outspoken on occasion, bordering on being a smart-ass, Stirling's inputs highlighted he possessed intelligence and a solid foundation. However, the process of changing a diamond from a rough stone into a brilliant faceted gem tended to be difficult and required a plethora of patience.

Cutting and polishing Stirling would be challenging, and Jake deliberated whether his temperament would achieve the best results. Though Jake did acknowledge he wouldn't be the only one to take part in the finishing, it would be a team effort, and as such, they all must buy in on their selection.

At this point, if he called for a vote, Jake believed Grant, Zach, and Dave would be in favor of extending the offer. Finn, although not wholly opposed to the idea any longer, had made some positive comments on the kid's skills during training but still sat on the fence. Jake assumed part of Finn's reluctance stemmed from his new role as team mentor, or in Finn's words, *'babysitter,'* for whoever became their newest member.

Jake also remained in two minds. He read Stirling's jacket multiple times and did a little digging of his own in the last seven weeks. The kid unquestionably had detractors, but Jake discovered most of them were of the older set, men likely to have been around when Zulu Team had been wiped out, or those mentored by men who served while the rumor mill ran unchecked and tempers flared. Input from newer leaders and many of Stirling's teammates was quite positive.

Long past judging Stirling by his parentage, Jake now struggled with something unexpected in relation to the young man. The keyword being *'young.'* Though raw talent exuded from the blond SEAL, Jake experienced an intense gut reaction when Stirling fell from the cargo net, much as he did when they arrived too late in the Argentinian jungle to stop Arcilla from impaling Stirling.

The sensation, both foreign and familiar, was unlike anything he had experienced when any teammate had been injured or killed. Jake wanted to understand this ambiguity before welcoming Stirling into the Zulu brotherhood, but he was no closer today to comprehension than he had been that day on the beach when the kid plummeted to the sand.

Shelving his thoughts, Jake focused on the mission at hand. The narrow street below and the surrounding houses remained quiet, as to be expected in the wee hours of the morning. Dave broke his concentration a few minutes later.

"So, how are things going with Jamie?"

Jake resisted the urge to groan, but he frowned.

"That good, huh?" Dave recognized Jake was going through a rough spot with his eldest son.

"Some days, I would take a colicky, screaming infant over an eighteen-year-old who thinks he's a man. He's been a handful and a half ever since graduating high school. Nothing Val or I say is getting through his thick head. Jamie came home drunk every weekend. Reached the point where I wanted to lock him in his room. Reason isn't working. He's too influenced by the shiftless crowd he is hanging out with now."

"I'm sorry, brother. Anything I can do to help?" Dave offered, glad he still had fifteen years before he reached Jake's issues.

"No. Val wants to send Jamie to live with her sister in Phoenix to give him a fresh start away from his do-nothing friends, but I don't think that will solve the issue. When we return, I'm going to talk to Jamie about the military again."

Grant chuckled. "You really think he'd join?" Having known James Marshall for years, a career in any of the armed forces seemed unlikely. Though Grant liked Jake's eldest son, in his opinion, the boy was more suited to creative endeavors where imagination and individualism were prized and encouraged.

Jake shrugged. "Not sure, but he needs to make a decision on a direction and take action instead of sitting around the house all day doing nothing. Military, community college, a trade school, hell, even making donuts at a coffee shop would be preferable to his inability to be decisive and do something."

"Ever thought of giving him an ultimatum? Find a job or go to school, or he's out of the house." Dave inquired.

"Crossed my mind. Getting Val to agree is another issue. She's always been softer on the kids than me. I don't understand why he is so indecisive and flighty. He's had Val and me as role models his entire life, and it's like he learned nothing from us."

Dave's gaze moved to Jake and back to his scope. "I wouldn't go so far, brother. Jamie's a good kid but struggling with deciding what he wants to be when he grows up."

"Well, he's eighteen. Time to decide." Frustrated by his son's lack of action, Jake raked his hands through his hair.

"You think the real Anwar will show, or is this another trap?" Dave changed the subject, recognizing his best friend would stubbornly dig in his heels if he suggested a softer hand or gave Jamie a bit more time to figure out his path.

For the next four hours, the three discussed a variety of topics as they logged the minimal comings and goings outside. As dawn approached, Jake rousted Finn, Zach, and Babcox to take over watch, allowing Stirling and Rob a few more hours of sleep.

25

Skunk Boy

Libya – Khames' Home

F INN leaned his back against the wall for support as he bent his knees and draped his arms over them, taking a short break from the scope to make log entries. Though with nothing much going on outside, his pen remained down as he stared at Stirling, who still slept. Jake said not to rouse the kid until at least two if nothing required him to wake before.

This reconnaissance gave Finn lots of time to think, and he reviewed every training scenario he observed in the last week. Try as he might, Finn couldn't identify one item that would jettison Stirling from consideration for Zulu. On the contrary, his presence on Sierra had a peculiar effect on the team's dynamics.

Never had he witnessed Babcox so engaged as a team player. Sierra Seven was inclined to be self-absorbed, which is one of the reasons they all eliminated him from the previous candidate selection. But Stirling must've said or done something that ignited Babcox's team spirit.

The others on the team, Devlin in particular, also appeared to listen when Stirling made a suggestion. A natural-born leader came to Finn's mind when he considered how Sierra Team reacted to Stirling during the drills. A rare quality, which Jake, Dave, and Rob also possessed. Though even with raw talent, the kid would need someone to sit on him so he didn't become too cocky.

Aggression, self-confidence, intelligence, perseverance, and ambition were traits all frogmen shared to some extent. Otherwise, they would've never made it through the rigors of the SEAL pipeline. And tier-one operators had a little something extra to make it through Green Team. However, restraint and maturity were also needed to function at Zulu's level.

He conceded the kid performed on par with their level in practice. However, Stirling remained less experienced than anyone ever considered for Zulu. Finn wondered if, at twenty-four, Stirling matured enough. With ample experience came eradication of immature notions, such as being invincible. *Can we risk this youngster having thoughts of being indestructible and doing something stupid that might end with him or one of us dead?*

That was the million-dollar question, which couldn't be answered without seeing Stirling in action. But that was the catch twenty-two. To obtain an answer, the kid must join them in the field, and if Stirling took unnecessary risks, someone might die.

"Got movement." Zach adjusted the scope.

Finn nudged Jake awake as he moved to view the video feed.

"Massi?" Jake asked as he roused Dave and indicated for him to do the same for the others still sacked out.

"Not certain. A group of five. Faces not visible," Finn relayed.

After Rob shook him awake, Max checked the time as he stood to stretch and couldn't believe he had been allowed to sleep straight through to one. He grabbed a water bottle and sipped as he listened to Marshall communicating with TOC.

As they continued to monitor, a truck halted in the street, and several crates were moved into the house before it drove off. They assumed the weapons delivery arrived, but Anwar didn't make an appearance. Activity on the narrow road continued unabated as the village's inhabitants went about their daily lives. Throughout the next eight hours, no one else entered or exited.

A little past nine, two cars arrived, and seven men disembarked. Manning the high-resolution camera, Max took a snapshot of a man illuminated in the entryway. "Got a positive ID on Massi."

Libyan Village

As prearranged, Babcox remained in Nader's home as overwatch while the others searched for Massi. In the middle of the stack, per Marshall's orders, Max prepared to enter the building with the rest of the team. His adrenaline pumped as McBride blew the breaching charge, and they rushed in.

When Dave, Rob, Grant, and Zach headed up the stairs to the second and third floors, Max went with Jake and Finn to clear the ground level. Moving down the hallway, with Max taking point, they cleared three rooms, schwacking five tangos. Halting at the last door in the back of the house, Max gripped the knob, ready to twist and push inward as Finn shifted to the other side.

Bullets peppered the wooden door from the inside, sending sharp shards and slugs flying outward. Max jerked backward as Jake yanked on the back of his vest, but despite Zulu One's action, several fragments embedded in Stirling's forearm and thigh.

"You hit?" Jake asked.

"No bullet holes," Max answered. Though the splinters stung, he ignored the minor injury.

Finn returned sustained fire. Afterward, they heard a thump and clank of a body and weapon falling. Kicking in what was left of the door, Finn entered, trailed by Max and Jake, as someone slipped out the window. By the time they crossed the room and peered out, the person was gone.

Both Zulu Two and Zulu Four reported no joy in locating Massi on their floors right before Jake followed Finn and Max out the open window as he contacted Lockwood. "Zulu One to TOC, the squirter must be Massi. Lost sight of him. Which direction did he go?"

"ISR shows three individuals exited the rear, and each went in a different direction," Bryan reported.

With a drone overhead, Draper provided the team with general directions since Massi could be any of them. Dave and Rob headed north, Grant and Zach went south, and the remaining three ran west towards the outskirts of the town.

"Our tango is not the HVT," Dave conveyed as Rob zip-tied the man they caught.

Max kept pace with Zulu One and Three as they chased their runner through the narrow maze of streets and alleyways. Elongating his stride, Max increased his speed and pulled ahead of the other two. With a fifty-percent chance this was Anwar, he didn't want the bastard responsible for Lucas's death to escape.

"Kid can run!" Finn puffed, hard-pressed to keep up with Stirling. He was a breacher and heavy weapons specialist, not a friggin' rabbit.

"Zulu Four to Zulu One. You gotta be following the right one. Our guy is a body double." Grant held out a hand to help Zach up after his incredible flying tackle. Together, they pulled one of Massi's men to his feet and headed back to the target building as Lockwood informed the team the Libyan Army arrived to secure the weapons.

Rounding a corner, Max grinned at how much of the gap he closed. His quarry now only ten feet or so away from him. He dug deep, his boots kicking up sand as he poured on speed. *Almost. Almost. Only a few more feet.* Victory nearly in his grasp, gunfire erupted in front of them.

Not far behind Max, Jake took the corner and gritted his teeth. *The young pup is damned fast.* Finn followed close behind him, but both dove for cover when AK-47s sent a barrage of rounds toward them. "TOC, troops in contact." When Stirling continued after Massi, he yelled, "Sierra Eight, get the fuck down."

Behind who he believed to be Anwar since the shots whizzed past him on either side, Max made one last-ditch attempt to stop Massi from getting away. He launched himself at Anwar, seizing him around the shoulders. They went down and kept falling when they should've ended up on the ground.

Jake couldn't believe his eyes. The kid was there one moment, jumping on their target, and in the next, he vanished. He didn't have time to contemplate how Stirling disappeared as the gunfire increased with Massi no longer an obstacle between them.

From their positions in adobe alcoves, Finn and Jake occupied what must be Massi's backup forces in an all-out firefight as Draper guided Dave, Zach, Rob, and Grant behind the heavily armed men. The fierce exchange of ammunition went on for several minutes before Zulu gained the upper hand, and the few remaining extremists surrendered or fled into the night.

As Zulu fought above, Max engaged in a battle of his own. He splashed down in something godawful, and his brain registered he must've crashed through rotted wood. Max didn't have long to regain his wits because Anwar rose in the waist-high lake of human waste, armed with a knife.

Max blocked the first strike, but his boots slipped on the slime and sludge, and the second one sliced through his dark plaid shirt, causing a nasty cut on his side. He dodged the third, barely. Regaining his balance, Max went on the offensive. Better trained in hand-to-hand combat than his adversary, Max disarmed Massi with little trouble.

When the knife dropped and disappeared in the cesspool, the HVT dove to retrieve it, or so Max thought. But he realized Anwar moved towards a three-by-three opening above the contents of the pit. Max lunged forward to drag Massi out and ended up getting kicked in the jaw.

Pissed off and covered in piss and shit, Max growled, grabbed Anwar's leg, and ripped the asshole from the tunnel. Anwar landed face-first in the foul waste, and Max held him under, yearning to drown the son-of-a-bitch. Reason and restraint returned in enough time for Max to haul Massi up before he killed him. Farris needed the dickwad alive to shut down the entire operation.

With his target somewhat subdued and busy gasping for breath, Max managed to zip-tie Massi's hands behind his back and shoved him to one side of what must be the town's septic tank. Winded but not wanting to breathe deeply due to the fetid air, Max ran a hand over his dripping hair to keep the crap out of his eyes. Searching for a way out, he listened on comms as Zulu routed Massi's minions.

Max realized he wouldn't be getting out on his own. The sides were straight, slick with putrid, decaying excrement, and the hole they created happened to be in the center and at least twelve feet above him. "Sierra Eight to TOC, how copy?"

"Good copy."

"Jackpot. HVT secured. Alive. Need assistance climbing out of a shithole."

"Say again, your last." Bryan peered at the monitor. The kid's voice and news filled him with relief. They witnessed Max falling, but Jake's needs took precedence until now.

"I'm standing waist-deep in shit and god-only-knows-what. Think this is the village cesspool."

"Copy. Stay put." Bryan groaned when he realized what he said and added, "We'll have you out of there as soon as possible."

"Roger." Max aimed his weapon at Anwar when he started to inch toward the drainage pipe again. Speaking Berber, Max said, "Don't move, or I'll put a bullet in your leg. Won't kill you unless infection sets in, and that would be a long and painful death."

Ghadames East Airport – Zulu Plane

Kira wished for schematics of the village's primitive sewer system, but things like that rarely existed for locales in which they operated. The only way to help at the moment would be to organize an area for Stirling and their HVT to wash and clean clothing because none of them wanted to fly for twenty hours with the stench of a cesspit.

She turned to Lockwood. "Sir, request permission to acquire items to facilitate a makeshift shower."

Bryan grinned at Draper. "You'd be doing us all a favor."

"Need any help? Stirling, the poor guy, has been through the wringer with ops related to the Massis. He deserves not to ride home in misery," Nicole said.

"Sure. Need to scrounge up some clothing for the HVT. Max should have a change in his bag." Kira hurried out to check with airport personnel about showers or at least a hose and spigot.

Libyan Village

The stinging in his side increased as Max waited for the guys to rig ropes, but he didn't dare press on the wound and introduce more bacteria than wading in the polluted water had already. Rob communicated to him the plywood he broke through was on its last legs and too unstable to hold anyone's weight. So, throwing down a line for him to tie to Massi wouldn't work.

Max wished to be first out of this cesspool, but he would be second after they hauled Massi out. The overwhelming stench caused both him and his prisoner to retch several times, adding to his misery. Max doubted he would ever feel clean and imagined the rank odor would seep into his skin and remain for days or perhaps months with his luck.

When the line dropped with a harness attached, Max moved closer to Anwar. Speaking in Berber, he said, "Don't try anything, or I'll leave you down here to rot." Receiving only a glare in return, Max fitted the harness without incident.

As Massi began his trip to the surface, the tension in Max's body started to uncoil, and his aches and pains made themselves known. He released a soft groan, realizing once topside, he must admit to the injuries because he had learned his lesson not to hide anything from Rob. And although minor, he needed to rinse them as soon as possible to prevent infection.

An unexpected splash of Massi into the raw sewage and shouts above pulled Max from his thoughts. He grabbed Anwar's arm, hauled the sputtering man out of the muck, and steadied him on his feet before keying his comms. "Whiskey Tango Foxtrot?"

"Rope snapped. Hang tight. This might take a while. We need to rig something else," Rob responded.

Max's eyes lit on the tunnel, just large enough for a man to crawl through. Switching to Berber again, he turned to Massi and asked, "Does that lead to an exit?"

Anwar spat, trying to rid himself of the disgusting liquid in his mouth before replying in his native tongue, "Yes."

"How far?" Max inquired.

Anwar glared but answered since he wanted out, *now*. "Unsure, but there is an access ladder at the end."

"Sierra Eight to Zulu One. I found a solution."

Frustrated by the amount of time it took them to find enough rope and jury-rig a pulley in the first place, only to have the damned thing break, Jake's tone came out a bit curt. "What?"

"There's a tunnel down here which the HVT indicates ends somewhere with a ladder. It heads north. Perhaps the asset knows where the manhole is located. If you get him on comms, I can ask him to point it out to you on a map."

"Copy. Stay put until we confirm you won't be coming up into a hornet's nest." Jake motioned to Dave. "Go to Nader's house so he can show us on the map if possible. Take Zulu Five to help Sierra Seven pack and carry the surveillance gear."

"Roger." Dave pivoted and waved to Zach to follow him.

Jake keyed his comms again, "Sierra Seven, find Nader and put him on your headset so Sierra Eight can speak with him."

Ten minutes later, with Max translating, the team obtained the position of the tunnel's outlet from Nader. Jake instructed Stirling to go ahead, and they would meet him there.

Max cut Anwar's hands loose because the man needed to crawl a quarter of a mile. He pointed to the opening. "You first. Try anything, and you'll regret it."

After Anwar entered the tunnel, Max pulled himself in and followed, his hands and knees squishing in stuff he'd rather not think about as he crawled. Though not claustrophobic, he cringed as the solid limestone walls surrounded him, and he gagged, fighting the need to hurl as the stench of excrement increased in the tight, enclosed space.

The meager light ahead, heralding his impending deliverance from this godawful sewer, drew Max like a shining beacon after what seemed like an eternity of navigating the darkness. Anwar went up first, and Max scurried after him. When he hauled himself out, he remained on his knees and sucked in fresh air … or, more correctly, less stinky air since the horrible stench saturated him.

Rob held out an uncapped water bottle to Max. "Rinse your mouth. Incredible first mission. You snagged one of the top twenty on the CIA's most-wanted list."

After taking a swig, swishing, and spitting it out, Max grimaced. "I'd rather someone else caught him. Got any antiseptic wipes?"

"You hurt?"

"A few splinters plus a cut on my side."

"From the plywood?" Rob queried.

Although hating to admit Anwar got the drop on him, Max decided the truth would be best. "Knife. Slippery down there and lost my footing when Massi came at me."

"Where?" Despite the unpleasant odor, Grant moved forward as he spotted the slashed section of Stirling's shirt. With gloved hands, he tugged the fabric away, revealing a slow oozing slash. "Vest and shirt off. Now!"

Bare from the waist up in no time flat, facilitated by Grant's trusty shears, Max stood stock still as Zulu's medic rinsed his knife wound with water, swabbed it with povidone-iodine, and applied a temporary dressing.

"Draper arranged someplace for you to wash, so the rest will have to wait until we reach the airport." Grant pulled off his gloves and shoved them in the trash bag with the other used items.

"Let's move out," Jake ordered as the vehicle the local military provided to transport them to the airfield arrived.

"Pepé Le Poop, you're lucky we don't leave any man behind. Though, I'm tempted to tie you to the roof," Finn teased, his nose wrinkling as he got blasted with a malodorous whiff of Stirling when the wind shifted.

"That's Pepé Le Pew, and if you weren't moving at such a snail's pace, you could've had the honors," Max retorted.

Enjoying the banter, Finn countered, "Only protecting our rear, Skunk Boy."

Giving Stirling a wide berth, Babcox noted dark splotches of crap clinging to Stirling's fair hair and jeans and couldn't resist the dig, "Your exterior finally reflects your skills ... shitty."

Unimpressed by Babcox's comment, Zach glared at him as he guided the blindfolded and restrained Massi to their transport.

Dave lowered the tailgate. "Sit here. You'll be downwind."

Max ignored Babcox as he eyed the truck. "Actually, I wouldn't mind being strapped up top. Not fond of my new Eau de toilet."

Happy the kid joked about his predicament, despite Babcox's asinine barb, Finn sought to return the repartee to jesting. "Hey, if you ride on the roof, we'll have shit on a shingle."

The guys groaned at first, then chuckled as Finn evaded the filthy glove Stirling tossed at him. When they loaded up, Max sat on the truck's tailgate while Finn continued his good-natured razzing. When Finn ran out of material, Max's thoughts turned to Cali. Thanks to her helping to break the ice the night they played pool with Finn, Zach, and Grant, Max realized McBride teased everybody, so he didn't take offense and laughed along, getting in a few humorous rejoinders of his own.

Ghadames East Airport

Max spotted the makeshift shower Draper set up next to a building a short distance from the plane. He couldn't wait to wash. As he hopped off the tailgate, he found Grant striding beside him as Zach escorted Anwar in the same direction.

"After you finish, I'll re-exam your wound, remove the deeply embedded wood fragments, and disinfect all the cuts." Grant halted at the tarped area, which provided a bit of privacy for the two men who would need to strip completely.

"Okay." Max bent to unlace what used to be his favorite boots. He would be tossing them now due to the stench.

Kira flashed a grin at Max as her gaze landed on his well-toned bare chest and muscular biceps. "Wish this could be a real shower, but a hose and a bar of soap will have to suffice."

"Thanks. Better than reeking for the next twenty hours."

"I'll leave you to it." As Stirling stood and began unbuttoning his jeans, Kira turned and ambled off, wishing she could get a peek of his entire well-built body.

26

Got Your Six

GRANT used tweezers to pluck out the last embedded splinter from the back of Stirling's thigh. He wanted to do this before they were airborne, but Max took longer than expected, wanting soap up and rinse off in triplicate. Draper caused a further delay in his plans when she trotted over to inform them, "Wheels up in five. Lockwood will explain why inflight."

Fortunately, none of the cuts appeared serious, not even the laceration on Max's side. Although deeper than the others, the knife wound possessed smooth edges and only required a couple of steri-strips to hold the gash together.

As he applied a topical antibiotic, Grant said, "Keep an eye out for redness, inflammation, or soreness. All indicators that you might need a course of oral antibiotics."

Max nodded, aware of what to watch for with cuts after wading in a cesspit for over an hour. Reaching for his uniform pants, he tugged them on before slipping his feet into his cross-trainers. Though not the best shoes to wear for a desert operation, he didn't pack another pair of boots, so he must make do with them.

While double-knotting his laces, Max glanced over to the detainees. Black masks blocked their vision, sound-proof earmuffs covered their ears, and their hands and feet were restrained with metal cuffs linked to a chain around their waists.

When he finished dressing, Max stood to join the team as they gathered around a makeshift table of cargo containers. Striding forward, running fingers through his damp hair, attempting to rake his unruly curls into submission, his gaze shifted to Zach.

Although Max caught the big fish, Zulu's dog handler captured the guy who spilled the beans on Massi's primary weapons stockpile. They would be making a pit stop in Algeria to blow the warehouse before word of Anwar's capture got out and someone else in the organization took over or moved the cache.

Jake eyed Stirling as he approached, contemplating whether to bench the kid. Though relieved Stirling hadn't been more seriously injured, Jake remained ticked off. Sierra Eight didn't immediately seek cover when the shooting began. He could've been killed. Unfortunately, they needed his sniper and possibly interpreter skills for this follow-on operation, but it didn't mean he couldn't express his displeasure.

His tone sharp and commanding, Jake declared, "Stirling, on this op, you *will* follow orders to the letter. No more stupid, showboating shit like running headlong into a barrage of bullets. I don't want to be the one informing your family you died."

Babcox smirked, glad Marshall took Stirling to task for his grandstanding. Stewart wanted to grab Massi to secure his place on Zulu, but the little shit got the glory—but also the dressing down he deserved. He didn't have anything to worry about. He was certain Zulu would pick him because Stirling was only needed for his language skills, which would fit right in with a support team role since they didn't often need an interpreter.

Taken aback by the undeserved reprimand, Max defended his decision but also carelessly revealed knowledge he held close to the vest. "My action was reasonable. They weren't shooting at Massi, and I was directly behind him. And I don't have any family, so no worries about who to notify. There isn't anyone."

Jake clenched his jaw, not expecting the response, especially the last part. Opening his mouth to lay down Marshall's law, he shut it when Lockwood spoke.

"Be that as it may, we need everyone's head in the game." Bryan needed to refocus them on the task at hand, so he squashed the discord before it grew. "Our intel is sketchy at best, but we don't want to lose this opportunity to abolish the Massi network and destroy the hoard of weapons. Lieutenant Farris, please relay the details you've uncovered about our target."

Turning a laptop towards the men, Nicole began to provide them the scant information she and Lester dug up.

After a thirty-minute planning session, Babcox silently fumed. He had been relegated to a support role instead of going on the mission. While Zulu and Stirling did a HAHO infil to a compound on the outskirts of a town in southern Algeria to blow the stockpile, he and Rob would land with the plane at In-Guezzam airport and drive local vehicles to the exfil point.

Marshall's decision to take Stirling made no sense to Stewart. He was a better sniper and a more experienced operator. They wouldn't be interrogating anyone, so Stirling's language ability didn't play a role. Also, Stirling's injury would be a liability, though that might benefit him if another Zulu member died.

Babcox wanted to plead his case and make his points that he would be the better choice, but he recalled the conversation he overheard about being a team player, so he decided to bite his tongue and bide his time, particularly after his earlier remark about Stirling bombed, and he got glares from Zach and Dave.

Besides, there was no way in hell Marshall would ever consider Stirling for Zulu. He was too young and too inexperienced, and more importantly, his father, Preston Stirling, was responsible for wiping out an entire team. No, the position would be his and his alone. He proved his worth during his stint in Sierra and, more recently, in training and the op in Tunisia. His photo would be free of darts during this selection process.

Jocked up and prepared for the HAHO jump, Max found it surprising Zulu traveled with all the necessary gear when it was not needed for the original mission. Draper certainly ensured her team would be ready for whatever might be required.

Max's gaze shifted to Marshall, who continued to pin him with steely eyes. He must've screwed up in talking back, and he still didn't quite grasp why the hard-assed team leader selected him over Babcox. They were both snipers, but Babcox had seniority on the support team, so by all rights, Sierra Seven should be going with Zulu, not him.

His thoughts wandered to his lapse of blurting out that he didn't have family. Max never shared that part of his life with any teammates. Sure, his CACO form listed his only living relative, Captain Athole, but if he could've left it blank, he would've because although they shared blood ties, Uncle Asshole would never be his family.

A tap on his shoulder brought him out of his reverie, and Max put on his game face as he nodded to Dave. It would be interesting to work with one of the best snipers in the SEALs. Katz's reputation preceded him. Max strove to break Zulu Two's records while in sniper school, and although he succeeded with one, Max hoped to learn more by observing Dave's techniques.

As Dave checked Stirling's straps to ensure all were correctly clipped and allowed the kid to do the same for him, Max's comment about not having any family floated in his mind. He pondered how anyone could go through life without people to love and who loved and supported him.

When the ramp started to lower, Dave shoved his non-mission thoughts in a box, said a silent prayer to keep them all safe, and focused on the task ahead. He pulled Stirling into line in front of him and waited for the green light to walk out the rear of the plane into God's magnificent star-lit sky.

A familiar rush of endorphins filled Max as he leapt out, and the wind blew in his face. He loved everything about being a SEAL, even if it meant he ended up in a cesspool.

This was better than he ever envisaged as a kid, but sometimes Max worried it was all a dream, and he would wake alone, locked in his bedroom without supper, and sporting a blistered behind from Athole's latest whipping.

Algeria

After touching down and stowing their chutes and oxygen masks, Max waited with the others as Jake made adjustments to their plan. The rare cloudiness prevented TOC from monitoring them on ISR, so instead of one sniper perch with a visual on their entry point, Jake decided to place Dave in the original position and him in a secondary one. This further confused Max since his linguistic ability wouldn't be utilized in the assault on Massi's weapons depot, but he kept his mouth shut.

Jake halted and turned to Stirling when they reached the steel girder satellite tower. Though not ideal to have his snipers work alone, he had to call an audible when the unexpected clouds left their exfil route without coverage. This position would not only give Stirling a view of Dave's location and three sides of the building but also provide the kid with the best possible concealment and keep him safer while working alone. "Up you go. Watch our six, and stay put until we rejoin you."

"Copy." Max released his grip on his rifle, letting it hang from its strap as Finn threw a hook line to the lowest crossbar and tugged to set the anchor. Max grasped the rope and began hauling himself upward.

After he reached his position near the top, Max wrapped his legs around a support beam and wedged himself in a corner. Concealed by one of the dishes, he braced his weapon on a bar and scanned the area as expected. Max keyed his comms and quietly reported, "Your path is clear."

"Zulu One to TOC. Passing Wolverine, Charlie Mike," Jake said as Dave took point, and they continued the mission.

"Good copy. Sierra One and Seven en route to exfil location." Bryan replied from within the plane as he marked off the checkpoint on the whiteboard. His gut still churned, worried this was another trap. He wouldn't put it past Anwar to prearrange with his minion to provide erroneous intel, which drew Zulu to their deaths. But at this point, he must trust Jake to destroy whatever weapons might exist and bring the boys home alive.

Algeria – Dave's Position

As the rest of the team waited in the shadows, Dave entered the two-story building with a terrace roof. According to the detainee's intel, this was Sayed Massi's home and would be empty since he had been captured months ago. With night vision in place, the eerie green glow showed no sign of inhabitants as he made his way through the ground level to the stairs.

The second floor also proved vacant, and Dave swiftly moved to the roof. Reaching the open-air terrace, he chose his spot. If he laid flat, the short wall decorated with triangular cut-outs ringing the edge would provide him a little cover and an unobstructed view of the target building's front.

Once secured, Dave surveyed the area through his scope. "Zulu Two to One. In position, all clear."

Dave maintained overwatch as Jake informed TOC he was passing Skunk right before they made entry. Grinning, he recalled Finn coming up with names of the smelliest animals on the planet as a way to tease Stirling. What Dave found encouraging was Max chuckled and suggested Hoatzin, a bird found in the Amazon, also known as the 'Stink Bird,' which produces a highly disagreeable, manure-like odor.

He tensed as concentrated gunfire and a flash-bang grenade erupted from within the building. The intel told them to expect at least six guards inside. Several minutes later, as the noise subsided and Jake's voice came over the headset reporting to TOC they were now setting the charges, Dave exhaled, releasing a long breath. It was too soon to call this a win. He didn't want to jinx them, but things appeared to be going as planned.

A thud behind him startled Dave. He twisted, and eyes widened in disbelief at the man lying outside the door. A second body fell not far from the first, both with perfectly placed holes between their eyes. A split second later, Dave realized what happened. Using the background noise provided by the explosion and gunfire to mask their approach, the tangos crept up on him unnoticed. Stirling just saved his life. He owed the kid a beer.

Algeria – Max's Position

In the zone, Max exhaled as he sent the skulker to his maker. While scanning, he had caught an irregular shadow behind Zulu Two's position and aimed at the silhouette on the off-chance someone managed to sneak up on Katz. When a man emerged with a weapon raised, Max didn't think—he acted.

About to activate his comms, the second one appeared, and again, Max took the shot without hesitation. He kept his scope trained on the doorway, unsure if Katz would be receiving more company but unwilling to allow anyone to get the drop on him.

Shifting his non-trigger hand to his commlink, Max depressed the button. "Sierra Eight to Zulu Two. Got your six."

Max understood the clipped "Copy" response and didn't expect any thanks. This was his job. No thank yous were required. As Katz returned to a prone position, covering the exterior to keep the area free of tangos, Marshall reported they were exiting and for Zulu Two to join them outside for exfil.

When Two left the rooftop, Max scanned the path Zulu would take to him and found it clear. He shifted to survey the route they would take to meet with Rob and Babcox. Thankfully, it, too, remained unimpeded. Swinging back to cover Zulu's departure, the night sky lit up with bright white for several seconds as the weapons cache exploded prematurely.

Men spilled out of surrounding buildings in various states of dress, many carrying AK-47s as they tried to figure out what happened. Yelling and bursts of gunfire ensued as someone spotted Zulu. From Max's perch, it was like shooting fish in a barrel. One tango after another fell lifeless to the ground, gifted with a slug from him.

With the prospect of being killed by an unseen sniper, the remaining tangos dove for cover. Max sent off a few more rounds as Zulu approached him, then scurried down the framework as they covered him. The six SEALs hauled ass to their exfil location and piled into two vehicles, which sped off before the tangos realized they were gone.

Zulu Plane En Route to Virginia

Coming down from his adrenaline rush, Max slumped in his seat in the middle of the plane. As missions go, he would classify this one as an unqualified success, which would cripple the Massi network and put a considerable dent in the arms trafficking.

Part of him believed he got payback for Lucas, but another piece told him revenge would never bring his friend back. Though Max did derive a slight sense of satisfaction, knowing his efforts tonight might save other innocent lives.

Yawning and stretching, Max winced as his movement pulled on his cut. His hand covered the wound on his side, providing support and pressure as he readjusted, trying to find a comfortable position. He eyed the hammocks swinging at the front and wished he could hang one, but as a support team member, he was relegated to the seats. Max shut his eyes, ready for some rest, glad debrief would take place sometime after they returned home. Footsteps coming towards him caused Max to lift his lids.

"Thanks for saving my ass. Damn-fine shots right through their light switches. You deserve this." Dave held out a beer.

The words and offer surprised Max. He accepted the unopened can and set it beside him. He was not in the mood to drink but said, "No thanks required. Just doing my job."

Dave lowered himself next to Stirling. "The thanks are from my wife and kids for making sure I'm going home to them. Jake's gonna have me running the hills for not being more aware and not noticing them as I cleared the house."

Max understood how Dave felt. If it were him, Max would also be kicking himself, but he suggested an alternative explanation. "Doubt you missed them upon entry. I didn't have a view of the rear, so it is likely they entered after you went up."

"Perhaps." Dave took a swig. "How's your side?"

"Fine."

His curiosity peaking, Dave asked, "What did you mean when you told Jake you don't have any family?"

"Only child. Orphan." Max kept his response short.

"No extended family?" Dave probed.

Not sure why Katz was interested in this part of his life, but realizing he couldn't brush him off without lying, Max admitted, "An uncle, but we've had no contact since I was fifteen, and I prefer it that way." Max closed his eyes and yawned purposely, hoping to stop further exchange.

"Sorry for prying. I'll let you rest. Thanks again." Dave rose and moved to where Jake sat with Lockwood as he let Stirling's admission roll around in his head. Pitching his voice soft so it wouldn't carry far, Dave said, "Kid is an excellent shot, and he handled himself well tonight."

Jake glanced over at Stirling, noting the untouched beer and that he laid across several seats. "Agreed."

"How much longer do you need to make a decision?" Bryan queried.

Shrugging, Jake lifted the bottle to his lips and took a long drink. "Not certain."

Dave shifted his gaze between Jake and Bryan. "I think it is time we discuss this as a team. And it is also time we're allowed to review his full jacket. We deserve to know what we are getting ourselves into if we pick him."

Nodding, Bryan said, "I'll speak with Kendrick when we return. If he approves, I'll provide you with Stirling's file. Now grab some rest." Bryan pulled the brim of his hat down and slouched in his seat, ending the conversation.

Both Dave and Jake finished their beers and sought their hammocks. When they landed, they must debrief and write up AARs before going home to their families, so grabbing sleep now seemed most prudent.

27

Matters of the Heart

Jake's Home

ANGER boiled just below Jake's surface. When he arrived home this evening after a grueling and intense discussion with his team, Val informed him their son went out with friends and was expected home by ten. At midnight, he encouraged her to go to bed since she needed to be up in the morning for their younger kids. Jake waited alone for Jamie to return, and the chimes of the grandfather clock in the entry marked each passing hour.

When the clock struck two, four hours after James should've been home, Jake struggled with a mix of relief and fury as he witnessed his eldest teen staggering up the driveway. The latter won when he went outside to confront him, and the alcohol fairly wafted off Jamie as his son came to a halt in front of him. "Out drinking again. Thought we agreed, this shit would stop."

"I am an adult. Can do what I want," Jamie slurred.

Jake crossed his arms. "Not while you're living under my roof. And at eighteen, drinking is illegal. Do you have any idea how worried your mother was when you didn't show up and didn't call? What the hell am I going to do with you?"

"Nothing!" Jamie attempted to push past his father.

"Hold up. Not so fast." Jake gripped Jamie's arm firmly.

"Let go, old man. I'm going to bed." Jamie tried to yank out of the vice-grip but couldn't.

"Not yet, boy."

"Not a boy!" Jamie retorted.

"Not a man, either." Jake steered Jamie towards the side gate.

"Where are we going?" Jamie stumbled along, his dad's grip keeping him upright. He regretted going along with his buddies tonight, but he was not about to admit that now.

Remaining silent, Jake maneuvered his errant son into the backyard. He released his hold, pointed to the ground, and ordered, "Drop and give me fifty push-ups."

"Not one of your men. You can't order me." He swayed as his eyes struggled to form one image of his pissed-off dad.

"No, I'm your father, which gives me greater authority. Drop. Now. Or you won't like the consequences." Jake's steel-blue eyes met his son's glassy, bloodshot, hazel ones.

Jamie gave a sloppy salute as he mumbled, "Yes, Sir." He went to his knees and flopped face first in the cool grass, passing out.

Growling, frustrated with the situation, Jake squeezed the back of his neck before crouching and peering at his boy. "Where have the years gone? You used to be so sweet and …" Jake trailed off, recognizing he couldn't lay this all at Jamie's feet.

He just didn't know how to relate to a kid so different from him, and his go-to methods that worked with his teammates only pushed him and Jamie further apart. Being a father was one of the hardest jobs he had, and lately, he felt as if he was failing his kids. Adapt and overcome were words he lived by, but nothing he tried produced the results he wanted with Jamie.

Though a tiny part of him believed Jamie deserved to sleep it off outside, Jake couldn't bring himself to be cruel to his son. Shifting to a knee, he turned Jamie over, sat him up, and picked him up in a fireman's carry. Making his way inside, Jake hoped his kid wouldn't leave a trail of puke for him to clean.

Twenty minutes later, Jamie was now undressed and tucked into bed with a trashcan near him. Jake stood in the doorway and sighed. "I'm not giving up on you, Son. We'll work this out one way or another."

Finn's Apartment

Flopping over on his bed, Finn groaned and stared at the big red 4:27 across the room. Sleep eluded him tonight, and he wondered if he should've gone to Glitter Girls as he had originally planned. At the last moment, he decided against it, opting for a sex-free night, hanging out with Grant, Zach, and Draper at the Barnacle.

Flinn believed the topic of their conversation made him restless. After they landed at the base, they did a quick debrief and wrote their AARs for both the Algeria and Libya missions. Then, everyone except Zulu left the room, and Lockwood provided them Stirling's jacket for them to review.

Each one, in turn, read the file, and then the discussion began. It was not like any deliberation they ever had, becoming quite heated as they each spoke their minds. The funny thing was, they were all in violent agreement and outraged.

As they dissected Stirling's records, comparing them against their observations while training, his performance during the missions, and his background dossier, some of the shit in his permanent record appeared to be wholly concocted.

When they coupled that with the faked AAR for the Argentina op and the beat down the kid received by a former teammate after Tanner's funeral, it became apparent Stirling got the shaft. He was on someone's shit list. Although that person remained unknown, they believed it must be someone with power and might go all the way to the top of command. Jake halted the examination at six last night and told them all to sleep on it, and he would be calling for a vote tomorrow, which was now today.

Finn eyed the clock again. 4:30. He now had five and a half hours left to make a decision. They all agreed Stirling met or exceeded the SEAL requirements, but Finn mentally ticked the boxes where the kid met his personal criteria. Solid team attitude, check. Sense of humor, check. True grit and heart, check. The only thing that still gave Finn pause was Stirling's age and the fact he would be the one responsible for mentoring Zulu Six.

Some days, Finn wished Grant had seniority and had been tapped for the Zulu Three position. The medic, although gruff at times, possessed more patience than he did and would be an excellent mentor. Hell, even Zach, their quietest member, might be a better choice for Three.

But this was his role, and Finn needed to base his decision on what would be best for the team, not him. Dave expressed a valid point when he said they should be considering the future of Zulu. And although he conceded Stirling might possess the right skills to one day lead Zulu, that day would be years from now.

Finn chuckled at the one-eighty turn in his thinking. When he first met Stirling, he most definitely judged him by his last name. Now, he realized the name must be more of an anchor than a silver spoon for the younger Stirling, and he had to work harder to prove his worth to others.

A sigh emitted as Finn's thoughts returned to particulars in the kid's background check. He couldn't imagine growing up all alone in a boarding school, but that is exactly what Max did from the time he was eight. They had all been impressed by his academic records, which, in hindsight, shouldn't have surprised them, given the number of languages Stirling spoke.

Truth be told, when he first learned Stirling joined the Navy at seventeen, Finn believed the kid might've dropped out of high school and gotten a GED to enlist. Finding out he was an emancipated minor brought up questions they couldn't answer. Dave did share with them that Stirling said he hadn't had any contact with his uncle since he was fifteen.

In a quandary, no closer to a decision now than yesterday, Finn growled. If he said yes, they might be bringing in a cocky young buck who would throw off team chemistry and bring a host of baggage along with him. With a no vote, because he desired a seasoned operator, Finn might deny Zulu a future team leader.

The bright red numbers now read 4:45. Unable to decide, he rolled over, pushed all his considerations into a box, buried his head under a pillow, and willed himself to go to sleep.

Cali's Apartment

Max shifted, lazily draping his arm over Cali's midsection, enjoying the skin-to-skin contact with an amazing woman whose beauty shone from inside out. Inhaling the lavender scent of her shampoo, Max nuzzled her neck and began to trail soft kisses across her shoulder as she slept.

Last night, he drove to Chesapeake and met Cali at Katsaros Gallery of Fine Art, where she worked. She invited him to be her plus-one at an alumnus fundraising gala for the local university's liberal arts department. He liked her boss, Dougal Flanagan, and several coworkers, but the jury remained out on a couple of her professorial acquaintances.

He got a distinct impression that his bruised and scratched face, scruffy stubble, and the fact he was a sailor made him inferior in the minds of the more pretentious people. When queried about what he did in the Navy, he deflected most folks, but when pushed by a few, he told them he worked in sewage disposal, which, as intended, ceased further inquiry. Though it added to their belief, he was beneath them.

Aware of his status as a DEVGRU SEAL, Cali almost gave him away when she giggled at his response and the expression of disgust on Frank Isaksson's face. Max didn't much care for the way Isaksson fawned all over Cali and insisted on calling her Calliope. Nor did he miss the sneers and snide remarks directed his way from the sociology professor who viewed all members of the military as warmongers.

Despite the few haughty people he mingled with, Max enjoyed the evening as Cali showed him around the gallery. He took delight in watching her eyes light up as she told him all about her favorite sculptures. The cherry on top of a fantastic night was being invited back to her place and, well, their incredible time in bed.

Max could deal with her hoity-toity acquaintances because their opinions of him didn't count one whit. Only Cali's mattered, and she appeared to accept him for who he was and wouldn't try to mold him into something he could never be.

Waking to kisses, which sent a tingling sensation to the tips of her toes and caused goosebumps on her arms, Cali sighed and turned in Max's embrace to face him. "Morning, handsome. What a fantastic way to wake." She melded her lips with his, savoring the connection.

Pulling a hair's breadth back, Max grinned. "Closer to afternoon. Just turned eleven."

Cali's eyes shot open. "Oh. Are you going to be in trouble for being late?"

"Nah. Rob said I'm off rotation for the next four days. I'm done with punishment." Max chuckled. "Little does he know I didn't view it as such."

"Wonderful. Dougal gave me today off. Now we can spend the whole day together, and I can have my way with you again and again and yet again." Cali leaned forward and captured his irresistible lips.

Max couldn't help chuckling. "Think you might be confusing me with a stud and overestimating my abilities."

Cali giggled. "Oh, you are undeniably a handsome stud. I'm sure you will be up for anything with a little coaxing." Her hand moved below the sheets and stroked him, swiftly bringing his cock to attention.

A sensual groan rolled out from the back of Max's throat as he thrust his tongue in her mouth in cadence with the movement of her hand. The notion of spending the day in bed, pleasuring one another, made Max happy, but all big-head thoughts ceased as Cali kissed down his torso and enveloped him in warmth.

Twenty minutes later, both now sated, Cali's head rested on Max's chest as she traced the outline of the bandage on his side with her fingertip. "Does this hurt?"

"Nah. Only a scratch."

Cali shifted and peered into his ocean-blue eyes. "Truly, or are you like my brother Gabe, whose leg could be hanging by a thread, and he would be claiming he could hike ten miles?"

Max kissed her forehead. "Honest. It's like a papercut."

"Those sting like a bitch." Cali smiled as Max chuckled.

"Yeah, they do, but I'm fine."

"I don't understand you or Gabe. Why do you put yourself in harm's way?"

Max gently moved a lock of Cali's hair behind her ear. "I don't think of it in that way."

"I guess you view your work as sewage disposal?" Cali used his words from last night.

"There is that element. We deal with the scum of the earth. But it's also about making a difference and creating a safer world. Saving the lives of people who end up in terrible situations and preserving our freedoms."

Cali nodded. "Freedom isn't free. Someone always pays the cost, like Lucas and his family."

The mention of Lucas brought a bit of sadness to Max's heart, and he changed the subject. "How about I take you out for brunch?"

Realizing she caused the flash of sorrow in Max's eyes, Cali regretted mentioning Lucas. "No. I'm going to make you my famous waffles. That way, we don't need to dress."

She slipped out of bed, comfortable in her skin, and sashayed towards the bedroom door before she turned and flashed him a bright smile. "You're welcome to shower while I cook. You'll find bandages and antibiotic cream in the medicine cabinet."

Max relished the view before him, and his mind was nowhere near showering alone. He stood and moved towards her, his eyes gleaming with devilment. "How about we shower together to conserve water? Then I'll help you in the kitchen."

"I like your plan much better." Cali seized his hand and led him into her bathroom.

Almost two hours later, while washing the dishes together in the nude, cracking jokes, trading kisses, and thoroughly enjoying themselves, Max's phone buzzed and destroyed the rest of their plans. He pulled on his clothes, gave Cali a quick peck on the cheek, and promised to call when he could before dashing out.

28

You're Out of Uniform

Sierra Equipment Cages

MAX rushed into Sierra's room, unlocked and opened his locker, then unbuckled his belt as he kicked off his dress shoes. Traffic from Chesapeake moved at a snail's pace, and the commute took almost fifty minutes. Noting his teammates were not there meant he arrived late.

Dropping his pants as he reached for his working uniform, Max realized he should've swung by his apartment first to grab another pair of boots. His choices now were his cross-trainers or oxfords. He chuckled at the thought of showing up wearing the shiny black leather shoes. Rob would think him seriously demented if he did. So, his only real option was tennis shoes.

He tugged on his desert digital trousers before shedding his button-down shirt and replacing it with his quarter-zip tactical shirt. Max sat on his bench, shoved his feet into his sneakers, and sped through tying them. As he shut his cage, he glanced at his watch and cringed. *Crap, I'm so late.*

Running down the hall, Max wondered why he had been spun up. Rob told him yesterday, after debrief, and before being sent to be thoroughly checked by the team doc, that he would have four days off rotation due to the knife wound. Not that Max needed the downtime, but he wished to spend today with Cali. However, duty called, and he responded as fast as possible.

Zulu Team Room

"He's late," Finn said as he swiveled in his chair.

"Perhaps traffic held him up. The woman he's been dating lives in Chesapeake," Rob offered from the back of the room.

Stirling entering cut off further speculation.

"Sorry. Got here as swiftly as I could." He moved to his usual place at the rear, and his eyes scrunched, noting only Rob from Sierra was in the room. Max came to a halt and faced the front, worried his delay might be an issue. That's when he noted Captain Kendrick in attendance.

The words Kendrick left him with when he spoke with him about joining Sierra came to mind. *Every man in my command is judged on his merit.* Max clamped down on his unease but couldn't stop his thought. *Great. Just friggin' wonderful. He gives me an opportunity, and I screw it up by being late.*

Marshall strode towards him with an inscrutable expression, which increased his anxiety. *Shit! He's gonna chew my ass right in front of the brass.*

Jake halted, standing less than a foot from Stirling. His gaze roamed from the top of Stirling's head to his feet before returning to lock gazes with him. "You're out of uniform."

A lead anchor dropped into the pit of Max's stomach. "Yes, Master Chief." He should've stopped there. Excuses were viewed with as much disgust as vomit, but Max added, "My spare boots are still at my apartment. I was not there when I received the page to come in."

Jake glanced down again and almost laughed. He hadn't noticed the shoes. What that said about him, he was not sure, but the line he chose to instigate his dialog had nothing to do with footwear. His hand whipped out and ripped off Stirling's Sierra Eight patch and dropped it to the ground.

Max blanched, and his eyes widened with shock. *What the hell did I do to be kicked off Sierra? Is he still pissed about me pursuing the HVT? Thought that was settled. Or is being late and wearing the wrong shoes enough to ruin my life?*

The flicker of disbelief and resignation that crossed Stirling's mien stabbed Jake in the heart, and he immediately regretted his course of action. He reached into a pocket and withdrew a piece of cloth as he said, "This belongs to you if you so desire. The choice is yours."

Max's gaze dropped to what Marshall held, and his throat constricted so tight no sound or air could pass as he viewed a Zulu Six patch. His heart rate increased as he lifted questioning eyes to meet Marshall's.

The room remained silent until Kendrick said, "Men under my command are judged on merit. You earned this opportunity. You possess exceptional skills, and we don't plan on wasting them. However, if you wish to remain on Sierra or wait for an opening on another team, you may do so without repercussion."

Sucking in a ragged breath, Max's eyes returned to the bit of fabric, which represented his dreams and the culmination of all his effort. In a millisecond, Max soared upward from the bottom of the Marianas Trench to the summit of Mount Everest. Soft and breathless, he said, "Once Zulu, always Zulu."

Intrigued by the kaleidoscope of emotions that raced through the ocean-blue eyes, Jake asked, "Is that a yes?"

Max scanned each man. Marshall's face gave nothing away, but he didn't think Zulu One would offer him this position if he didn't agree. Dave gave him a nod as if encouraging him to say yes. Finn appeared almost constipated, so there might be some discord with him. Grant casually leaned on the wall with an open and relaxed expression. Zach scratched Rocketeer's ears while affecting a friendly countenance. Lockwood and Kendrick he couldn't read, but Rob grinned like a cat who ate the canary.

"Well?" Jake prompted.

"I'm in." Max took the patch from Marshall and attached it to the Velcro field on his left sleeve. A beaming smile spread across his face. Somehow, someway, despite all the hurdles placed in front of him, Max managed to follow in his dad's footsteps.

"Welcome to Zulu." Jake extended his hand.

Max shook his new team leader's hand as Captain Kendrick approached. When Marshall released his grip, Max redirected his gaze to his father's friend, the man he suspected was responsible for his change in circumstance and likely a stalwart champion in his corner.

"Preston would be proud of all you've accomplished. Your mother, too. Welcome aboard, Stirling."

"Thank you, Sir. I'll do my best not to disappoint."

Kendrick nodded. He doubted Maxwell would ever fall short, but he didn't voice his opinion. "Well, I'll leave you to it." He turned to Jake. "Your team will have two weeks for integration training unless duty calls."

"Understood, Sir."

Bryan stepped forward and offered his right hand to Max. "After you move your gear to Zulu's equipment room, stop by my office to sign the paperwork to make this transfer official. Good to have you on Zulu."

"Copy. Thanks."

When the officers left, Jake said, "There are six primary rules to being on my team. First, never lie to me. Second, your phone is to remain on and always charged. Third, notify Lockwood and me if you will be more than thirty minutes away from the base.

"Fourth, no excessive alcohol consumption because we are always on call. Fifth, I'm the first person you contact if you are in a situation that will prevent you from responding to a spin-up. Sixth and equally important as the others, never hide injuries. They can be a liability to the team."

"Roger."

"Take today to set up your cage, and be here at nine tomorrow morning to run through some drills." Jake shifted to the side as his second in command approached.

Dave grinned as he strode towards their new guy with an outstretched hand holding a shot of whiskey. "The first drink is on us, Brother. Tomorrow, bring a case of beer. Oh, and my wife is arranging a welcome barbeque. It will likely be next Sunday."

Max accepted the glass as rule number four crossed his mind. *Well, one shot isn't excessive.* He swallowed it in one gulp and grinned. "I look forward to meeting your wife."

Eyeing Stirling's footwear, Finn now accepted his role as mentor and determined to do his damnedest to ensure the daring young gun didn't go get himself killed before their plans to shape him into a future leader came to fruition. "Make sure you're wearing proper boots tomorrow, Kid. Don't want you tripping on your laces."

"I'm twenty-four. Not a kid," Max retorted.

"You are compared to us," Grant smirked as he pushed off the wall to offer a fist bump to Max.

"Well, we could always call you Skunk Boy," Finn quipped as he rotated his chair and tipped his hat back, enjoying teasing the newbie.

Max groaned as everyone else chuckled. He probably wouldn't live that one down for a while. He'd been called worse than Kid, so the more prudent action would be not to rock the boat right after climbing aboard.

Rising from his seat, Zach headed for Max as Rocky trotted beside him. He held out a Zulu Team patch, grinned, and said, "Welcome to the pack."

Smiling, his facial muscles would likely be sore tomorrow from overuse. Max reached for the red and blue shield framed in gold, which bore a golden trident and a black and white orca with an exaggerated mouth full of dagger-like teeth. "Thanks."

Rocky circled his new packmate, recalling the scent he tracked several months ago. Satisfied he liked the smell of him, Rocky nudged the human's leg, seeking a pet.

Zach chuckled. "Rocky doesn't normally warm up so quickly to new people. Scratch behind his ears, and he'll be your buddy."

Crouching, Max came eye-to-eye with the Malinois. He always wanted a dog, and Dad promised to buy him one when he turned ten, but that never came to pass. "Hey, Rocky. Who's a good boy?" He held out his hand for the pup to sniff, then petted him.

When Max straightened up, Rob patted his back. "Sierra's got dibs on you for one more night. We're going to the Barnacle for a bon voyage party." As Jake gave him the stink-eye, Rob laughed. "Won't let him get shit-faced. Just a little fun with the guys before I let you adopt my boy."

Max rolled his eyes at the remark. "Full-grown man here. Can take care of myself, and no one's adopting me."

"Au contraire, mon frère. Team's family. You're our newest addition. Once Zulu, always Zulu," Dave stated.

Rob tugged on Max's arm. "Let's go sort your stuff out so you can sign the paperwork, and we can celebrate."

After Max and Rob exited, Jake released a sigh as he scanned his remaining teammates. "He's gonna be a challenge, isn't he?"

Finn laughed as he kicked his feet up on the table. "Told you so. Gonna take a village to raise him right."

"No doubt he deserves to be Zulu Six, he more than qualifies." Dave resumed his seat and mused aloud, "You think whoever is making his life hell will mess with him now that he's on Zulu?"

"He's ours now. We'll watch out for him." Jake went to the fridge and pulled out a beer but put it back and selected an energy drink. Although they were off duty today, he didn't want alcohol on his breath when he returned home to talk with Jamie.

"If you don't need us, Rocky and I are going to take a run. He's been cooped up in the base kennel too long." Zach voiced a command to his canine after Jake nodded, and they left.

Grant started for the door but paused when Dave asked where he was off to. "Going to chat with Dr. Irving to find out if I need to carry anything special for Stirling in my medkit and review his file to familiarize myself with his baselines. Also, going to check if the results of the blood workup are back. Max spent a long time in that cesspit with open wounds."

"You expect a problem?" Jake inquired.

"No, but better safe than sorry." Grant hurried out.

Jake sighed again, wondering if he made the right selection for Zulu. *Only time will tell.*

Sierra Equipment Cages

Still riding high, yet a little nervous about how his Sierra teammates would take the news, Max halted at the door to their equipment room. He left here only twenty minutes ago in a rush, and now he strolled back with Rob, who told him the guys would be waiting for him inside to help him pack his gear and move it to Zulu's room.

Rob noted the hesitation. "Most will be happy for you."

"Most?"

"Some will be a bit envious but will recognize they selected the right operator and be glad for you. However, one member continuously eyes any open spot on Zulu as his, despite being cut from prior selections. The latest being the previous process when they chose Axel.

"Doubt enough time has elapsed for him to correct anything which concerned them. Marshall is quite thorough and sets exceedingly high standards. He also critically assesses the input of all his men. It isn't always unanimous but damned close.

"And if Jake believed team alchemy would suffer, the offer isn't made. So, rest assured, Marshall thinks you'll fit with Zulu." Rob chuckled and patted Max's back. "Just be prepared to be razzed mercilessly and go broke buying beer."

"So, the case tomorrow isn't the only one I'll be buying?"

"Not even close." Rob snickered as he pushed the door open and waited for Max to enter before him.

"We catch a spin-up?" Scott asked as he rested his forearms on the tall workbench in the center of the area.

"Nope." Rob stopped beside Max.

Terrance huffed. "Damn, not more training. Thought you were done punishing Stirling. Was enjoying a lazy day by my pool."

Devlin shifted his gaze to Max when Rob only grinned. "Hey!" He strode forward and grabbed Max's left arm. "Shit, no. This can't be right, can it?" Excitement filled his eyes as Devlin peered at his teammate, or more correctly, former teammate.

"Yeah. It's right," Max said.

Devlin dragged Max around by the arm, turning him so the others could view the patch. "He's Zulu Six! I win the bet. Hand over the twenties, suckers."

Scott, Terrance, Orlando, and Rakeem gaped at the designator patch as Stewart glowered. Four hands willingly reached for wallets, withdrew bills, and slapped them into Devlin's hand while simultaneously heaping congratulations upon Max along with claps on his back and fist bumps.

Leaning against his cage, Stewart Babcox silently fumed and refused to pay up or offer any best wishes. He tried to wrap his head around how, when, and why Zulu, Marshall, in particular, would've selected Maxwell Stirling, the son of the man who killed an entire team. He came to one conclusion. *Stirling stole Zulu Six from me.*

As Babcox remained quiet and the well-wishes died down, Max said, "You wagered I would be offered Zulu's open spot?"

"Hell yeah!" Devlin glanced over at the sourpuss Babcox and decided to wait until later to collect from him.

"Why? How? When?"

Devlin flashed a *no-duh* expression at Max. "The moment they all gathered around you at the cargo net after you fell. Well, not exactly then, but when you got back, and they watched every training session, it became clear they were scoping you out."

A sheepish smile came to Devlin's face as he admitted, "And I might've accidentally overheard Marshall loudly expressing his desire to Lockwood that whoever beat the hell out of you must be punished. If he weren't considering you, he would've let Rob do the bellowing. While Marshall can be overbearing, demanding, and a pain in the ass to work for, he goes to bat for his men. Nobody fucks with them."

"You had insider knowledge. Not a fair bet. I want my twenty back." Terrance reached for his money.

"All's fair in love and war." Devlin twisted, evading Terrance.

A chase around the table ensued as Max processed the fact he had no clue this entire time, but the pieces began to fall into place.

The reason they designated him the second sniper during the follow-on mission to destroy the weapons stash and relegated Babcox to a support role made sense now. They wanted to witness his performance under fire. Saving Dave and clearing their exfil path most likely influenced their decision.

Rob's whistle put a halt to Terrence's pursuit. "Devlin, you can buy the first round tonight with your ill-gotten gains. For now, let's help Max pack up his stuff."

When Devlin agreed, Max unlocked his cage, and everybody except Babcox began loading his gear on a trolley someone had brought into the room between the time he changed earlier and returned to tell everyone his news.

Max noted Babcox sulked in the corner and deduced the person Rob mentioned must be the other sniper. If roles were reversed, Max would be disappointed too. So, he decided to give Stewart space to lick his wounds and come to terms with being passed over.

Once everything was loaded, the guys headed home after determining to gather at the Barnacle at eight due to several prior commitments. Max grinned as he pushed the laden trolley down the hallway. After storing his equipment and signing the transfer documents, he would still have time to enjoy dinner with Cali before meeting them. Today couldn't get any better.

Zulu Equipment Cages

Max stopped near the only empty cage, well, almost empty since a couple of shoeboxes sat on one shelf. When he stepped inside to take a closer look, his ever-present grin grew, and he chuckled as he read the short note from Draper. In the future, be better prepared. Always remember to pack a spare pair.

Opening one box to examine the contents, Max wondered how she found out his preferred brand and size. "Without a doubt, I owe Draper a case of beer."

"Would prefer a bottle of wine." Kira smiled when Max turned. "I hear congratulations are in order."

"Thanks. Any particular type?"

Kira shrugged. "I like Merlot."

"You got it. Thanks for the boots, arranging a shower in Libya, and the stuff when I got the arrow in my backside."

"All part of my job. Make a list of any other equipment you require, and I'll ensure you get it." Kira placed the batteries Dave requested on the table before heading for the door. "See ya around." Kira waved and exited.

After the team's logistics specialist left, Max hurried to store and organize his items so he could spend as much time as possible with Cali before meeting up with the guys. As he withdrew the last item from his pack, Max paused.

Though old and scratched with faded paint, Max treasured the small wooden box and its contents. It was all he had left of his family. The few things he squirreled away before Uncle Asshole tossed or sold them like everything else his parents owned. With care, he lifted the lid and gazed at the picture tapped to the top.

Max's grandmother took this photograph on his fifth birthday. Preston stood beside Lois in front of the Mustang, with an arm draped across her shoulders, pulling her close, while his other one held Max on his hip. All three of them wore bright smiles. This had been Max's world … a happy family … before both parents and his grandma died.

His gaze moved to the trinkets in his box. A tiny blue and white ceramic owl that belonged to Grandma. Mom's silver locket with his baby picture on one side and a photo of Dad on their wedding day on the other. Max's eyes watered as he stared at his dad's trident ring. Wiping the liquid from his eyes, Max inhaled deeply as he closed the box with reverence and longing before setting it in a place of honor on his shelf.

When Max finished organizing his gear, he scanned the room, wondering which cage had been his father's. With a sense of pride, Max focused on Zulu's menacing orca painted on the far wall, grinned, and murmured, "I did it, Dad."

Thank you for reading
ZULU SIX

Please consider leaving a review or rating.

For details on all Laura's novels, sneak peeks of work in progress, and to sign up to be notified when her next book is released visit
www.lauraactonauthor.com

Strike Force Zulu's missions continue in

BLOOD BONDS

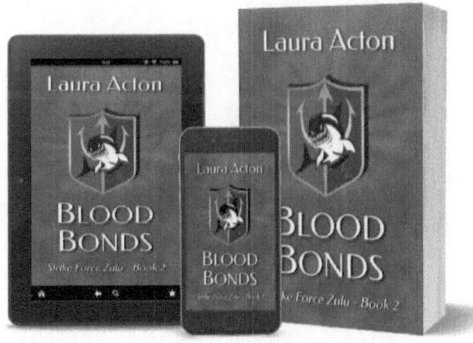